Praise for TH

"Fast-paced and engaging, *Trapped in the Cascades* converges three separate storylines, each ripe with malicious intent and life-threatening repercussions. These are woven into a nail-biting finale with Luke McCain and his faithful companion, Jack, fighting off dangerous weather conditions and the ticking timer towards death if they are unsuccessful. A five-star read!"

–J.C. Fuller, author of *The Rockfish Island Mysteries*

"I kept turning pages in *Trapped in the Cascades* long after I should have been doing other things, but as I followed Luke and Jack through biting winds and snow, smelling pine crushed underfoot and hearing the pop of pine sap from the fire, I couldn't put the book down. Phillips is a great storyteller who can weave clever mysteries and plot twists that particularly appeal to people who love the outdoors but will please anyone who likes a good thriller."

–Dalyn Weller, author of the *Apple Valley Ranchers* series

"I had almost given up reading novels ... then I picked up *Creature of the Cascades*. Here is something you don't see every day. Rob Phillips writes real places into this page-turner, and he is not averse to taking risks with humor, suspense and wordplay. I was hooked from the first jump."

–Gary Lewis, TV host and author of *Fishing Central Oregon*, *Fishing Mount Hood Country*, and *John Nosler Going Ballistic*

"Rob Phillips takes you on another fun romp into the wilds of Washington State as Luke McCain works … to figure out who or what is killing pets, livestock, and wild game in the South Cascades. Is it Sasquatch as some believe or is it something else?"

–John Kruse, host of *Northwestern Outdoors* and *America Outdoors Radio*

"*Cascade Manhunt* is the fifth book of Rob Phillips' Luke McCain series, and I believe it to be his best work . . . . As a retired Washington

State undercover Fish and Wildlife detective, I found Rob's book to be spot-on. I simply couldn't put *Cascade Manhunt* down and am already thirsting for Rob's next book."

–Todd Vandivert, retired Washington State Fish and Wildlife detective and author of the Wildlife Justice series

"Poaching big game . . . check. A loveable yellow Lab . . . double check. Computer hackers from India . . . WHAT! That last item is the big checklist twist in outdoor writer Rob Phillips' latest novel, *Cascade Kidnapping*, the fourth in his Luke McCain series. As in all of Phillips' books, *Cascade Kidnapping* reinforces healthy respect for the outdoors and laws that protect it."

–Bob Crider, retired editor and publisher, *Yakima Herald-Republic*

"This is crime fiction at its finest–the perfect blend of a compelling mystery, a fabulous setting, the best dog ever, and a very likeable hero you won't forget."

–Christine Carbo, award-winning author of the Glacier Mystery Series

"*Cascade Vengeance* takes readers on a thrill ride through the dual worlds of drug dealing and big-game hunting deep in Washington's Cascade mountains. Rob Phillips uses his extensive knowledge of the region to tell the fast-moving tale . . . on the way to the story's harrowing and heartbreaking conclusion."

–Scott Graham, National Outdoor Book Award-winning author of *Mesa Verde Victim*

"*Cascade Vengeance*, the second book in the Luke McCain series, is another hang-onto-your-hat, nonstop action episode with Luke, a Washington State Fish and Wildlife officer, his FBI girlfriend Sara, and Jack, his loyal yellow Lab. I felt like I was riding shotgun in Luke's Ford pickup, bouncing along forest service roads where very bad guys might be lurking."

–Susan Richmond, owner of Inklings Bookshop

CASCADE WITNESS

Book and cover design by Kevin Breen

ISBN: 978-1-957607-35-1
Cataloging-in-Publication Data is available upon request

Manufactured in the United States of America

Published by
Latah Books, Spokane, Washington
www.latahbooks.com

The author may be contacted at yakimahunter@yahoo.com

CASCADE WITNESS

A LUKE MCCAIN
NOVEL

ROB PHILLIPS

LATAH
BOOKS

For Terri

CHAPTER 1

He didn't think of himself as a murderer. Or a serial killer. He thought of himself as a savior. An angel of mercy. Someone who helped others move from this life to a better life in the next, whatever that might be. Similar to Doctor Kevorkian, only he wasn't just assisting people who wanted to leave their earthly bodies; he was helping those who needed to die and just didn't know it. Because he thought of himself as Kevorkian and because he was an actual physician, he went by the street name of Doc.

Dressed in an old green Army coat and green wool pants, wearing a pair of black Danner boots, Doc pushed his shopping cart along Second Avenue in downtown Seattle. His outerwear was carefully selected from a Goodwill store in Portland. His undergarments, however, were the finest REI sold—a heavy, wool base layer of Merino long underwear and shirt. A second layer—a slim, down jacket by Patagonia worn under the Army coat—kept him quite comfortable as he moved along in the often chilly and wet late-winter weather of Western Washington.

When it really rained, he would pull on a Polyurethane Helly Hansen raincoat. Like his other coat and pants, the raincoat was dark green, keeping him dry while still looking unkempt and shabby. Doc also often wore an old, beat-up leather hat, with rabbit fur lining and ear flaps. The hat looked like it could have been worn by Eddie Rickenbacker during an aerial battle against the Red Baron in World War I.

His shopping cart carried various items, including a puffy sleeping bag loosely rolled up, along with a blue tarp crammed into one corner, and other less useful things. Underneath the sleeping bag, in the bottom of the cart, was a lock box that could be opened in a second by reading Doc's fingerprints. The box included a few tools of his trade, including syringes and vials of oxycontin, heroin, and fentanyl that, when placed into the human bloodstream in the correct amounts, would mercifully end a person's life quite quickly, whether they wanted to die or not.

A Springfield 911 pistol in .45 caliber, fully loaded and ready to fire, also sat in the box. While he'd had to pull the handgun on a couple of occasions to get out of a sticky situation involving overzealous or drug-addled freaks in the camps he was visiting, he had yet to fire it for protection.

Both of the men who had given him crap during those altercations unfortunately died of overdoses in the days that followed. One of the men, who had tried to attack Doc at a small camp under one of the I-5 overpasses, came around in a last moment of lucidity, looked at Doc, and said, "Hey, you're the dude I . . ." Doc pushed the plunger of the syringe, and the man was gone. For good.

Doc was taller than average, just over six feet. But when he pushed his cart around the dozens of homeless encampments, he would slouch, walking slowly, giving the illusion of an older man.

With a three- or four-day growth of salt-and-pepper beard, and his longish graying hair pulled over his ears and eyes, Doc blended nicely into the ever-growing homeless population around Puget Sound.

The irony was Doc wasn't homeless. He lived in a very quaint and perfectly nice house in an area known as Queen Anne Hill. The four-thousand-a-month rental was covered via an automatic payment from a bank account at U.S. Bank, set up under a fictitious name.

After each of the merciful deaths of one of the folks he had chosen to rescue from this life, Doc had slipped away from the homeless camp, made his way to his quaint little home, and slept quite soundly. Unlike the folks he spent his days with, Doc would enjoy a hot shower, a tasty dinner, and then, after reading or watching some television, he would retire for the evening.

He paid particular attention to the local news, either at six o'clock or eleven. Occasionally, he would see a report about a homeless person who had overdosed in one of the homeless camps, but most of the time, the local news people left well enough alone. Frankly, most of the people in Seattle or other cities in the region couldn't give a rat's ass about the mentally ill and the addicts that made up the homeless population in the area. The local politicians gave the occasional lip service to the homeless situation, but they had no clue as to how to solve the issue.

"It's a problem that can only be solved by more affordable housing," the mayor said in one of the reports Doc saw.

Doc actually laughed out loud when he heard the blathering leader of the city say such a stupid thing. Even if there were ten thousand free homes available to the people who were living in tents in the city parks and along the freeway, it would not solve the problem. Oh sure, there were the occasional few living in cars who had lost jobs and could no longer afford their rent. But with just about every retail store and fast-food place in the metro area screaming for help, Doc thought getting a job was very attainable if someone wanted to work. Plus, with several federal and local government programs available to get people into affordable housing, someone who wanted to work and needed a place to stay could make it happen.

Doc saw it day in and day out. The elected officials would too, if they ever spent more than three minutes in the homeless camps. When they were at the camps, with a TV camera following them around, it was all for public relations purposes. A photo op and a sound bite, and then they were gone.

He had given a great deal of thought to the issue and had determined that the problems ran so deep, there would never be a quick fix. Doc believed the issues with the homeless, the drug addiction and the mental health problems, began with the deterioration of the family structure. The huge numbers of single-parent homes and families without fathers participating in the raising of the children was, he believed, at the heart of the problem.

Doc wasn't a religious man. If he had been, he might have had more remorse and guilt about what he was doing. But he did believe that people who participated in organized religion also had fewer issues with drugs, alcohol, and homelessness. Religion, he believed, was a good thing. It just wasn't for him.

No, there would be no instant fix, particularly with the government involved. So Doc had taken matters into his own hands. He was single-handedly whittling away at the homeless problem. The only issue being, he was having trouble keeping up. For every person he sent to a better life in the nether-world, five more people popped up at the various and assorted camps.

After a year, Doc had upped his game. He was, as he thought of it, euthanizing a needy homeless person about once every two weeks. Sometimes he'd take two out in a week, and sometimes he'd wait a month.

He continued to be very careful and was now working from Olympia to Everett. Doc figured if he spread his work out over three counties and several cities, the overworked police and social workers would never put two and two together. His plan was working quite well. In a twelve-month period working around

Puget Sound, Doc had sent twenty-two people to the hereafter.

Added to his victims in Los Angeles, San Francisco, and Portland, he had now killed ninety-one people who had been living on the streets and in homeless camps. He never checked the records for who was the worst serial killer in U.S. history because he didn't believe he was a serial killer. He believed he was more akin to an angel, putting seriously ill people out of their misery. Because, really, wasn't it inevitable? They were going to die at some point in the near future. Either from a real overdose or for some other medical issue due to the beating their organs had been taking from years of alcohol and drug abuse.

Yes, Doc was doing them a favor. He believed it wholeheartedly. He would keep working at his mission as long as he could before the authorities caught on to what was happening. And if they did, well, he'd just move on. He'd done it before and would do it again.

* * *

Kristen Gray had grown up believing she was going to save the world. She knew from the time she was little that she was put on this earth to help people. When there was a person sitting next to the stop sign on the road to the grocery store with a "Homeless, Please help" sign in his or her lap, Gray would beg and plead with her mother to give the poor person a dollar. And if the person at the stop sign had a little dog, well, Gray would jump out of the vehicle if her mother or father didn't stop to help with some cash.

A dean's list student at the University of Washington, Gray received her BA degree in social welfare and her master's degree in social work, with a specialty in integrated health and mental health. Short and fit, Gray looked like she could be an Olympic gymnast. With short brown hair, dark brown eyes, and a small nose sprinkled with a few freckles, she appeared to be much younger than her twenty-six years. In fact, more than once, high school guys had hit on her when she had been at the mall near where she lived.

Gray was now working on her PhD, and her dissertation was going to be based on her on-the-ground observation and interaction with the thousands of people who were living in one of the hundreds of homeless encampments in and around the Puget Sound area. She planned to be out there with the people for a full year. Her observation would include keeping track of how many times officials and social workers from the city, county, or state made contact with the population. It was impossible to be in all places at all times, so oftentimes she would follow a social worker as they left the office to see where they went, who they contacted, and what they did to help.

Because of who she was, Gray had the constant desire to assist the people she met. Unfortunately, because she was a poor college student, it was tough for her to buy the next needy person she ran into something to eat.

One day, as she tailed one of the social workers in her car, she spotted some people at an encampment off I-5 who were all huddled around in circle. Despite the brief view she was afforded, one woman stuck out to Gray. She looked to be in hysterics, pulling at her hair and crying. The woman, who may have been about her age, Gray thought, was rail thin and dressed in several layers of clothing. She kept looking down at the ground in the middle of the huddle, then raising her head in obvious pain.

Gray had been at that very camp just two days earlier, so she knew how to get there. She took the next off-ramp and got around to a side road and headed back to the camp. She parked her car, a 2015 Honda CRV, and headed to the camp.

When she arrived, there were fewer people in the huddle, but there were still several standing in a circle and looking down. The woman Gray had seen from the freeway was sitting on a nearby rock with her face in her hands. She was young, with long, straight blonde hair, maybe twenty-one or twenty-two, slender, with a face that at one time had been very pretty. Now, dirty and with muddy stripes down her cheeks from the tears, she looked older and very tired.

Kristen walked over to the woman, introduced herself, and said, "Is everything alright?"

The woman looked up at Gray, tears in her eyes, and said, "Toby." Then she pointed at the group still standing in a circle.

"Toby?" Gray asked as she looked over at the group. When she did, she saw a person lying on the ground, curled up in a fetal position. "Is something wrong with Toby?"

"He's dead," the woman said. "He's my boyfriend. We were going to get married. And now he's dead."

Gray got up and walked over to the group of four men and two women standing and looking at a man, who, based on the ashen coloring in his face, was most assuredly dead. Still, she knelt and felt for a pulse. Nothing.

"Did anyone try Narcan while he was breathing?" Gray asked.

"He hasn't been breathing for a while," one of the men in the group said. "I saw him just like this when I woke up this morning. Hasn't moved an inch. I thought he was still sleeping, but when I saw him still layin' here, I called for Magic."

"Magic?" Gray asked.

"Yeah," the man said with a head bob toward the young woman on the rock. "That's Magic, Toby's girlfriend. She checked him and started screaming."

"Okay," Gray said. "I need to call the police, so if any of you don't want to be here, you better pick up and get going."

"Cops don't do nuthin' to us," another man said who was wearing a heavy wool coat and gloves with the fingers missing. "They come by and talk to us now and again, but they don't do nuthin'."

"This is the fourth person to die in this camp in the last couple months," said a woman with no front teeth, bundled up in a bright purple down jacket, and a Seattle Seahawks stocking cap pulled down on her head.

Gray thought about that for a minute. Homeless people died occasionally, but to have four in one camp die seemed odd to her.

"Were they all overdoses?" she asked the woman in the Seahawks cap.

"That's what the cops said, but one of the guys, the Duckman, he never did drugs. He said drugs were demon spirits. I think he was supposed to be on some prescription drugs for whatever was getting at his brain, but he wouldn't even take those."

"The Duckman?" Gray asked.

"Yeah, that's what everyone called him. Don't know his real name. He liked going to the park down the road to feed the ducks. Those birds would come flocking to him anytime they saw him coming. He went to a couple of bakeries every morning and dug all the stale bread out of the dumpster and took it to the ducks. He was a nice guy."

Gray called 911 and reported the dead man.

* * *

When the Seattle police officers arrived, they came over and checked on Toby, confirming what everyone else knew. He was, in fact, dead.

"Anyone see what happened?" asked the officer, a tall, sturdy Black man named Jones, who could have played defensive lineman for the Washington Huskies in his younger years.

He got no response, which was pretty normal in these situations.

"You called it in?" asked the second officer, a woman with brown skin and black hair stuck up under her hat, and a very business-like look on her face. The name badge on her blue coat read "Donley."

"Yes, I did," Gray said. "I guess no one has a phone because I think they knew he was dead for a while. I saw the young woman crying as I went by on the freeway and pulled in here."

"The woman?" Jones asked.

"Yes," Gray said. "Her name is Magic. Or at least that's what the others around here call her."

Both officers were looking around.

"We know Magic," Donley said. "But I don't see her."

Gray looked around too.

"She was just here. Guess she didn't want to talk to you guys."

"We'll run her down," Jones said, then asked Gray for her information.

"You a case worker or something?" Donley asked.

"No, I'm doing a study on the homeless for my doctoral degree at U-Dub. I know some of the people too, although I've only been around for a few weeks. Magic and Toby are new to me."

The two officers just stared at her until Jones finally said, "You're a brave little lady to be down here all by yourself. You need to be careful."

Donley just smiled at her and nodded her head in agreement.

"I'll be fine," Gray said. "Say, did you know a guy who lived around here called the Duckman?"

"Yeah, we knew him," Donley said. "Tragedy. Everyone liked him. And the birds over at the park miss him, I believe."

"Was an autopsy done?" Gray asked.

"Don't think so," Jones said. "But in just about all these camps if someone dies, it is almost always an overdose of something."

"The others here said he wasn't a user," Gray said.

"I was here after the call came in," Jones said. "He wasn't shot, or knifed, or hit on the head with a rock. Didn't smell like alcohol. So unless he died from a heart attack, it was an overdose."

CHAPTER 2

Over the years that Luke McCain had been patrolling the wilds of Central Washington, he had watched the homeless problem continue to grow. There was a lot of lip service by the local politicians about wanting to work to get the problems solved, but Luke felt it was going to be a momentous task. You couldn't just throw up a few fences or build a shelter. The issues with addiction and mental illness wouldn't be solved nearly that easily.

Back when he was first transferred to the Region 3 office in Yakima, Luke would find the occasional angler who'd decided to open the fishing season on one of the local rivers too soon. And in the fall and winter, when he would check on duck hunters who were floating the Yakima River, those were the only people he would see. Now, however, as he walked that same stretch of the river, he ran into one homeless camp after another. Some of the camps were inhabited, while others were abandoned, with trash scattered everywhere. More than once, he retrieved some big garbage bags from his truck and cleaned the trash from the riverbanks. Rarely did he see anyone fishing this stretch of the river now, during the season or not. Most people, including all but the most avid anglers, avoided the areas where the camps were.

About once every six months, one of the warming fires the homeless people had going would get out of control and burn up the brush and trees along the river. Other fires had burned nearby playgrounds and picnic equipment. Dealing with the people in the camps wasn't really part of Luke's job description, but it was a fact of life. They were where he needed to be looking for possible poachers and lawbreakers, so it was inevitable that he would interact with them.

Wearing a badge got him plenty of respect from most people, including those living in the camps. Being nearly six-foot-five and very fit didn't hurt either. Luke's approach to his job, and to life in general, was to be nice to everyone until they weren't nice to you. And he treated everyone with the same respect he hoped they would give him, homeless or not.

Even though he wasn't around the camps as much as other folks, Luke recognized some of the people. One morning as he walked along the river with his yellow Lab, Jack, looking for a couple of guys who were supposedly fishing out of season, he saw one of the men he'd gotten to know over the past two years.

"Hey, Moon," Luke said when he saw the man who was probably in his late 20s or early 30s but looked like he was fifty. Moon was in a ragged pair of short pants, Converse tennis shoes with no shoelaces, and a heavy leather coat. Luke couldn't tell if the man was wearing a shirt, but most days he didn't. Moon's sandy-colored hair looked like it had just been through a minor tornado.

"Hey, Luke," Moon said. Then he said, "Hey, Jack!"

The big yellow dog went over to Moon, tail wagging, and let the man pet him.

"How ya doin', boy?" Moon asked as he scratched Jack's ears.

"How are you doing?" Luke asked.

"Aw, ya know," Moon said. "I'm okay."

Over the months, Luke had offered to connect Moon to some kind of social service that might help him with his addictions. He tried not to harp on it, but he would often remind Moon the offer was always out there.

Moon and many of the other people Luke saw in the different camps had cell phones. They were given to them by some social service agency in hopes, Luke thought, that if they had a phone maybe they would call for help, either in getting treatment, or from authorities if they were in danger. And he hoped some might even use the phones to call home to let their loved ones know they were still alive, if not okay.

Luke had given Moon his card with his phone number, even helping the man program his number into his phone, and said, "Call anytime, day or night, and I'll come help. And if I can't, I'll make sure help comes right away."

Moon seemed appreciative but had never called.

"So," Luke said, "a bike rider on the pathway up there was through here a little while ago and said he saw two men fishing in the river. Did you see anyone fishing?"

Moon scratched his head through the mop of unkempt hair and said, "You know, now that I think about it, yeah, I saw a coupla dudes fishing up the river a ways."

"You remember what they looked like or what they were wearing?"

Moon stood, head bowed, and thought about it for a minute.

"One guy had a red hat on," he said to Luke. "And they both had fishing poles in their hands."

Luke laughed to himself and said, "Okay, that helps. Thanks, Moon. You call me when you decide you need help."

Moon just gave a backhanded wave and wandered back over to an old lawn chair, the kind with the nylon webbing, and sat down.

As Luke walked up the river, looking for the two fishermen

with fishing poles in their hands, he wondered about the man he knew as Moon. He didn't know if Moon was the man's first name, last name, or if it was a nickname. And he wondered what it took for someone like Moon to get so far down that they were okay with living in a cheap tent down by the river.

Luke hadn't walked two hundred yards downriver when he spotted two men standing up to their knees in the Yakima River. The men were wearing chest waders, had on fishing vests, and as Moon had described, they had fishing rods in their hands.

"How ya doing, fellas?" Luke asked.

The men, who were standing about ten yards apart, turned in unison, and when they saw Luke and the badge on his chest, they frowned.

"We're doing okay," the man in a red San Francisco 49ers hat said. "Not catching anything, though."

"Can I get you guys to come over here for a minute?" Luke said.

Both men reeled in their lures, turned, and sloshed over to where Luke was standing, with Jack sitting by his side.

"You have your fishing licenses?" Luke asked.

Both men nodded and started to dig down into the waders to get to their wallets.

"What you fishing for?" Luke asked as the men were digging.

"Trout," the other man said, who was wearing a black Las Vegas Raiders hat.

"Yeah, there are some nice trout in here," Luke said. "The only problem is this part of the river is not open for trout fishing."

"It says it is in the regulations," 49ers cap said.

"Can you show me?" Luke asked as he took the men's licenses from them.

"Well, I don't carry the regulations on me, but I read that the Yakima River is open year-round to trout fishing."

"Some parts of the river are, but not this part," Luke said as he read their addresses. The men were both from Oregon and had purchased out-of-state fishing licenses.

"We read this story in one of the fishing magazines about the great trout fishing in the Yakima River, and how it was open year-round, and decided to come give it a try," Raiders hat said.

Luke looked at their lures. They were using single barbless-hooked spinners, which were legal on the Yakima River ten miles upstream, where it was open for fishing all year long.

"Listen," Luke said. "I believe you made an honest mistake here. Sometimes our regulations can be a bit difficult to decipher. Grab your gear and come with me. I'll get you headed in the right direction to where you can fish."

"Gee, that's pretty nice of you," 49ers hat said.

"Nice looking Lab you have there," Raiders hat said. "I have a chocolate Lab. Great dogs."

"Well," Luke said, "this one can be great, but most of the time he is just looking for something to eat."

Jack wasn't paying attention; he was up the trail sniffing for something.

They walked by Moon's tent, and Luke noticed the man was no longer sitting in his webbed lawn chair.

"You guys have the same homeless problems we do down in Portland," 49ers hat said. "But we have it about a hundred times worse."

Luke didn't say anything and just kept on walking. When he and the men were back into a parking lot near the nature path, Luke told them how to get up into the Yakima Canyon where it would be legal to fish.

"Thanks, officer," the man in the Raiders cap said and gave Jack a couple of pats on the side.

"Good luck to you guys," Luke said and headed for his truck.

He was just about to open the door when he heard someone calling his name.

"Luke! Luke! Help!"

Luke turned and saw Moon stumbling his way, waving an arm. He turned and ran to the man, who fell to his knees just as Luke reached him.

"What is it, Moon?"

"There's a woman down by my camp who needs help!"

"Okay, can you show me?"

Moon struggled to his feet and started back the way he'd come. "I think she's OD'd," Moon said.

"Is she still breathing?" Luke said as he pulled his radio mic off his shoulder and called for an ambulance.

"Yes, still breathing, but she's not good," Moon said breathlessly.

"Do you know her name?"

"Not her real name," Moon said. "She showed up a couple days ago. I never talked to her, but one of the other women said her name is Magic."

CHAPTER 3

When Doc walked into the camp, no one gave him a second look. He looked like one of them, so he must be one of them. He had been through the camp several times over the past six months and had sent two deserving people to the life beyond. One man and one woman. Both were miserable, sitting in their own waste, smelling of urine, begging for money, scraping together just enough change each day to buy a hit of something that would satisfy their need for the next twenty-four hours.

He had watched each of them off and on, and when the opportunity arose, he poked them with his special cocktail, and they died within seconds.

Unfortunately, as he was putting the woman out of her misery, he had been watched. He had looked all around and believed he was in a spot where no one could see him give the woman the shot, but when he turned, he caught someone peeking out of the top of the zipper on a green and yellow tent.

Doc had no idea if the person who saw him was a man or a woman, but he needed to make sure they didn't speak to anyone about what they'd seen. He started for the tent, but three men came strolling into the camp, talking and laughing, and sat in chairs not far from the tent.

He couldn't take care of the problem right now, but he would have to do it soon in case the person in the green tent started blabbing about what he, or she, had seen.

It took him two more trips through the camp to find out who lived in the green and yellow tent.

"Oh, that's the Duckman," a woman with no front teeth said when he asked about it. "He's probably over at the lake feeding the ducks. He gets up early and goes to get bread to feed those damn birds. Maybe I should quack like a duck."

The tooth-deprived woman cackled at her own joke. Doc laughed too, thanked the woman, and went on his way. He'd be back.

He caught up with the Duckman three days later. It was early in the morning, and no one in the camp was stirring, except for the man who liked to get up early to go collect the stale baked goods thrown in the dumpsters at two nearby bakeries.

The Duckman was not feeble and drug-addled like his other victims. The man was fairly fit and agile, and he wasn't going to go down without a fight. Doc wrestled with the man, finally got the needle in his arm, and was just laying him down in the dirt when someone said, "Hey, what are you doing there?"

Doc looked quickly over his shoulder, saw a young man coming through the door of a nearby tent, and took off. He didn't run, but he walked quickly. Luckily, he had parked his car nearby, and he was in it and gone before the young man caught up to him.

"Shit!" Doc said to himself as he drove down I-5. This thing was getting out of hand. Now he would have to kill the young man or risk him telling the authorities what he had seen.

Doc watched the daily paper and the local TV news, but he didn't see anything about the three people he had killed in the one camp. Evidently, the authorities just believed it was a string of bad luck. Maybe the addicts got a particularly strong batch of whatever they were putting into their bodies.

✳ ✳ ✳

It wasn't easy killing the kid. Doc stayed around the camp longer than he wanted to, but he needed to make sure no one could identify him as the man who was wrestling with the Duckman.

He changed his normal "homeless" costume from Army green to an old leather-sleeved letterman jacket without any letters on it and a purple University of Washington ball cap that looked like it had been sitting in the diamond lane of I-5 for a week, then he watched from afar. Doc identified the tent where the kid lived and watched as he came and went. He had seen a young woman hanging around, but he wasn't sure if she was with the young man or just another resident of the camp. The two talked with each other frequently, but Doc never saw any signs of affection between them.

The kid looked to be in decent shape, especially compared to some of the other residents in the camp. It would be much more challenging to stick a needle in him.

Plunging a hypodermic needle into the young man's neck would work, but no one ever shot themselves up in the neck.

He believed his best bet to take the kid down was to surprise him and do it in the cover of darkness. Doc had a bottle of ether in his little bag of goodies and decided that holding a cloth doused in the anesthesia would be his only way to give the drugs to the kid in a spot where officials would believe he had overdosed.

His plan worked, but not to perfection. Dressed all in black, Doc waited behind a tent next to the kid's tent. He watched and waited as the young man talked to two other men. Finally, the two men turned and headed to other tents down the way, and Doc watched as the kid walked away from his tent and toward some blackberry brambles.

He realized the young man was going to urinate before heading to bed, so he pulled the rag out of his bag, poured the ether on it, and quietly walked up behind him. Just as the kid was zipping up his pants, Doc grabbed his face from behind with the ether cloth in his left hand, wrapped his right arm around the young man's neck, and pulled him down.

The surprise of the attack, and the kid having both hands occupied with the jeans zipper, was probably the only reason he was able to get him down as quickly as he did. The kid fought, grabbing Doc's right arm to try and pull it away, but the ether was just too much to overcome.

Once the kid was down, Doc found that the coat the young man was wearing was too thick to stick a needle through. He didn't want to take the time to unzip it and wrestle it off, so he stuck him in the neck with his deadly potion and watched as the young man took his last breath.

It was a risk to use the ether, Doc knew, but after he had done the deed, he realized it was really the only way he was going to be able to subdue the kid. If the officials did an autopsy and analyzed the young man's blood, they would certainly find the ether in his system. But from Doc's experience, the authorities would rule the death as just another senseless overdose by a known drug addict and not spend much time or effort in trying to determine how he had died.

Before he left the camp, Doc looked around. This time he was confident no one had seen what he had done. Thankfully, he thought, this was the last witness to take out, and he could move on with his work.

After killing the young man, Doc drove back to his house, showered, and changed into his homeless costume. An hour later, he was sitting on the edge of a concrete abutment under the bridge, near the tents where he had overtaken the kid. As the first light of morning started pushing the darkness away, he could see the young man still lying right where he'd left him.

Doc kept his head down, the hood of his Army coat pulled up and over his World War I hat, holding a wine bottle stuck in a brown paper sack. Just another long-lost alcoholic who had been up drinking the night away. No one paid an ounce of attention to him, nor did they notice that under the hood he stared at the dead man and the few people who were now starting to stir in the camp.

After watching for almost a half hour, Doc saw the two men the kid had been talking with right before he'd killed him come wandering by. They looked at the body but went on down the line of tents and talked to a woman. A short time later, the men came back, and as they got to the body, one man, dressed in an oversized Seattle Mariners sweatshirt, dirty white sweatpants, and sneakers with no laces, bent down and said something to the kid on the ground. When he got no response, the man shook the kid and then turned and said something to the other man. The second man, dressed in a long gray overcoat and a felt cowboy hat, knelt and also shook the kid.

When he got no response, he stood and started yelling, "Magic! Magic!"

Doc watched as several people stumbled out of the nearby tents. Was "magic" a code word that they used in this camp to notify the others about someone's death? That couldn't be right, could it, Doc wondered.

Then he watched as the girl he had seen talking to the kid come out of his tent. She looked sleepy and confused. When she got to where the young man lay, she put her hands to the sides of her head and dropped to her knees.

The girl put her head on the kid's chest and then started to push on it, like she was doing CPR. After a few minutes of watching her trying to revive the kid, the two men stopped her and talked to her. She started to scream and shake her head.

"No! No! No!" the girl yelled. She called out a name. "Toby! Oh God, Toby!"

Then the young woman collapsed.

Doc watched the young woman sob, and he was about to leave when he saw another young woman come into the camp. She was not part of the tent camp, Doc could see. She was dressed casually, and although she seemed small in stature, she had an air of authority about her. She walked over to the body, talked to the people standing around, and then pulled out her phone. To call the authorities, Doc knew.

He had been in dozens of camps around the area, but he had never seen this woman before. He watched as she walked over to the crying woman and talked to her. Then he saw her looking around. Doc ducked his head and hoped she hadn't seen him looking at her.

A few minutes later, the cops showed up, and everyone was talking with everyone. Doc stood and watched. He was getting the bad feeling that the girl who had tried to revive the dead kid was more than just a friend. Had the young man told her what he'd seen? Was he going to have to deal with another potential witness? And who was this other young woman? What had she learned?

As Doc was thinking all of this, he stared at the young woman who had called the police. He should have been quicker, but he was lost in thought. As if she knew he was watching her, the girl turned and stared right back at him. Their eyes met for an instant, and then Doc dropped his head. He looked out of the corner of his eye, and as soon as the girl turned her head, he turned and walked away.

* * *

Hearing that this was the fourth death in this camp in the past two weeks was disturbing to Kristen Gray. She had run across the occasional overdose in her studies, all after the fact, and there didn't seem to be any pattern or reason for who or where the people died. But after talking to Magic, she'd learned that the two most recent deaths involved men who supposedly were either off drugs, or who had never had a drug issue. That was really strange.

"Will the medical examiner do an autopsy on this man?" Gray asked Officer Donley.

"Can't say," Donley said. "Most of the time they don't."

"Before she disappeared, Magic told me that her boyfriend was off drugs," Gray explained. "She said they both hadn't used anything in months, and they were going to get married."

"I guess we could request an autopsy if we believe there's been some foul play," Donley said. "But if he was killed by some kind of violence, being shot or stabbed, for instance, we'd see evidence of that."

Gray thought about that for a bit.

"And," Donley continued, "if he was killed by someone who shot him up with something . . . well, that would be almost impossible to prove. Especially with a known junkie."

She watched as the EMTs put the man named Toby on the gurney to be transported to the medical examiner's vehicle. What had happened to Toby, she wondered, and where had Magic gone?

As she looked around for the woman who had been crying on the rock, she scanned the other people in the crowd. They were all watching as the gurney was pushed up the hillside, except for one man. A guy wearing an old Army coat with the hood up and holding a bottle of booze was staring right at her.

The man gave her the creeps. He was too focused, too alert. Even though he wore the clothing of a homeless person, he didn't *look* like a homeless man.

She looked away from the man but then decided she would try to get a better look at the face. When she looked back, the man had turned and was walking off in the opposite direction. Gray thought about going after him but decided she needed to find Magic, so she dropped it. She would keep her eyes open for the man who she was beginning to think might be an imposter.

CHAPTER 4

They heard the ambulance in the distance as they hurried to where Moon had seen the woman named Magic.

"She's right up here," Moon said, breathing so hard he could barely speak.

Luke scanned the brush along the river and finally spotted a young blonde woman lying in the green grass right at the water's edge. She looked unconscious or even worse, dead. She wasn't moving, and Luke couldn't see her breathing.

He rushed over to her and knelt. He grabbed her wrist and could feel a faint pulse. Then he saw her chest rise as she took a breath.

"She's still alive," Luke said. Then he asked Moon, "Can you watch her for just a minute while I go direct the medics?"

Moon just nodded as Luke, with Jack on his heels, ran back up the trail to get the EMTs.

He met the two medics, a woman and a man, just as they were getting on the nature path. The man was packing a large red medical bag, and the woman had on a backpack.

"This way," Luke said and turned to run back. As he jogged along with the EMTs right behind him, he said. "A woman, maybe mid-twenties, probably drug overdose. I felt a light pulse, and she was breathing slowly."

The two didn't say anything, just jogged along until they arrived at the spot where the woman lay.

Luke stood back as the EMTs went to work on the woman. They asked Moon a couple of questions, but he couldn't help, he said, because he had never talked to the woman before, just had seen her the last couple of days wandering along the river. He said he thought she was camping in one of the spots just up the river.

After spending a few minutes with the woman, the EMTs got her talking and then sat her up. Luke couldn't hear what they were saying, but they hadn't given her a Narcan spray. They had a blood pressure cuff on her right arm and were checking her lungs with a stethoscope.

Finally, the woman EMT stood and came over to Luke and Moon. "She says she hasn't had any drugs for months," the EMT said. "We think she's maybe just really weak from not eating for a few days. And even though there is water right here, she is very dehydrated."

"That's good, I guess," Luke said.

Moon just stood there, again scratching his wild mop of hair.

"We'll take her to the hospital. She may need an IV to get her going again. She saw you were a cop of some kind and would like to talk to you."

"Okay," Luke said. "Now? Or should we wait until she's doing better?"

"Now," the EMT said. "She seems to believe someone is after her."

Luke watched as the male EMT headed back to the ambulance to get a gurney. Once he was out of sight, Luke walked down to where the other EMT was again checking the woman's vital signs.

When the EMT gave him a head nod, Luke knelt to talk to the woman. He could see she was young but had been living a tough life. She had tangled dishwater blonde hair that fell just past her shoulders. Her face was pretty, Luke thought, but it currently was covered in streaks of mud and dirt. She was extremely thin and reminded Luke of pictures he'd seen of women with eating disorders.

"Hi," Luke said. "I'm Officer Luke McCain. The EMT said you wanted to talk to me?"

The woman didn't say anything for a minute, then her eyes started to fill with tears.

"He killed my boyfriend," the woman said. "And he's going to kill me, I'm sure of it."

"Let's start with your name," Luke said.

"My name is Magic. My boyfriend's name is, or was, Toby. We were living in one of the camps over in Seattle, and Toby happened to see this homeless guy doing something to the Duckman."

"Who is the Duckman?" Luke asked.

"An older man in our camp that always fed the ducks at the park. Really nice guy."

"Okay, and your boyfriend Toby saw this homeless man with the Duckman. Did something happen?"

"Yeah, the Duckman died. The cops came and said it was an overdose. The funny thing is the Duckman didn't do drugs. He might have needed something for his brain, he was kinda different, but he was really nice and never did drugs that any of us saw."

"But he died of an overdose?" Luke asked

"Yeah, and Toby saw this other man doing something to the Duckman, and now Toby is dead."

"Did Toby do drugs?" Luke asked

"Toby and I were getting clean. We hadn't used anything in almost four months. We wanted to get married, but because we had no money, we stayed in the camp where we knew we'd be safe among friends. Or where we thought we'd be safe."

"And Toby died of an overdose?"

"I don't know," Magic said. "That's what the cops will think. They figure anyone who dies in a camp dies from an overdose."

"So you think the man who did something to the Duckman also did something to Toby?" Luke asked.

"We were talking about the Duckman, and Toby was convinced this man gave him a shot of something that killed him," Magic said and started to cry again.

"And now Toby is dead," she said after wiping her tears, smudging brown over her cheeks.

"And when was this?" Luke asked.

"Two or three days ago. I've lost track," Magic said.

"Did you see the strange man around again?"

"No, but what else could have happened? I went to sleep while Toby was outside talking to some other guys in the camp and then, when I woke up, someone was calling my name. I went outside the tent, and Toby was just lying there, dead."

When Magic asked what else could have happened, Luke thought that maybe Toby had decided to take a hit of fentanyl and, bang, he was dead.

"Then what did you do?" Luke asked.

"I cried," Magic said. "Then this young woman showed up, maybe from DSHS, and called the cops. I got outta there because if the man who killed the Duckman and Toby knew that me and Toby were living together, he'd think Toby told me about the man, which he did."

The EMT rolled the gurney down the path and stopped just above where Luke and the other medic were tending to Magic.

"Can you help me get her up the hill to the stretcher?" the woman medic asked Luke.

Luke didn't hesitate for a second. He scooped the woman up, barely believing how light she was, and carried her through the grass and brush, up a trail to the paved pathway, and put her on the gurney.

"Listen," Luke said to Magic. "You go with these folks to the hospital. I'll come check on you shortly, and we'll see what he can figure out."

"Okay, thanks," Magic said, still with tears in her eyes. "We were going to get married." Then she started to sob.

* * *

Luke watched the EMTs slide the gurney with the woman into the back of the rig, close the double doors on the ambulance, climb into the rig and drive away, red lights flashing. Magic had been pretty convincing, and he thought about what he should do next.

Luke whistled for Jack, and they headed for his truck. Luke just happened to know the local special agent at the FBI office in Yakima, so he decided to go have a chat with her.

When he was in his truck and rolling toward the FBI office, he figured it would be best to call first versus arriving unannounced.

"Hey there," Sara said when she answered her cell phone. Luke would normally call that number, as he figured if she was busy, she would just ignore the call and he would know to not bother her right then. Which happened about half the time he called.

"Hey, any chance you'd have a couple minutes if I stopped by?"

"Sure," Sara said with a question in her voice. "Everything alright?"

"Well, I'm not coming to ask you for a divorce if that's what you're worried about," Luke said with a chuckle.

Sara laughed too and said, "Dang, the pool boy and I were just talking about how we might get rid of you."

"Are we getting a pool?" Luke asked. "I might just change my mind if we're getting a pool."

"What is it then?" Sara asked.

"I'll tell you when I get there. Might be something for you in your professional capacity."

Sara, Luke's wife, was a special agent with the FBI. They had met several years before when both were working on a case that involved a serial killer dropping dead women's bodies in the Cascade Mountains.

Luke wouldn't admit it to her, but for him it had been love at first sight. Sara was tall, fit, and beautiful, with dark hair and eyes to match. She was the smartest person Luke had ever met, and every day he was thankful she had come into his life. He truly believed he was the luckiest man in the world to have somehow gotten her to fall in love with him.

Mostly, Sara's work involved helping with serious crimes on the Yakama Indian Reservation. She had helped solve several cases of missing and murdered women, and because of her success, she had been offered promotions that would take her to San Francisco, Denver, or other bigger cities around the country. Luke had told Sara he would be willing to give up his job as a Washington State Fish and Wildlife police officer if she wanted to take one of the offers. Fortunately for him, she had told him she was very happy with her job in Central Washington.

Luke loved his job as a game warden, and especially loved spending his days along the rivers and patrolling the Cascade Mountains. He didn't tell her this, but every time Sara passed on one of the job offers in another state, he was relieved.

When he arrived at Sara's office in downtown Yakima, she was on the phone. She looked up, saw him coming through the front door, smiled, held up a finger to say "give me a minute," and looked back at her computer screen.

Luke found a chair in the outer office and sat down. He could hear Sara talking, and it sounded like whoever she was conversing with had a lead on a suspect in a multiple murder that had occurred on Yakama Nation lands the previous summer.

He and Sara would share what they could with each other on cases they were working, but Luke knew there were some things his wife legally could not tell him about, and he was good with that. There had been things on cases he'd pursued that he hadn't shared with her as well.

They liked to talk about cases when they could, and there were times when Luke had suggested something that had helped Sara, and vice versa. A year before, Luke had been investigating a series of weird mutilations of domestic animals around the area and had finally figured out who the perpetrator was. When he went in for the arrest, the suspect had shot Luke in the chest with a handgun, and only his Kevlar vest saved his life.

Sara had wanted to go with Luke the night he was shot and was mad at him, and herself, for not being there when it had happened. After much discussion, Sara got over it, but anytime he was out on a stakeout, watching for poachers, she worried. And he worried too about her when she was running down a possible suspect.

"You don't need to worry about me," Sara had once told him as she pointed to a pistol target that she had taped to the side of the refrigerator. The target had four holes, each touching the other, in the 10-ring. Luke knew she was an excellent shot with her service pistol. Much better than him. But still he would razz her about the target.

"I could do that prone with a rifle too," Luke said after she pointed at the target.

"You know I shot that with my pistol."

"Maybe from five yards," Luke said.

"Twenty-five yards," she corrected. "Listen, do you want to put some money on it?"

Other times, he would accuse her of stealing some other shooter's target. Or even sticking holes in it with a blunt-tip arrow. But truth be told, if he ever were to get into a serious situation where guns were needed, he would want no other person by his side.

Luke heard Sara tell whoever it was on the other end of the call goodbye, and then she stuck her head out the door and said, "Hey, sorry about that. How may I help you, officer?"

CHAPTER 5

"So, you don't want a divorce then?" Sara asked with a coy grin on her face after Luke got seated.

"Jack would miss you too much," Luke said.

"And?" Sara asked.

"Well," Luke said and then hesitated. "If truth be known, I would too. But I'm not telling anyone."

"As long as we have that all settled," Sara said. Then she got up from behind her desk and walked around to Luke. "Stand up here for a minute, mister."

Luke did, and Sara wrapped her arms around him and give him a long kiss.

"That was nice," Luke said after the kiss. "But aren't such things frowned upon by the federal government? Especially in an official FBI office?"

"I think they'll let it slide just this once," Sara said. "Now, what's going on that you need to come see me in the middle of the day?"

Luke told her the story of talking to Moon, and then him yelling for help, and Luke finding the young girl next to the river before calling the medics.

"Her name is Magic, and she told a pretty wild story of someone killing some people, including her boyfriend, in one of the homeless camps over in Seattle."

"I assume you believed her, or you wouldn't have called," Sara said.

"She's pretty believable. I really think it might be worth you going and talking to her. The ambulance took her to Memorial. The medics said she was probably dehydrated and possibly hypoglycemic."

"Okay, but you should come too," Sara said. "You told her you were coming, so you should come."

"I'll meet you there," Luke said as he was standing. Before he left, he went over and kissed Sara again. "Since they're letting these things go today," he said with a grin and turned to go.

Sara didn't say anything. She just smiled, grabbed her coat, and followed Luke out the door.

* * *

It took a few minutes to figure out where Magic had ended up in the hospital. She had been in the emergency room, but the doctors wanted to watch her for twenty-four hours to make sure she was properly hydrated and to keep an eye on her blood sugar levels. So they decided she should be admitted and had put her in a room on the third floor.

After signing in as visitors, Luke and Sara rode the elevator up to the third floor.

"Poor girl," Sara said. "She's got no one to be with her. And if what she told you is right, she has to be grieving the death of her boyfriend."

"She looks young, but a little bit hard too," Luke said. "My guess is she's tough. Has to be to live in those camps."

They walked to room 317, and Luke looked in. Magic was in a hospital gown, lying on the bed with an IV stuck in her right arm. A nurse was checking a machine next to the bed.

"Knock, knock," Luke said.

Magic looked up and recognized him. She looked relieved, he thought.

"Can we come in?" Luke asked.

Magic looked at the nurse. She turned and saw the badge on Luke's shirt, nodded, and moved around him and out the door.

"Hi, Magic," Luke said as he moved into the room. "How are you feeling?"

Magic shrugged and then looked at Sara.

"This is Sara McCain," Luke said. "She is an FBI agent and is interested in talking to you about the deaths of your boyfriend and the other man in your camp."

Magic shrunk back into the bed, and tears filled her eyes, as if for a moment she had forgotten about Toby.

Sara moved around Luke and walked over to the side of Magic's bed.

"I'm so sorry to hear about your boyfriend," Sara said. "When you feel up to it, I would like to talk to you more about what happened in Seattle. Could we do that?"

Magic just nodded her head.

Luke handed Magic a tissue from a bedside box of Kleenex. She took it, dabbed at her eyes, and blew her nose.

"Am I safe here?" she asked, looking at Luke.

"Yes, you are," Luke said. "We're going to make sure of it."

"Would you mind if I sat and talked with you for a few minutes?" Sara asked.

Magic hesitated and then said, "Yeah, that would be okay, I guess."

Luke pulled a card out of his shirt pocket and handed it to Magic. She looked at it but didn't seem to make the connection of Luke and Sara sharing the same last name.

"You are with the best FBI agent in the country," Luke said. "But if you ever need anything, there is my number. Call anytime, twenty-four hours a day."

Magic just kept looking at the card and then nodded.

"Get to feeling better," Luke said, touched Sara's shoulder, and walked out of the room.

"He seems really nice," Magic said when Luke was gone.

"He is nice," Sara said. "And very good at his job. But he is a wildlife officer, and what has happened to you and your friend is more in my area of expertise."

Sara could see Magic staring at her.

"So, do you feel well enough to tell me the story that you told Officer McCain?"

Hearing Luke's last name triggered Magic. "Isn't that your last name?" she asked.

"Yes, it is. Officer McCain is my husband."

Magic didn't say anything.

"So, could we talk about what happened in Seattle?" Sara asked again.

"I guess," Magic said.

"Okay, but first, let's start with your name. Your first name is Magic, but what is your last name?"

"Magic is just my nickname. My real first name is Madison."

"What is your last name? And where were you raised?"

"My last name is Harris, and I was raised in Chico, California."

"How old are you?"

"I'm twenty-three. My birthday was last week."

"How long have you lived in Seattle?"

"About two years. I met Toby in Portland, and we moved up to Seattle when we decided to get off drugs and get married."

Magic went on to tell Sara her story. She said she was raised by a single mother who brought men home on a fairly regular basis. Each of the men, according to her mom, was going to be their savior. But each of them, Magic said, turned out to be jerks who couldn't hold a job and who treated Magic and her mom like crap.

Some were alcoholics, some hit her and her mother. Her mom would boot the guy out, and within weeks a new guy with different issues would be living there.

"She sure knew how to pick 'em," Magic said. "The last one came into my room one night and started touching me. I told my mom, and the next night she shot the guy."

"She did?"

"Yep, shot him right in the stomach with a shotgun. Blew his guts all over the place."

"Oh my gosh," Sara said. "What happened then?"

"The cops came and took her away. Said it was murder and locked her up. I told them what the douchebag had done to me and that she was just protecting me, but they didn't seem to care."

"Where is your mother now?" Sara asked.

"Still in prison, I guess. We had no money for a lawyer, and the public defender was fresh out of college and in way over her head. My mom never had a chance. This was six years ago. I had nowhere else to go, so I just took off."

"When did the drugs start?"

"I had been smoking some pot in school with my friends, but after seeing Mom shoot Darrel, and knowing I was on my own, I wanted something else to ease the pain. Someone gave me some ecstasy, and then I just went for whatever anyone had."

"And the next thing you knew, you were hooked."

"Yes, and I liked it."

"You are lucky to still be alive," Sara said.

Magic said nothing. She just dropped her head and started crying again. Finally, she said, "Toby wasn't so lucky."

Sara wanted to redirect the conversation to how Magic believed Toby and some other man had been killed in Seattle, but she decided the girl needed a break.

"Listen," Sara said, "is there anything I can get you or do for you? Are you hungry?"

"I am," Magic said. "They said they would be bringing me something to eat soon."

"Okay, let me go check on that," Sara said. "We can talk more later."

"Are you leaving?" Magic asked.

"Just to go check on your lunch. I'll stay as long as you want."

The girl smiled slightly. Maybe the first time she had smiled in days, Sara thought.

"I'll be right back," Sara said.

Sara checked in at the nurse's station and was told that lunch was on its way. Then she took two minutes to call Luke.

"Hey, how's it going?" Luke said after answering his cell phone.

"Okay, but I still need some time with her. Not surprisingly, she has had a troubled past. But she seems to be opening up. I know it's not your job really, but would you mind going back down to the river to see if you can find where she was sleeping and gather up whatever belongings she might have? I don't want her to have to go back there."

"I can do that," Luke said. "I'll see what I can find and let you know."

Sara clicked off and watched as an orderly with a rack full of food trays came rolling up the hall, stopped at Magic's room, and carried a tray in.

When Sara entered the room, the orderly was moving a table over in front of Magic, with the tray of food already loaded. Sara couldn't tell what the food was, maybe some warmed mystery meat. She looked at Magic's face and could tell that whatever it was, it was not appealing to her.

Just as the orderly was leaving, a nurse came in and checked a bunch of numbers on the machine next to Magic's bed. She then took the almost-empty IV bag off a hook attached to an arm coming from the wall, pulled the line out of it, removed a new full bag of clear liquid from a drawer, attached the line to it, and hung it back up on the hook next to the bed. Sara and Magic watched as the nurse went about her duties, and then the nurse turned to Magic and asked if she was doing okay.

"Yes, fine, thank you," Magic said.

"Your numbers are looking better, and you'll definitely feel better after you eat," the nurse said and turned to leave.

"I don't know about that," Magic said half under her breath as she poked her fork at the unidentified meat in the gravy.

"Doesn't look very appetizing, does it?" Sara said.

"I've seen better looking food come out of the garbage cans behind the restaurants in Seattle," Magic said.

"What if I run out and grab you something and bring it back?"

"Could you? Would they let you bring it in?"

"I'm an FBI agent. What are they going to say?" Sara said. "What would you like? A hamburger and fries? Pizza?"

"All of the above," Magic said.

Sara smiled, learning that Magic wasn't picky when it came to her take-out options. Any hamburger place would be great, she told Sara. She wanted a chocolate milkshake and fries too.

"What about the pizza?" Sara asked.

"Maybe for dinner?" Magic said hopefully.

"I think we can arrange that," Sara said. "I'll be back as quickly as I can with your food."

Magic thanked Sara and smiled again. It was a sad smile, Sara could see. But at least it was a smile.

CHAPTER 6

Doc spent the better part of two days looking for the girl. He took a chance and wandered back through the camp where he had killed the three people and didn't see her. He was reluctant to ask anyone about her. Instead, he mostly watched from afar, hoping to see the girl come back to the camp. But he never saw her.

After working his way through several other encampments and not seeing her, he wondered if she had totally left the city. That scared him. If she had left town that quickly, there was a good chance she knew what the boy had known—that someone had killed the man who fed the ducks.

But could she identify him? Had the boy seen enough to tell her what he looked like? He couldn't take that chance. He had to find her and get rid of her. But this time he would do it without anyone watching.

On one of his watches during the second day after killing the kid, Doc saw the young woman who had been in the camp shortly after they found the body. He thought she was a college student. But now that he looked at her, he thought maybe she was a DSHS field person or a volunteer from one of the homeless shelters. She was talking with several of the people in the camp. She had a clipboard and was taking notes. Who was she?

He wondered if this young woman knew the girl. Would she know where she was? Then he thought about her looking at him the morning of the killing. She had looked right at him, right into his eyes. She knew what he looked like and would definitely remember him. He would have to be careful around her.

* * *

Kristen Gray could not figure out what had happened to the girl called Magic. She had been there with Toby, the boy who had died, and then she was gone. Magic had been very distraught. And she had said some things at the time that were disturbing.

Gray tried to remember the exact words. Something like, "How could this happen? Toby wasn't using drugs anymore." And then she said something about a duck man and that the same thing had happened to him.

When she couldn't find Magic after twice going back to the camp, Gray decided to do some checking on how the boy had died. The girl said he was not using, but really, how else would someone that age, with a history of drug abuse, die?

She checked in her notes for the name of the woman officer who had come the morning that Toby had died. Donley was her name. She had a number for Donley, so she reached for her phone and punched in the numbers.

"Donley," a woman's voice said by way of answering the call.

"Yes, Officer Donley, this is Kristen Gray. We met the other morning at the homeless camp where the young man named Toby was found dead."

"Oh yes. The U-dub student doing research on the homeless.

How can I help you?"

"Do you know if the autopsy on Toby has been completed?"

"I don't think there is going to be an autopsy," Donley said. "His eyes, skin color, and a few other obvious signs showed he had most likely died of an overdose. Since he had no known family, no one was pressing for an autopsy, so I believe the medical examiner just put the cause of death as an overdose."

Gray said nothing.

"Were you expecting something different, Ms. Gray?" Donley asked.

"No, I guess not, but it just seems weird to me that four people, including three in a ten-day span, all died in that one camp."

"It is a little unusual," Donley said. "But you should know, as someone who is spending time in the camps, the lifestyle of the people living there is not conducive to longevity. Deaths happen, unfortunately."

"The girl they call Magic told me that Toby wasn't using anymore and hadn't been for some time. And the man that fed the ducks, he never used drugs according to the people who live in the camp. Yet he too supposedly died of a drug overdose."

"What can I say?" Donley said. "That stuff is all around them, and we all know that one hit of some bad fentanyl can kill anyone."

"I guess," Gray said. "It just seems like more than a coincidence to me."

"I'll tell you what," Donley said. "We'll make an effort to spend more time in that camp and do a little more checking around. If we find something of significance, I'll give you a call."

"I would appreciate that," Gray said.

She thanked Donley for her time and hung up. The officer said they would do some more looking, but Gray knew the fact of the matter was local law enforcement already had plenty on their plates. Following up on the unsuspicious deaths of some homeless people was not going to be high on their to-do list.

Gray really wanted to talk to Magic again. She decided to

make one more pass through the camp to see if anyone might know where the girl had gone.

* * *

A woman in black sweatpants and a dirty Seahawks jersey was sitting near where Toby's lifeless body had been found. The name on the back of the jersey was Wilson. Some disgruntled fan had most likely thrown the shirt away or donated it to Goodwill after the popular Seahawks quarterback Russell Wilson had left Seattle for big money in Denver.

Gray wasn't much of a football fan, but everyone in Seattle knew who Russell Wilson was. She walked over to the woman who looked up and smiled at her with a toothless grin.

"I remember you from the other day," the woman in the jersey said. "The day that Toby died."

"Yes, I was here," Gray said. "I remember seeing you as well. Do you like the Seahawks?"

"I root for them, but baseball is my favorite," the woman said with another smile. "I met a Mariners player once over at the mall."

"Which one?" Gray asked, although she knew less about the Seattle major league baseball team than she did the football team.

"I can't remember," the woman said. "He was a pitcher, I think."

"My name is Kristen," Gray said. "I'm doing some research on camps like yours. Would you mind talking to me for a few minutes?"

"Got any money?" the woman asked.

"No," Gray said. "Frankly, I'm just a college student."

"That's okay," the woman said. "I just thought I'd ask. So, whatchoo wanna know?"

"First, I'd like to know your name."

"My name is Mary, but people around here call me Moms. I guess because I'm one of the oldest women in the camp, and without any teeth I look like Moms Mabley."

Gray had no idea who Moms Mabley was, but she made a mental note to look it up when she had a minute.

"What would you like me to call you?" Gray asked.

"Moms is fine."

"What is your last name?"

"Let's just leave it at Moms. Not that my family is lookin' for me no more, but I don't want my old man to find me."

"Your husband?" Gray asked.

"Yeah, mean son of a bitch, he was. Not that he'd be lookin' for me neither. But I never want to see his cheatin,' lyin' ass again."

"How long have you been here?" Gray asked.

"In Seattle? Or in this camp?"

"Both," Gray said.

"I came to Seattle from Portland after that asshole husband of mine kicked me out of the house nine years ago. I had a job but still couldn't afford no decent place to live, so I stayed at the Mission for a while."

"Why didn't you stay there?" Gray asked.

"Because I started drinkin' again, and they don't want no alcoholics livin' there. So I got me a tent and moved down here. It ain't bad really, except for now the people livin' here seem to be dyin'."

"That's what I wanted to talk to you about," Gray said. "I spoke to Magic the day that Toby died, and she said that three other people in this camp had died recently."

"We all been talkin' 'bout that," Moms said. "It's scary. Right before Toby died, the Duckman died. Cops said it was an overdose, but the Duckman, he didn't do no drugs."

"I was talking with the police today," Gray said. "And they said that Toby's death was due to an overdose too, but Magic said he wasn't using anymore."

"Nope, he wasn't," Moms said. "We never saw him use nothin'. Him or Magic, neither one. They were goin' to get married. Did you know that?"

"Magic mentioned that to me, yes," Gray said. "It is all very sad. Magic was very sad. I've been trying to check on her. Have you seen her lately?"

"No. Not since Toby died. She just disappeared, like magic. Hey, do you think it was magic, 'cause that was her name?"

"I really don't know," Gray said. "Did you ever talk to her about where she came from?"

"I think she said she was from California," Moms said. "Don't know nothin' 'bout her family."

"I've looked in several of the camps around Seattle, and she isn't in any of them," Gray said. "Did she ever say anything about going someplace else?"

"I remember her and Toby talkin' about gettin' out of this rain," Moms said. "They was talkin' about going to someplace warmer and dryer, but I don't know where."

"Was anyone else here in the camp close to Magic?"

"Only Toby," Moms said. "They was really happy together. Poor girl. I hope she's okay."

"If I find her, I'll tell her you were concerned about her welfare."

Moms just smiled a toothless smile and waved as Gray walked away.

"Go Hawks!" Gray said, but that got no response from the woman in the Seahawks jersey with Russell Wilson's name on the back.

* * *

Doc observed the camp from behind a bridge abutment a hundred and thirty yards away, dressed in his letterman jacket and a cowboy hat pulled down low. He watched the college girl talk to the woman in the Seahawks jersey. He wondered what they were discussing. Were they talking about the man or kid he had killed? Or were they discussing the girl that had disappeared?

He watched the women talk for ten minutes and then saw the younger woman get up and walk off in the other direction. She looked in his direction as she stood to leave, but she didn't seem to recognize him.

When she had been gone for a good five minutes, Doc slowly

stood and walked toward the camp. The woman in the Seahawks jersey was still sitting there in an old metal folding chair. He ambled into camp but did not look at her. He didn't want to make it obvious he was coming to talk to her.

Doc stopped at the Duckman's green tent, peered inside, and then around the camp, as if looking for the man.

Moms saw Doc coming and watched as he looked inside the tent and then around the area.

"Who you lookin' for?" Moms asked the man in the letterman jacket.

"The man who feeds the ducks," Doc said. "I met him here a couple weeks ago."

"Sorry, honey, but he dead," Moms said.

"What?" Doc said, trying to put real surprise in his voice.

"Yep. Five or six days ago. Overdose, the cops say."

"No," Doc said. "I don't believe it." Then, after thinking about it a few seconds, he said, "How about the young girl that was here—sort of pretty, blonde hair, about twenty-five?"

"Whatcha want with her?" Moms asked.

"Nuthin' really. She was just nice to me, and we talked for a while. Thought I'd say hi to her too."

"She gone," Moms said. "Her boyfriend died, and she took off. No one's seen her since."

"Did she say where she was going?" Doc asked.

"Nope," Moms said abruptly. Doc worried she was getting a bad vibe from him.

"Okay, well I hope she is okay. Sorry to hear about the Duckman. Have a good day." Doc turned and started walking back the way he came.

"You want me to tell her who was looking for her?" Moms asked.

"No, that's okay," Doc said with a wave and kept right on walking.

CHAPTER 7

Luke had fielded some strange calls in his twenty-three years as a fish and wildlife police officer, including one regarding some domestic animals being skewered on tree branches high off the ground in the forests in his patrol area. Folks began thinking bigfoot was involved with those.

But the call he received while driving to work the next morning was right up there with the weirdest. The man on the phone was asking about ownership of dinosaur bones that were discovered on public land.

"Say that again," Luke said after the guy asked the question.

"Is it legal to take dinosaur bones off state-owned land?" the man asked.

"I've never been asked that before," Luke said. "My first inclination is to say no, it is not legal, but I need to do some checking."

Luke knew that arrowheads and other Native American artifacts were not to be removed. And it was illegal to remove petrified wood from state land, so it would seem dinosaur bones would fall in line with those items.

"Well, I've heard of a guy who says he has found some bones," the man said. "He thinks they're from a brontosaurus or something. I know him well enough to know he's going to sell the bones if he can."

Luke remembered that there had been some mammoth bones discovered out in the Wenas Valley in the past decade, so there was a chance this man had stumbled onto some ancient bones somewhere in the area.

The caller's name was Derek Day. He gave Luke his phone number and the name of the guy who claimed to have found the bones.

"His name is Quentin Nash," Day said. "You want me to tell him he can't take the bones?"

"You might let him know that you believe it is illegal, yes," Luke said. "Any idea where these bones are located?"

"Somewhere up on the L.T. Murray," Day said. "But he won't say where beyond that."

The L.T. Murray Wildlife Area is located northwest of Yakima, mostly in Kittitas County, and covers approximately 118,000 acres of cheatgrass and sagebrush with some coniferous forest and riparian habitat along several creeks and the Yakima River.

As Luke thought about it, he realized that depending on where Nash found the alleged bones, they might be only a few miles from the mammoth dig site in the Wenas Valley. So it was quite possible the bones were mammoth bones.

"If you hear any more about what Mr. Nash has planned for the bones, give me a call," Luke said.

Day agreed to try to learn more and call Luke back if he heard anything. Luke thanked him for the call and clicked off.

He was in his state-issued truck when the call from Day came through. Luke didn't know how the man got his cell phone number, but over the years he had handed out hundreds, if not thousands, of business cards with his information on them. So calls came into his cell phone semi-frequently from people he didn't know.

That was fine with Luke. He didn't mind the calls unless they woke him from a dead sleep in the wee hours of the morning. Usually, the calls from unknown numbers came from people who had questions about certain game laws or were asking about wildlife in the area. Occasionally, the callers wanted to give him information that might lead Luke to a poacher.

Luke liked taking all the calls and tried to help anyone who had a question. He knew the laws and happily answered those questions. Many times, he could answer questions about the wildlife in the area, but when someone asked him about something he didn't know, he would refer them to the biologists in the Region 3 office.

He was always amazed at the callers who offered tips and leads about lawbreakers. They came from all sorts of sources. Snoopy neighbors, relatives, hunting partners, spouses and ex-spouses—they all were happy to drop a dime on someone they thought was breaking the law.

The calls all started out similarly. The person on the other end of the line would say something like, "I probably shouldn't be calling, and I really wouldn't want him to know I called, but my neighbor is skinning another deer in his backyard. He's done three in the last week. I thought deer season was over last month." It was those kinds of calls from the public that helped Luke and his fellow officers catch many criminals. Not always, but often the tips would lead to an investigation that would ensnare the lawbreakers.

As was the case with most law enforcement officers, Luke had quickly become acquainted with the habitual lawbreakers. When he saw them out and about, he paid particular attention to them. He knew almost all the reoffenders by name, but Quentin Nash did not ring a bell.

When he got to the office, Luke fired up his desktop computer and googled the Wenas Valley mammoth discovery. According to the story Luke found from the *Yakima Herald-Republic*, some people were having work done on their driveway, and the construction crew dug up the leg bone of a Columbian mammoth. The story went on to say the mammoths lived in Washington State seventeen thousand years ago and were the ancestors to modern-day elephants.

How someone wandering through the L.T. Murray might dig up a mammoth bone was another question altogether.

Next, Luke walked into his captain's office to get his take on the whole dinosaur bone situation.

"I believe it is illegal," Bob Davis said after Luke asked him about removing the bones.

Davis was a former college football player and still had the physique of a defensive lineman. He had brown hair going to gray and a big bushy gray mustache. He looked like a cross between actor Wilford Brimley and Andy Reid, the coach of the Kansas City Chiefs.

"That's what I thought," Luke said. "Do you think I should call someone? They had a team from the university up in Ellensburg work on the site where the mammoth was found."

"Let's wait and see if this Nash fella actually has found some bones," Davis said. "Maybe try to run him down?"

"Will do," Luke said and headed back to his desk.

He had just sat down when his cell phone rang again. He looked at the ID on the screen. Sara was calling.

"Hey," Luke said.

"Hi. I just met with Magic again. The doctor said she is doing much better and is ready to be released. The only problem is she has no place to go but back to one of the camps down by the river."

"Did you tell her I grabbed her stuff and we have it?"

"Yes, and she would like to get it. But I don't want her going back to the camp. I don't think it is safe for her."

"What do you want to do?" Luke asked.

"Would you mind if I offer to have her stay with us in the guest room for a while?"

"Fine with me, although you are finally going to have to make a decision on some of your stuff that's stored in there."

"We can get that figured out. I'm not sure she will even want to come and stay with us, but it's a much safer option. I talked to her again about the whole situation in Seattle, and she is convinced that someone killed her boyfriend and the man in the camp that fed the ducks."

"But she didn't see anyone do it and can't ID the person, so she should be safe from him if there is such a person," Luke said.

"Just knowing there might be someone out there who killed those men puts her in some danger," Sara said. "She's smart enough to know that. That's why she caught a ride to Yakima as fast as she could."

"I'm fine with whatever you think," Luke said. "Hope she likes dogs."

"I'll let her know about Jack," Sara said. "But you know him— he'll work his way into her heart in a matter of minutes."

"He'll be happy to keep her company at the house," Luke said.

"Let's see if she'll agree to come home with me," Sara said. "We can figure out the other stuff later."

"Sounds good," Luke said.

Sara said, "See ya tonight" and was gone.

After he set his phone down, Luke started thinking about having another woman in the house. He'd been a bachelor for a long time, and it was a bit of an adjustment when Sara had moved in. He loved her dearly and was happy that they were together, but he hadn't realized that females came with so much stuff.

Sara, as a professional, had at least two dozen suits. Most were pantsuits, but she had dress suits too. The FBI had a pretty tight set of guidelines on what their agents were to wear in the field and in the office, and she had enough to cover at least two weeks' worth of work if she were to be away from home.

Then came all the stuff women need for personal purposes. Luke had a razor, some shaving gel, a toothbrush, toothpaste, and a hairbrush in the bathroom. Everything else that was in the drawers and on the bathroom vanity was Sara's. It wasn't that much frankly, because Sara didn't want or need much makeup or hair product, but even still, she had tripled the number of items in their bathroom.

Adding another woman into the mix would definitely create some challenges, although with Magic living in a camp for the last however many months, she probably wasn't going to leave much of a footprint.

When Luke had finally located Magic's personal items, after checking three other camps along the river, he found very few items in her backpack. She had a sweatshirt, two pairs of socks, two t-shirts, and one pair of short pants. Luke didn't count the underwear, but there were at least a couple of extra pairs along with a pair of flip-flops. Everything else she owned, she was either wearing when he helped her at the river, or she had probably left behind in her rush to get out of Seattle. Luke wondered what Magic was going to do when the weather got colder, or when it rained, which she must have had to deal with already in Seattle.

Surprisingly, Luke did find that Magic had some money. As he looked to see if there was some kind of identification in the pack, he found an envelope with almost two hundred dollars in it. Even more shocking was the money was still there after she had left the backpack in the camp.

Luke had recruited Moon to go with him to the different camps, and after they'd found Magic's backpack and saw the money, he asked Moon about it.

"There's kind of a code in the camps," Moon said. "People don't mess with other people's stuff or they get kicked out. Or worse, they might get a beating. Her money was as safe here as it would be in some bank."

Luke raised his eyes and nodded as if he understood, but he really didn't.

"Well, I'm glad they left her backpack alone so we could get it back to her," Luke said.

* * *

He found an address for Quentin Nash in the Washington State driver's license records. Or at least he assumed it was the man he wanted to talk to. It seemed to be an uncommon name, and since there was only one Quentin Nash listed in Yakima County, Luke figured it had to be his man.

The information for this Quentin Nash told Luke that the man had dark hair, brown eyes, was fifty-one years old, stood over six feet tall, and weighed two hundred and thirty-five pounds. The driver's license photo showed Nash with black hair, a black beard, and heavy black eyebrows that furrowed as he squinted at the camera. It was like he was pissed because he had to have his photo taken.

Nash's address was listed as Selah, but Luke knew from the listed road name that Nash lived out of town and probably wasn't that far from where the Wenas mammoth dig had taken place.

Looking a bit deeper into the records, Luke found that twenty-three years ago, Nash's wife had gone missing. The Yakima County Sheriff's detectives had done a thorough investigation and had searched Nash's residence and surrounding property, but they'd found nothing.

Nash's estranged in-laws were convinced that their daughter hadn't just packed up and left town, believing that Nash had done something to her, but neither they nor the police could come up with any proof.

"Interesting," Luke mumbled to himself as he wrote down the address in his pocket notebook.

After taking care of some other emails and returning a couple of phone calls, Luke was ready to head into the field. Being in the office, going to meetings, and filling out reports was a necessary part of his job, he knew, but his real love was being outdoors. Luke spent as much time as possible during his workday out and about, checking on hunters and anglers and doing the real work of protecting the fish and wildlife in Central Washington.

He thought about calling to see if Quentin Nash was at home but decided to just drive out to his place and arrive unannounced.

Calling might save him a trip because if Nash was like most other fifty-two-year-olds, he was probably at a job someplace and not at home. But if he was home, Luke wanted to see how he might be greeted by just showing up out of the blue.

As it turned out, Nash was at home, and Luke quickly found out how the man felt about a law enforcement officer arriving unannounced.

CHAPTER 8

S he knew it wasn't really her duty to check into it, but Kristen Gray was just inquisitive enough to want to know how Toby had died. She believed Magic when she said her boyfriend, her fiancé, was no longer doing drugs. And if that was truly the case, how had he died? She decided to check into it further.

Gray had never been to the King County Medical Examiner's Office before, but after looking online, she found out that she had been very close. The office was located on the second floor of Harborview Medical Center, a hospital she had been to more than once while visiting relatives.

She found a spot in the hospital's visitor parking lot and headed to the entrance. As a mere college student, and not related to Toby, Gray knew she really had no business asking for information about his death, but she was willing to give it a try. The question was, what was the best way to approach the situation?

As she walked to the hospital's entrance, she thought about telling the medical examiner's staff that she was Toby's cousin. But the more she thought about that, she worried that they might just turn his body over to her for the handling of his remains. She definitely was not prepared for that, emotionally or financially.

She finally decided to fib just a little and tell them she was a good friend of the dead man and see where that might lead. Gray didn't even know his last name. They would surely ask that of a good friend of his.

Unsure of where this was going to lead, Gray steeled herself and headed for the elevator.

"How may I help you?" a woman behind a counter asked after Gray pushed through a glass door with King County Medical Examiner painted on the upper half. The woman had dark hair that was streaked with gray and a slim face that wore a businesslike expression. She had a name tag pinned to a white lab coat that read Liz Maxwell.

The office smelled like cleaning solution, made up mostly of ammonia, Gray thought. The desks were all metal, sturdy and industrial-looking, like from the 1960s. The chairs matched. An instrumental version of "The Girl From Ipanema" was barely audible coming out of a speaker somewhere in the ceiling. One other younger woman, maybe a tech of some kind, sat at a desk in the far corner of the main office area.

"I'm here to follow up on the death of a friend of mine," Gray said. "He died two days ago in one of the homeless camps down by the football stadium."

"Do you have his name?" Maxwell asked.

"Yes, his name is Toby," Gray said. "I never knew his last name, and I'm not sure anyone else did either. That was one of the questions I was going to ask of you—if you learned his last name."

"Let me check the files," Maxwell said as she moved back to a desk with a computer monitor perched on it.

"How old?" Maxwell asked.

"I would say mid-twenties," Gray said.

Maxwell tapped a few more keys on the computer keyboard.

"The only younger male deceased currently in our possession is listed as a John Doe."

"Does it say he died of an overdose?"

She clacked a couple more keys and said, "Yes, it does."

"But you didn't do an autopsy?"

Click, click, click. "No, no autopsy has been done."

"And none is scheduled?" Gray asked.

The woman looked at the computer monitor. "No, there is not."

Gray thought about it for a minute and then asked, "What would need to happen to get an autopsy done?"

"We would need a valid request from a member of his family or a police agency," Maxwell said.

Again, Gray paused to think. "What will happen to his body if nobody claims it?" she asked.

More clicking on the keyboard, and then Maxwell said, "The body was placed in the morgue yesterday morning. We'll try to locate family to see if they want to pick up the body for burial. If no one claims it, the body will be cremated."

"Where is the morgue?" Gray asked

"Downstairs," Maxwell said. Then she looked at Gray and said, "Is there something else going on here?"

Gray decided to lay it all out on the table. She told the woman who she was, that she barely knew the man who was lying somewhere back in the autopsy area, and that she had been in the camp shortly after he had died. Then she told her about the young woman named Magic, and what Magic had told Gray about someone possibly killing the man she knew as Toby, along with another man who lived in the same camp.

Maxwell listened and then said, "My, that is quite a story."

"Is there anything I can do?" Gray asked.

"You need to talk to the police," Maxwell said.

"I did," Gray said. "But they seemed uninterested in the whole thing. Dead addicts in homeless camps are way too common, and they have better things to do with their time."

Maxwell just listened and said nothing.

"Would it at least be possible for me to see the body?" Gray asked. "At least I would know it is Toby, and that might help you or others identify him."

"I'll need to check, but I think that would be okay," the woman said and picked up the receiver on a phone on the desk.

The woman talked quietly to whoever answered the call, so Gray couldn't hear what was being said. The call ended fairly quickly, and Gray thought it was going to be a no-go.

"Follow me," Maxwell said and pointed Gray to a swinging gate at the end of the counter.

The two women walked to the back of the office, past the other lab-coated tech sitting at a metal desk, through a metal fire door with a small, narrow, vertical window inserted in it, and down a long hallway. They walked past three doors, all closed, and then turned to a larger set of double doors. Maxwell reached for a key card attached to a retractable device affixed to her belt, pulled it out, and ran it through a reader next to the door. A half-second later, there was a buzz, and the doors opened inward automatically.

They walked through the doors to a wall of stainless-steel doors. There were identical doors, four across and two high. Each door, which was about four feet by four feet, was numbered. The woman in the lab coat went to the door with the number four on it, pulled the heavy latch handle, and opened the door. Then she reached in and pulled a seven-foot gurney out of the compartment.

Lying face up on the gurney was the same man Gray had seen just two days before. It was the young man the girl named Magic had been kneeling over. It was Toby.

Gray was slightly surprised to see Toby still in the same clothes he had been wearing the day he died. On all the television shows she had seen, the body of a deceased person in a morgue was naked. If the medical examiner had determined it wasn't necessary to do an autopsy, they must have decided to hold off on undressing Toby's body.

"That's Toby," Gray said. "I wish I could tell you his last name."

"Toby is a start," Maxwell said. "I will get this to the police officer in charge of the case. They can run a missing person's report for anyone named Toby."

"Or Tobias?" Gray said.

"Yes," Maxwell said. "I'm sure they will try all possible derivations of Toby."

"How long will you keep his body here?" Gray asked.

Maxwell glanced at her smartwatch. "We normally only keep bodies for forty-eight hours longer, and then they are sent for cremation."

"Even if you don't know what the family's wishes might be?"

"We only have so much space," Maxwell said.

"Is there anything I can do to get you to hold it for a while longer? I know his fiancé, and I'm trying to run her down now. And, as I mentioned, there is this issue of a possible homicide."

"I will talk with the M.E.," Maxwell said. "If there is no urgent need for the space, we might be able to hold the body a bit longer. It would help, though, if you could get a police request."

"I'll see what I can do," Gray said.

✳ ✳ ✳

Sara McCain called the Seattle Police Department and asked for the officer who had investigated the death of the man she only knew as Toby at one of the homeless camps down by the football stadium.

"Can you give me any more information?" the person who answered the call asked.

"Yes, my name is Sara McCain, and I am an FBI special agent calling from Yakima," Sara said and gave the person on the other end of the line her ID number. "Other than that, I have a very scared girl here who says she believes someone killed her boyfriend, a young man named Toby, three days ago. And I would like to talk to the investigating officer or officers."

"Yes, ma'am," the man's voice said on the other end of the line. "It might take me a few minutes. Could I take your name and phone number and have the officer give you a call back?"

"No, I'll wait, thank you," Sara said. She knew that a call back almost never came because police officers have a hundred balls in the air, and the one closest to falling to the floor would get the most attention. She figured her call wasn't even one of the balls in the air.

She listened to dead air for a moment, and then a computerized voice came on and told her that her call was important and to please continue to hold.

The message played every thirty seconds for four minutes and thirty-seven seconds, according to the time on Sara's cell phone, and then a harried woman's voice came on the line and said, "Agent McCain, sorry to make you wait. I'm Officer Jan Donley, and my partner and I were the ones who took the call about the dead man at the homeless camp the other day."

"Can you tell me what happened?" Sara asked.

"911 got a call from a woman who said there was a dead man at one of the camps," Donley said. "She didn't know the physical address because, well, there isn't any at any of the camps, but she described it to the emergency operator who then put the call out. My partner and I were close to the football stadium and knew where some of the camps were, so we took the call."

The officer went on to tell of arriving at the camp and finding the dead young man.

"Who placed the call to 911?" Sara asked.

"A young woman who had come into the camp to see what was happening," Donley said. "She is a student at the university here and is doing a study on the homeless people. I have her contact information in the report file."

"I'd really like to talk to her if I could," Sara said.

"Give me a second," Donley said. Sara could hear keys clicking on a keyboard, a pause, and more keys clicking.

"Here it is. Her name is Kristen Gray," Donley said and gave Sara the phone number. "She's a little bit of a thing. I remember my partner and I were worried about her safety, hanging around in the camps, but she said she'd been doing it for a while and has had no problems."

"Great, thanks," Sara said. "I'll call her. And do you know the young woman named Magic?"

"Yes, we've seen her in the camp a time or two," Donley said. "Evidently, she and the dead man were living together. Ms. Gray said she saw Magic sitting on a rock crying when she got there. But when we arrived, Magic was gone. We were dealing with a dead body and trying to get as much evidence on what might have happened, so we didn't spend much time looking for her."

"Well, she ended up over here in Yakima, and she is understandably upset," Sara said. "She is claiming that someone killed her boyfriend, Toby."

"It had all the signs of an overdose," Donley said. "It's a tragedy, but it happens occasionally in these camps."

"Magic claims that both she and Toby were clean, and had been for a while, and that he had seen someone struggling with another man in their camp who ended up dead. A man they called the Duckman."

"Yes, another overdose," Donley said.

"She thinks the man who was struggling with this Duckman fellow might have come back into the camp and killed Toby because he could identify the man."

"We hadn't heard that," Donley said.

"Did the medical examiner do an autopsy on Toby or this Duckman?" Sara asked.

"Let me check," Donley said and again started typing away at the keyboard. "No, it looks like neither of the bodies were autopsied. The cause of death on both is listed as an overdose."

"Are either of them still at the morgue?"

More keyboard clicking and clacking. "Amos Carl Haynes, the man they called the Duckman, was cremated a week ago. No one has picked up the remains. Toby, last name unknown at this point, is still in the morgue."

"Thank you, Officer Donley," Sara said. "Can you give me your direct line, or a cell number, in case any other questions pop up?"

Donley gave Sara the numbers and said, "I'm happy to help. And I hope Magic is doing okay. She seems like a nice girl."

Sara thanked the officer again and clicked off.

Then she dialed the number for Kristen Gray.

CHAPTER 9

He had searched at five other camps within a three-mile radius and still could not find her. And he had spent an uncomfortable amount of time watching the camp where he had killed the young man. If the girl was around, she most likely would come back to her tent at some point to get her personal items and to chat with the friends in the camp. Or so he thought. Maybe she had come and gone during one of the times when he hadn't been watching the camp? He didn't know.

Doc really needed to find the girl. If the kid had told her what he had seen the night he had killed the old man who fed the ducks, she might be able to identify him. And if she'd told the police about what the kid had seen, then there was a chance they would start looking for him. They might even start to put two and two together, and then he could be in serious trouble.

After watching the camp for the better part of two days, he decided to risk going back in and chatting with one or two of the residents to see what he might find out. This time he would be in full homeless gear, no letterman jacket or cowboy hat. He'd be back to the bulky raincoat and the leather pilot's cap.

The woman who had been in the Seahawks sweatshirt seemed to always be around. She might know something new. He looked around and didn't see the woman but instead a man in a brown jacket with a fleece collar sitting on the old metal folding chair where the woman usually sat.

Doc slowly worked his way down the path under the freeway and looked at the ground, like he was looking for something.

"You won't find no money there," the man in the coat said. He was wearing gray sweatpants, stained in places, and a blue Mariners hat. He had a week's worth of gray stubble on his face. "Nothing good gets missed for too long."

Doc just kept looking at the ground, kicking at some rocks in the dirt, like he didn't hear him.

"You're wasting your time," the man said, waving his hand like he was shooing a fly.

Finally, Doc looked at the man. He was smiling. Smiling with a big gap in his front teeth.

"I've seen you around here before," the man said. "What camp you live in?"

Doc gestured with his thumb back over his right shoulder. "That way," he said with a gravelly voice and dropped his head back to the ground. He was dressed differently than when he had talked to the woman a few days earlier, and he wanted to sound different too.

"What you want down here?" the man asked. "I seen you before, hovering around, watching in here. You lookin' for someone?"

Doc kept his head down and said, "I met a young girl here once. Some man hit me up at my tent and said he was looking for his daughter. Described the girl that lives here 'bout perfectly. I didn't tell him I saw her, but I wanted to see if she is interested in seeing her daddy. That's all."

"She ain't been around since Toby died," the man said, shaking his head. "She and the boy were going to get married. She was real broke up about him dying."

"And she just disappeared?" Doc asked.

"We heard rumors where she went," the man said. "But no one knows for sure."

"I forgot her name," Doc said.

"Magic," the man said. "Her name is Magic."

"Yeah, Magic," Doc said. "That was it, but that wasn't what her daddy called her."

"Well, that's the only name we knew her by. No last name or nothin'."

"And where do you think she went?"

"I got no clue," the man said, shooing another fly.

"You said there were rumors?"

"Yeah, but who the hell knows. Some said she went to Spokane. Some said she went to Portland. Some said she went to Yakima. No one knows for sure."

Doc thought about that for a moment. If she had left town, maybe the girl named Magic wouldn't be an issue.

"Well, if you see her, tell her her daddy is looking for her."

"She gone," the gap-toothed man said. "I don't think she wants nobody to find her."

* * *

"Hi, this is Kristen. I can't take your call right now. Leave a number, and I will get back to you as soon as possible."

Sara listened to the recording and then said, "Hi, Kristen. My name is Sara McCain. I am an FBI agent in Yakima, and I have some questions about the young man named Toby who was found dead in one of the homeless camps there in Seattle the other day." She left her number and asked Gray to call.

Sara pushed end, set the cell phone on her desk, and turned

to her computer monitor to call up her emails. Within forty-five seconds, her phone started buzzing and skittering on the slick desk surface. The girl had had just enough time to listen to the voicemail after not answering the call because it was an unlisted number.

"This is Agent McCain," Sara said.

"Seriously," Kristen Gray said. "Are you really an FBI agent?"

"Yes, I am. Is this Kristen?"

"Yes, ma'am," Gray said. "And you are the answer to my prayers."

"How so?" Sara asked.

Gray went on to tell her the whole story, from the time she saw the people in the homeless camp around Toby's dead body, to talking with Magic, to speaking with the police, and then taking it upon herself to try to determine if the officials had done an autopsy on the young man.

"I was haunted by what Magic had told me that morning, that she thought Toby had been killed by someone who wanted him dead for witnessing another murder in the camp. Now I can't find Magic anywhere, and the medical examiner is about to cremate Toby's body."

"That is why I'm calling you," Sara said. "I've been in contact with Magic, and I wanted to look into this a bit further."

"You have to stop the cremation and get an autopsy," Gray said. "The woman at the medical examiner's office said that the police could request an autopsy. The local cops are convinced it is just another overdose, but it sure couldn't hurt to check."

"Do you happen to have the phone number for the person you talked with at the medical examiner's office?" Sara asked.

Gray said she did, and after quickly scrolling through her phone contacts, gave the number to Sara.

"They'll surely do the autopsy for the FBI, won't they?" Gray asked.

"I'll do my best," Sara said.

"How is Magic doing?" Gray asked. "She was so brokenhearted.

I went to talk to the police in the camp the day Toby died, and she just disappeared."

"She says she is afraid that the man who killed Toby would come for her next," Sara said.

When she heard that, Gray suddenly flashed back to the man who was staring at her from under the bridge. There was just something about the guy. He was dressed for the part, but still he stuck out from the others in some imperceptible way. And when he saw her looking at him, he turned and left, quickly. Too quickly for an old timer hampered by all the aches and pains from sleeping on the ground. And he was creepy.

"If there is such a guy, I might have seen him," Gray said.

"Really?" Sara said with interest. "Can you describe him?"

Gray gave her a general description of the man, who could have been one of a hundred at the different camps around the Puget Sound.

"I know that doesn't help much, but there was just something about the guy. I see homeless people all the time in my studies. This guy was different. He seemed too self-conscious maybe, or like his entire appearance was put-on. I don't know if I'm explaining it right. I've been around hundreds of homeless folks during my graduate work, and no one has ever made me feel unsafe just by looking at me. Except him."

"Would you know him if you saw him again?" Sara asked.

"I don't know," Gray said. "Maybe."

"Magic said one other man in the camp, the man that Toby thought was killed by this guy, didn't use drugs either, but the police said he died of an overdose."

"She mentioned that to me too," Gray said. "And that there were two other people in that camp who had died there recently. Like I said, I'm in and around those camps frequently, and it just seems really weird that four people, including two who supposedly hadn't been using, would just die."

"Most of those people don't live very healthy lives," Sara said. "And one hit of some bad fentanyl can kill anyone."

"That's what the Seattle police said," Gray said. "And I agree with that. But it just seems that it is an awfully strange coincidence that two men in the same camp, neither one using, would die of an overdose."

"Let me see what I can do," Sara said. "I'll call the medical examiner's office now and ask them if they will do an autopsy."

"I hope we're not too late," Gray said. "They told me they only hold bodies for forty-eight hours and then they cremate them. I begged them to hold Toby for a while longer, and I think they were going to try."

Sara assured Gray that she would call immediately and then would call her back when she knew for sure what was going to happen.

"Thank you so much, Agent McCain," Gray said.

"You are welcome," Sara said. "And please, call me Sara."

"Thank you, Sara," Gray said. "And good luck."

*** * ***

It took a few minutes to get through to the right person at the King County Medical Examiner's Office because the woman who Kristen Gray had spoken with was off for three days. And even though she had left notes about her meeting with Gray and the discussion about trying to hold Toby's body for a little longer, nobody had read them.

"So does that mean his body has been cremated?" Sara asked the man on the other end of the line.

"Well, I don't know," the man said. "Let me check."

Again, Sara heard the familiar clicking of keys being tapped on a computer keyboard.

A minute later, the man said, "No, it hasn't been cremated yet, but it's set to go next."

"I need you to put a stop to that," Sara said with some urgency. "We have a credible source saying this man may have been the victim of a homicide, and we need to have an autopsy done as soon as possible."

"We'll need to have an official request for that to happen," the man said. "In writing."

"I can email you something right away," Sara said. "Will that work?"

"We have forms that need to be filed and then those will need to be approved by a medical examiner."

"I'll happily do whatever needs to be done, but we need to put a hold on the cremation. Can you do that?"

The man on the other end of the phone paused and muttered something Sara couldn't understand.

"Listen," Sara said. "Let me talk to a medical examiner."

"She's very busy," the man said. "So I'm not sure I can reach her."

"Tell her it is the FBI calling and it is very important. I am making a serious request to get that cremation halted. If I can't talk to someone who can put a stop to it and initiate an autopsy, there are going to be some serious consequences. Please try to get her on the phone now!"

"Yes, ma'am," the man said.

"I'm not a ma'am, I'm a special agent. Please address me as such."

"Yes ma . . . er, special agent. Hold on one minute."

Unlike the Seattle Police Department, the King County Medical Examiner's Office played some music for the people who were put on hold. Sara listened to a Hall & Oates song, "Private Eyes," and was enjoying it when it ended abruptly and a woman's voice came on the other end of the line.

"Special Agent McCain, I am Doctor Joyce Hanson, a King County medical examiner. Michael said you need to put the stop on a pending cremation and you are requesting an autopsy?"

"Yes, Doctor Hanson. Thank you for taking my call. We have new information on this situation, and we believe this young man may have been murdered."

"Can we get some written authorization?" Hanson asked.

"Yes, I can get you all the paperwork you need, but it sounded like the body was next up for cremation, so I need to get it stopped."

"Certainly," Hanson said. "I'll put a stop to it right now and get Michael to email you the appropriate forms. I will try to start the autopsy later this afternoon. Would you like to be here for it?"

"Thank you, doctor," Sara said. "Unfortunately, I'm in Yakima right now. But could you call me after you have done the autopsy?"

"I will call you as soon as we have any results," Hanson said. "Let me switch you back to Michael, and he will get you the forms."

"Do I need to follow up to make sure things are stopped and started as requested?"

"No, that won't be necessary," Hanson said. "I will be in touch. Hold for Michael."

After giving her email address to Michael so he could send her the proper forms, Sara called Kristen Gray.

"Hopefully, I caught them in time," Sara said after Gray asked how she did with the medical examiner's office. "They have agreed to do the autopsy."

"That's great! Thank you so much, Agent McCain."

"Sara, please," Sara said. "And I will call you Kristen."

"Deal," Gray said. "Any idea when there might be some results?"

"The medical examiner assigned to it thought she might do the autopsy later today, but I am guessing the blood analysis and whatever else they do might take some time for results. Maybe a few days."

"Okay," Gray said. "At least something is being done. Will you tell Magic what is happening?"

"Yes," Sara said. "At some point."

"She was convinced that Toby wasn't taking drugs and would not have OD'd," Gray said. "And after listening to her and seeing the look in her eyes, I believed her."

Sara thought about the short visit she'd had with Magic in the hospital. She agreed with Gray. Magic was convinced, and she was very convincing.

"We'll get an answer," Sara said. "Hopefully."

"Hopefully," Gray said.

"I'll call you as soon as I hear anything," Sara said.

CHAPTER 10

"Get the hell off my property!" the man on the porch yelled. "Now! And don't come back!"

Luke double-checked the address he had in his notes and then looked at the man. He had the driver's license photo of Quentin Nash, but the man on the porch looked nothing like the man in the photo. The Nash in the photo had a thick mop of jet-black hair and a matching beard covering a full face. Luke hadn't been able to see Nash's body in the photo, but the information on the driver's license said he was fairly heavy, over two hundred and thirty pounds.

The man Luke was looking at now might have weighed a hundred and sixty pounds with a couple of big rocks in his pockets, and his face was thin. Short, thinning gray hair covered the man's head, and there was no sign of a beard. The man looked sickly, possibly near death.

"Are you Quentin Nash?" Luke asked.

"None of your damn business," the man said. "Get the hell outta here."

"I just wanted to chat with Mr. Nash for a minute," Luke said. "Only a couple of questions."

As he talked, Luke looked around the place. It was a typical country house. A stick-frame rambler, probably built in the 1970s. But it was in a serious state of neglect. The paint on the siding was cracked and peeling. The roof was missing a shingle here and there. An old walk-behind gas lawn mower sitting in front of the garage door looked like it hadn't been started since George Bush was in office. But the lawn had been mowed, at least sometime in the last month.

An old brown Chevy pickup, 1980s vintage, sat just off the driveway. All four tires were inflated, which could mean the truck still ran. And the license plate had current tabs. Luke read the plate number and repeated it in his mind three times. He would write it down on his notepad as soon as he could.

There was an old rusting wheelbarrow tipped over to one side near the front porch and a few tools—including a rake, a shovel, and a pickax—leaning against the trunk of an old apple tree that grew on the side of the house. The tree hadn't been pruned in years and looked about as sickly as the man on the porch.

Nothing that might possibly be a mammoth bone was anywhere in sight.

"Last warning," the gray-haired man yelled. "I'm going to call the sheriff if you don't leave now."

"I'm leaving," Luke said as he stepped back to the driver's door of his pickup. "Tell Mr. Nash I'd like to talk to him please. Nothing serious. Just a couple of questions."

The man on the porch just glared at Luke as he climbed into the truck, fired it up, backed around, and drove out of the driveway.

When he got onto the county road, Luke stopped, dug out his notebook, and wrote the license plate number down. Then he found the phone number for Derek Day, the man who had called in the tip that Nash was digging up mammoth bones on public lands. He punched the numbers into his cell phone and waited for a ring on the other end.

"Yeah, hello?" Day said.

"Mr. Day, this is Luke McCain, the game warden you called about the mammoth bones."

"Yeah, how you doing?" Day said. "Mammoth bones? I thought they were dinosaur bones."

"I guess technically mammoths weren't dinosaurs," Luke said. "They were around here after the dinosaurs, but still thousands of years ago."

"Uh, okay," Day said. "Whatever. Did you talk to Nash about diggin' 'em up?"

"That's why I'm calling," Luke said. "I went to the address I had for Mr. Nash, and a guy who didn't come close to matching the description I had for Nash came out and ran me off his property."

"Can they do that?" Day said. "You're the law. Can't you go where you want and talk to whoever you want?"

"Only if we have reason to believe there has been a crime committed," Luke said. "Or if we have a court-ordered search warrant. I was only on the property for a few minutes, but I saw no proof that there were mammoth bones anywhere around there."

"Well, all's I know is he's supposed to be lookin' to sell some dinosaur bones that he dug up out there on the L.T. Murray."

"Have you actually seen or talked to Nash lately?" Luke asked.

"Well, no, but I do know him. We used to work together over at the Tree Top juice plant in Selah."

"How long ago was that?" Luke asked.

"Ah geez, I guess that was about fifteen years ago."

"So, you've not seen him since then?"

"No," Day said. "Er . . . I mean, yes, I've seen him several times over the years, at the grocery store and the hardware store. You know, like that. But we wasn't best buddies or anything."

"Did you know his wife went missing about twenty years ago?"

"Yeah, he said something about that when we was working

together at Tree Top. Called her an old hag, and she just up and disappeared. Didn't seem to be too broke up about it."

"Did he ever say what he thought happened to her?" Luke asked.

"Nope. Just said the hag went missing, and that was that."

"So, just to get this straight. You heard he was digging up dinosaur bones, but he didn't tell you that himself?" Luke asked.

"Yeah, I heard it from a guy who knows a good friend of Nash's."

"So, thirdhand?"

"I guess," Day said. "From Nash's friend to the other guy, and then to me. Yeah, that's three."

"And you didn't hear from any of those guys that he might be selling the bones?"

"No, but I remember when I was working with him at the juice plant, he was always scamming to try to make more money. I know for a fact he was selling some elk and deer horns, and he's not much of a hunter, so who knows where he got them."

Luke put his hand up to his forehead, closed his eyes, and rubbed his temples like a person who was dealing with a headache.

"Okay, here's what we're going to do," Luke said after thinking about it for a minute. "Don't contact Nash. If you can find out who the guy was who originally heard he was digging up the bones on the L.T. Murray, get me that guy's name. If you can't get his name, don't push it. And I'll do some checking around elsewhere."

Derek Day said he would do just that. Luke thanked him for his time and ended the call. As he drove back to the office, he thought about the whole deal. He'd like to know more, but legally there wasn't much else he could do. When he got a little free time, he would drive out to the wildlife area and look around, but unless he heard something else, the mystery of the mammoth bones would have to remain unsolved.

* * *

Luke was just about back to his office when Sara called. She told him about what she had learned after talking to the people in Seattle.

"Well, that's good you caught up to the university girl," Luke said. "Sounds like she is just as convinced as Magic that there was some foul play involved in the boyfriend's death."

"We'll hopefully know a lot more after the results of the autopsy are finalized," Sara said. "Oh, and I talked to Magic. She has reluctantly agreed to come stay with us for a while."

"Great," Luke said, but he didn't sound quite as enthusiastic as he might have.

"I can't let her go back to the river," Sara said after hearing the hesitation in Luke's voice.

"No, no," Luke said. "I don't want her to go back there either. It will be fine."

"It won't be forever," Sara said. "I just feel like having a real roof over her head will be good for her healing, both physically and mentally."

"I agree," Luke said. "You are a good person, Sara McCain."

"It'll be fine," Sara said. "So, what have you been up to?"

Luke told her all about the call on the dinosaur bones and the visit to Quentin Nash's house.

"That sounds kind of weird," Sara said. "Was the guy hiding something?"

"Oh, probably," Luke said. "But you know the law, so I'll leave him alone. There is one other thing about the guy that is somewhat interesting."

"What's that?" Sara asked.

"His wife mysteriously disappeared twenty-some years ago. Evidently, her parents are convinced that he had something to do with it, but according to the reports I read, the sheriff's detectives searched pretty much every inch of Nash's place and found nothing that would indicate he had anything to do with her disappearance."

"Still doesn't mean he didn't do it," Sara said matter-of-factly.

"No, it doesn't," Luke said.

"And that wasn't Nash who came out and yelled at you?"

"I don't know. The guy on the porch was the right height, but if it was Nash, he's dealing with cancer or something else that made his hair turn gray and caused him to lose a bunch of weight."

"Maybe it was a brother, or his father?"

"I guess," Luke said. "It was hard to tell."

"So, what are you going to do?"

"I'll go out to the L.T. Murray and poke around, but that is big country. Someone could dig up a hundred mammoths, or bury a thousand bodies out there, and no one would know."

"It sounds like someone knows something about the bones, or that guy wouldn't have called you."

"Yeah, we'll see," Luke said. "So, when are you bringing Magic to the house?"

"I'm going to get her at the hospital this afternoon, as soon as they release her."

"Should I plan on cooking dinner?" Luke asked.

"That would be great," Sara said. "Maybe some salmon. I think we still have some salad fixings, and we can have some baked beans."

"Done," Luke said. "See ya tonight."

"Yep," Sara said, and then she was gone.

* * *

Back at the office, Luke took care of some emails and phone calls and filled out reports on contacts he had with anglers on the Yakima River during his morning patrols. But as he worked, he kept thinking about his visit with whoever it was at Quentin Nash's place. It was weird. Rarely had he been asked to leave someone's property without at least having a chance to talk to them. Something was going on.

He decided to drive back out to the Wenas before heading home, to do a little more looking around. The houses in the area where Nash supposedly lived were not close together like neighborhoods in the city, but there were some homes within a quarter-mile of each other. Ideally, one of Nash's neighbors could shed some light on who may have yelled at Luke.

Driving up the county road, Luke looked at each of the houses he passed. Most sat on five-acre plots, and some were on ten acres. Some had fenced pastures with a horse or two, or a couple of cows grazing away. The houses all looked newer than Nash's. Or maybe they were just maintained better.

In the distance, he could see Nash's house, and there was a neighboring house just coming up. Luke turned into the neighbor's driveway and found a woman pruning one of about thirty rose bushes that surrounded the front yard. The flowers were in full bloom, in an array of colors from peach to pink and yellow to red.

The woman stopped and stood when she saw Luke pull in. He stopped the truck and got out.

"Hi there," the woman said as she looked at the WDFW Police emblem on the door of Luke's truck. "Can I help you?"

"Maybe," Luke said. "I'm Luke McCain, an enforcement officer with the Department of Fish and Wildlife."

"I can see that," the woman said as she pointed her hand pruners at Luke's truck. "I'm not a hunter or an angler, so I know you're not here after me."

"No, ma'am," Luke said. He could see her smiling. "I'd like to chat about your neighbor if you have two minutes."

"Okay," the woman said, stretching the word out and ending it an octave higher than she started it.

"You didn't ask which neighbor," Luke said.

"I'll play along," the woman said. "Which neighbor would you like to chat about?"

"Which neighbor do you think I'd like to chat about?" Luke asked.

"I'm guessing Nash," the woman said.

"That'd be the one," Luke said. "And what made his name come to mind first?"

"Lucky guess," the woman said as she placed the hand pruners on the porch and pulled a pair of pink gardening gloves off her hands.

Luke chuckled and asked her name. She said it was Sarah Stout. He wondered if her middle names were Cynthia and Syliva but decided he should let it go. She'd probably had plenty of people make the connection with the old Shel Silverstein song about the girl who forgot to take the garbage out.

Stout looked to be in her 50s or possibly 60s. She was short, maybe five foot two or three, fit, and had a pretty, tanned face. Her shortish brown hair was streaked with gray, and her eyes were a light brown.

"What can you tell me about Mr. Nash?" Luke asked.

"Well, he's a bit of a loner," Stout said. "Comes and goes at weird times. But he's never been a bother, you know, like some neighbors can be. He has no barking dogs and doesn't complain about anything I'm doing over here. He just minds his own business."

"Just for my information, what does he look like?" Luke asked.

"He's a big guy, dark hair and beard."

"Have you seen him recently?"

Stout paused as she thought about it, then said, "Probably a couple of weeks ago. What is this all about anyway?"

"Have you seen an older man there—gray hair, skinny?"

"Occasionally, I've seen a man I thought might be Nash's father over there. But not recently."

"Well, someone of that description ran me off earlier today," Luke said.

Again, Stout paused and thought about it, and then just shook her head.

"Did you live here when Nash was married?" Luke asked.

"Yes," Stout said. "His wife was a nice lady. Didn't seem to be a good match for him, but what do I know. She just up and disappeared one day."

"Any thoughts on that?" Luke asked.

"You mean, do I think Nash had anything to do with her disappearance?"

"Yes, do you think he might have been involved with that?"

"One way or another, he was," Stout said. "She either left to get away from him, or he got rid of her. I thought the sheriff investigated all that way back when."

"He did," Luke said.

"So, what do you think?" Stout asked.

"I know nothing about it," Luke said. "I just found out about it when I was reading some old reports about Nash. I never heard of the guy or the investigation until today."

"So, this has nothing to do with Lynn's disappearance?"

"No, not really. We have a report that Nash has been digging up mammoth bones on public land and may be trying to sell them. I'm just trying to get a handle on the guy."

"Mammoth bones?" Stout asked. "Like they found a few years ago on that place over on South Wenas Road?"

"That's what we think," Luke said. "The guy who reported it said, 'dinosaur bones,' but more than likely they are mammoth bones. Ever see something like big white bones around Nash's place?"

"No, but frankly I don't waste a whole lotta time looking over there. I really don't care what he's doing. What I can tell you is he is not much on keeping the place up, and that pisses me off because it is hurting the value of my property. Not much I can do about that."

The two chatted for another few minutes, but Luke learned nothing else about Quentin Nash. He thanked Sarah Stout for her time, gave her one of his cards, and asked her to call if she ever saw anything going on at Nash's place that was out of the ordinary.

"What's ordinary?" Stout asked with a laugh as Luke climbed into his pickup. "Everything he does seems to be out of the ordinary. I'll call if I see something really weird, but like I said, I don't spend much time watching what's going on over there."

CHAPTER 11

The boy awoke, rolled off the mattress on the floor, stood, rubbed his eyes, and listened. He heard nothing. That meant he would be getting himself breakfast and ready for school. No big deal. He was used to it. He just hoped his mother was not home.

She had left with a man, whom the boy had never seen before, after dinner, such as it was. As she walked out the door, she'd said, "I'll see you in the morning, baby," but he knew that was a lie. She had told him that repeatedly after leaving him alone night after night. Most mornings, she was nowhere to be found. On the rare morning that she was home, she was passed out on the couch.

He hated seeing his mother like this, knowing that she was an addict and was doing who-knew-what to get her drugs.

To his surprise, the boy walked out into the living room and found his mother on the couch. She looked like she was dead. Her sweatshirt was stained with sweat and booze, and she had obviously lost control of her bladder and her bowels.

He walked over to check to see if she was alive. The stink of the mess in her pants, and the mixture of the alcohol and sweat on her clothes, was sickening. After a few seconds, he saw her chest raise slightly. She was breathing. She was alive. He was actually disappointed. He wished she was dead.

Even as a boy of eleven, he knew this was a horrible way to live. If he'd known how to put her out of her misery, he would have sent his mother to a better life right then and there. Instead, he left her passed out on the couch, stewing in her own feces and urine and sweat, and went to school, more determined than ever to make good grades so that he could build a better life for himself.

* * *

Doc thought back to that day often. The day he had the revelation. He would become a medical doctor and heal the people he could heal. The others who were incapable and unwilling to help themselves get better, people like his mother, he would send to a better life, ending years of misery.

He was in his third year of postgraduate work at Emory University School of Medicine in Atlanta when he sent his very first person to the great beyond. He and a team of five other med students were volunteering at a homeless shelter, and there was one particular man who would beg to be euthanized.

"Please, Doc," the man would say. "Please. I miss my wife and children so much. Please put me down."

The man, who looked to be in his sixties but was probably much younger, was nothing but skin and bones. He said he had been a successful businessman in the area, but after his wife and two kids were killed in a head-on car collision, the other car driven by a drunk driver, he had spiraled out of control.

The drug habit, he said, started as a way to numb the pain and to help him sleep. But soon the doctor's prescriptions hadn't been enough. He started getting pills from a guy he met at a coffee shop, and when those stopped working, he tried heroin. Then it was too late. He was hooked. In a matter of two years, he had lost his job, run through his savings, his retirement, and because he hadn't made payments on the house, the bank foreclosed, and he was out on the street.

Doc hated seeing the man like that. And every time the man saw him at the shelter, he would approach and plead for him to do something to put him out of his misery.

"I miss my family so much, Doc," the man said. "You have to help me. That's what doctors do, right? If you don't help me, I am going to kill myself."

Two nights later, in an alley three blocks from the homeless shelter, Doc found the man passed out on the concrete. Doc slipped a needle into his arm and pushed the plunger, sending a lethal amount of sodium pentobarbital and phenytoin sodium into his vein. The same drugs used to euthanize dogs killed the man in a matter of two minutes.

As Doc walked away, he felt no remorse. In fact, he felt a rush, a thrill that he had never felt before. He thought back to his days living with his mother and remembered her on the couch, passed out in her own filth, and wished he could have done the same for her then.

It had been inevitable that his mother got hold of some bad fentanyl. He was thirteen at the time. Her death made him work harder in school, and a decade later he was well on his way to becoming a physician. Two decades later, he had become an angel of death, having already sent over three dozen people to a better place.

* * *

It had taken him a little more than a year to figure out a modus operandi for his work. His first few clients, patients, victims—he didn't know how to categorize them—were sent from this life to another by a man dressed in black. All of them had been seen by him as patients where he volunteered on his days off. They came in for free medical and dental care. Every big city had several of these places. Some were Christian missions; others were funded by coalitions that assisted those in need.

In short order, it had become clear that finding the people who needed deliverance became too risky if he was the treating physician. Not that people were putting two and two together, but someone certainly could. And at some point, they probably would. He needed to do something differently.

Later, after he graduated from med school, he left Atlanta and took a job as an emergency room doctor at the Long Beach Medical Center in Los Angeles County. There, he developed his alter ego, dressing as a homeless person on his off days, working the camps, finding the people who were the most destitute and in pain, then successfully assisting them to a peaceful end.

After four years in LA, he packed his bags and moved up the coast to San Francisco, taking another ER job at the University of California, San Francisco Medical Center. In a matter of months, the rate of overdoses in the homeless camps around the Bay Area rose a whopping twenty-seven percent. Yet no one took even a minute to consider what might be causing the increase.

Of course, it wasn't a what, but a who, causing the uptick in overdose deaths.

He wasn't sending people to a better life on a regular basis. Sometimes he would go two or three months between kills. Other times, he might find two people in a week who he deemed ready for a new life in the hereafter.

It went like that for almost six years in San Francisco and some of the smaller cities in the area. Oakland was a real hotspot. It was also where he faced his possible death and a probable beating one Sunday night.

He was working through a camp, watching for someone in need of his services while pushing a Target shopping cart, when three young Hispanic men stopped him and started to harass him.

"Where you going, old man?" the shortest of the three said. "You steal that cart?"

Doc ignored them and tried to push the cart around them. One of the other men stuck his foot out and blocked the front wheel, stopping the cart from moving.

"We're talking to you, old man," the short guy said.

All three of the men were wearing wife-beater undershirts, baggy denim shorts with legs that went down almost to the tops of their socks, and blue bandannas wrapped around their heads. They had tattoos on their hands, arms, chest, neck, and one of the men had some on his face.

None of the three seemed to be armed, which was a mistake, because Doc was. He had a short-nosed, Smith & Wesson Model 642 .38-caliber revolver tucked into the front of the cart under a coat. It was purchased at a gun show in Reno, Nevada for three hundred dollars, cash, no paperwork, no registration, for just this very purpose.

"What do you want?" Doc asked, keeping his eyes down, not looking the men in the face. He slowly moved his right hand under the coat balled up in the cart.

"We want what you got," Shorty said. "And we want it now."

"I have nothing you want," Doc said. "Just some dirty clothes and my sleeping bag."

"How about we take a look anyway," Shorty said and grabbed the side of the cart to tip it over.

Doc grabbed the pistol from under the coat just as the man threw the shopping cart to the ground. The three men all were watching the cart and didn't notice that he had slipped the pistol out. He dropped his hand with the gun to his side.

"Look through that junk," Shorty said to the man with the face tattoos.

The man did and found nothing more than some clothes, a sleeping bag, and an empty wine bottle.

"This is disappointing," Shorty said to Doc. "Where's your drugs? You all carry a toot or two in your carts."

"Not me," Doc said.

"No, but you got it somewhere, right?" the little man said. "Guess we gotta look harder. Take off your coat and your pants."

The third man stepped at him, and Doc brought the pistol up.

"I don't think so," he said, pointing at the shortest man's head. "Back off!"

"Hey, hey. Take it easy, old man. We're not going to hurt you," Shorty said.

"That's right, you're not," Doc said.

The men looked at the pistol and the hand that was holding it. It wasn't the shaking hand of a feeble old homeless man; it was steady as a surgeon's. Then they finally really looked at the man who was holding the gun. They looked at his face. They looked in his eyes. They didn't see fear or senility. They saw death.

"Okay, old man. Take it easy," Shorty said again, raising his hands, palms out. "We're just having some fun."

"Go, now!" Doc said and pulled the hammer back on the pistol.

The three men turned to run away, and as they did, Shorty said, "But we're coming back, and we're coming for you!"

Not that he was all that worried about the gangbangers, but the next day Doc submitted his resignation at the hospital, loaded up his SUV and a cargo trailer he had rented, and headed north up Highway 101.

It took him only two weeks to find a job as an ER doctor at the Providence St. Vincent Medical Center in Portland. Three weeks later, he found his first victim, a suffering, pitiful woman that reminded him of his mother, in a homeless camp under the I-405 freeway.

And so it went for three more years. He lost track of how many people he euthanized in that time. They were all pitiful souls that were suffering extensively in this life.

Ironically, because Oregon is one of just a few states where terminally ill patients may legally end their own lives if they choose, Doc provided the drugs and training to assist seven terminally ill patients to die with dignity, as the state law calls it. Better with dignity, for sure. His other victims had no idea what the word dignity even meant.

The next summer, when a bunch of idiots started rioting in Portland, Doc decided it was a good time to pick up and move on, so he went up I-5 and settled in Seattle. Again, finding a job in an ER department—this time at Harborview Medical Center—was no problem. His experience in the other cities made him an easy hire at the busiest trauma center in the Northwest.

He took time to settle into his new job and to find a nice townhouse in Queen Anne Hill. A month after arriving, Doc was shuffling through the homeless camps along the freeway, in the parks and under the bridges looking for more people to save. Everything was going great until the man who fed the ducks saw him kill the woman, and then the boy saw him kill the man. It was probably time to move on again and start up somewhere else. Boise maybe, or Denver. But he liked it in Seattle. He had settled. If he could find the girl named Magic, and at least learn what she knew, everything would be okay.

He really needed to find her, and he thought he knew how he might do so.

CHAPTER 12

"He's beautiful," Magic said as she rubbed Jack's ears. The big yellow dog had come up to her the second she came through the front door.

"That's Jack," Sara said. "He'll try to worm his way into your heart, but he has ulterior motives. Once he thinks you like him, he'll be pestering you constantly for a bite of whatever you are eating."

"Too late," Magic said as she knelt and gave Jack a big hug. "He's already stolen my heart."

Jack just stood there and let the girl love on him, as if he knew it was something she needed. Every time she squeezed him, his tail would wag.

"A Labrador retriever, right?" Magic said with a smile. "I always wanted one but never was in the right place in my life."

Sara looked at Magic. It was the happiest she'd seen her since they'd met.

"Yep, he's a Lab. And he's a great dog. He goes out with Luke on his patrols lots of times and has helped catch some bad guys here and there."

"Is that right?" Magic said to Jack in a voice one might use if they were talking to a baby while continuing to rub his ears. The big dog looked like he was loving every second of it.

"We've got you in here," Sara said as she started down the hall to the guest room.

Magic stood and followed. Jack followed Magic.

"I'd be happy on the couch," Magic said. "You didn't have to give me a room."

"This a guest room, and you are our guest," Sara said and turned. "And here is the bathroom. We only have one, so we'll have to share."

"That's no problem," Magic said as she looked at the bathroom.

"Luke will be home in a little bit, and he is planning on cooking dinner for us. Hope you like salmon."

Magic didn't say anything. Sara could see her thinking.

"I can't remember the last time I had salmon, but it is one of my favorites," Magic finally said.

"Great," Sara said. "Now, make yourself comfortable. Luke has your backpack from your camp and is bringing it with him. Take a nap, or take a shower, or if you want to just sit and chat, I'm here for you."

Again, Magic hesitated, thinking. "I would like to talk to you, but I would love to take a shower first. Would that be okay?"

"That would be fine. Towels are in the cupboard next to the tub. And I have body wash and shampoo in the shower. Help yourself to whatever."

Magic started for the bathroom and then stopped. "I have no clean clothes," she said. "Any chance I could wash these?"

"Throw them out into the hall, and I'll get them in the washer," Sara said and then went to get an old pair of her sweatpants and a sweatshirt. "You can wear these until the clothes are clean and dried. Tomorrow, we'll go get you a few new things."

Magic smiled and thanked Sara. Then she headed for the bathroom. Two minutes later, Sara heard the bathroom door open, then a pile of clothes thump down in the hallway, and then the door close.

The shower ran for almost half an hour. Sara smiled. She wondered how long it had been since Magic had had a good shower. Days? Weeks? Whatever. It didn't matter. Hopefully, it was washing some of the grime and pain from the past several days away. The dirt, she knew, would be easy. The memories would be much more difficult.

Luke drove into the driveway just as Magic was getting out of the shower. Sara knew her husband was home because she saw Jack get up and go to the back door. That was the door Luke almost always used to enter the house when he got home from work.

"Hey, boy," Luke said to the dog as he opened the door.

Sara could hear the dog's tail thumping against the walls and Luke's legs. She walked in from the living room and gave Luke a quick kiss on the lips.

"I'm glad to see you too," she said to Luke. "But I can't wag my tail."

"This is better," Luke said and kissed her again.

"Good response," Sara said. "Magic just got out of the shower. I'm guessing she will be ready for dinner soon. Salmon is thawed and in the fridge."

"Let me change quickly, and I'll get the grill going," Luke said as he headed for their bedroom with Jack following.

Magic came out of the bathroom just as Luke was coming down the hall. She surprised him. He knew she was in there, but she looked like a completely different person. Her hair was wet, and her face was clean and shiny. She looked ten years younger than she had when he had helped her at the river the day before.

"Hi," she said softly, looking at Luke and then looking away in embarrassment.

"Hi," Luke said. "I'm going to change clothes and then I'll get the fish on the grill."

"Thank you for having me here," Magic said.

"We're happy to have you," Luke said. "But you're going to have to stop wearing those sweats."

"Luke, stop," Sara said. "Don't listen to him. My husband is a kidder. And unfortunately, he went to school at Washington State University. Those sweats you are wearing are from the University of Oregon, where I went to college. He's just jealous because we kick WSU's ass in just about every sport known to man."

Magic looked down at the green and yellow sweatshirt with the UO on the front. Then she looked at Sara like she had no clue what she was talking about.

"Don't worry about it," Sara said. "You're fine. He's just kidding." Then down the hall at Luke, she yelled, "And he's jealous!"

There was no response.

"C'mon," Sara said to Magic. "We'll sit in the living room and let Luke do his thing with dinner. Can I get you something to drink? We have iced tea, Pepsi, and good old water straight from the well."

"Water is fine," Magic said. "The doctor at the hospital told me to drink as much as I could."

Sara told Magic to go sit in the living room and went to get the water. Jack followed Magic, and when Sara came into the room with two glasses of water, Magic was sitting cross-legged on the floor in front of the sofa, and Jack was sitting in her lap.

"He thinks he's a Pomeranian or something," Sara said. "Just push him off if he's bugging you."

"Never," Magic said to Jack as she scratched his sides and belly.

Sara sat down and started to say something when her phone buzzed in the kitchen.

"Sorry," Sara said to Magic as she stood and went to get the phone. "It's my work phone, so I need to take it."

Magic just nodded and turned her attention back to Jack, who was now prone on the floor and enjoying every second of the rubbing, scratching, and petting that he was receiving.

"This is Agent McCain," Sara said after sliding the answer button on the phone's screen.

"Agent McCain, this is Joyce Hanson with the King County Medical Examiner."

"Yes, doctor, thanks for calling. I assume you have some results from the autopsy?"

"Nothing final, but you may be right about the young man's death. We found needle marks in his neck, which is totally incongruent with what we find in other overdose deaths. Most of the time, they administer the drugs via their arm, thigh, or in between their toes."

Hanson paused for a beat and then said, "And it looks like there was another chemical in his bloodstream. It is uncommon to find other substances in the blood of an overdose victim other than the drugs that killed them. We haven't identified the substances yet, but we should know tomorrow."

Hanson paused for another few seconds to let her information sink in. Then she said, "I'll be providing the Seattle Police Department with the official results as soon as we have them, but I wanted you to know what we're thinking based on the preliminary examination."

"Thank you, Doctor Hanson. We really wanted to believe what the young man's fiancé was telling us, and now we know she was right. I'll reach out to the SPD detective tomorrow and see where we go from here."

The women each said good evening and clicked off.

Luke, now in blue Levi's and a WSU pullover, wandered through the kitchen where Sara was on the phone and heard the last of the conversation.

"Good news?" Luke asked.

"I'm not sure if it is good or not, but it sounds like Magic may be right that Toby was murdered."

"Oh, wow," Luke said. "So, what happens from here?"

"Let's talk later. Go get the salmon on the grill."

* * *

They were just finishing up with dinner when Magic said, "I can't remember the last time I sat down at a table and had dinner like this."

"It looks like you liked it," Luke said.

Magic had had a double helping of the sockeye salmon Luke had grilled, along with a good-sized serving of salad and beans.

"I loved it, thank you so much. The only time I've had salmon is when I've scrounged it out of the dumpster behind one of the restaurants in Seattle. Then it is cold and who knows what else has ended up on it."

The young woman hadn't talked much during dinner, only speaking when Luke or Sara had asked her a question. Then her answers were usually made up of a word or two. In between, Luke and Sara talked about Luke's day, about going to Quentin Nash's house, the weird old man who ran him off the place, and the conversation with Sarah Stout, Nash's neighbor.

Magic listened intently and even laughed a couple times at Luke's story.

Sara knew that the dinner and the conversation were considered normal to most people, but she guessed workday catch-ups hadn't been part of Magic's life in a long time, if ever.

"So, you think you are going to go try to find where he's digging up the bones?" Sara asked Luke.

"If I get some time in the next couple of days, I'll run out there and see if I can find something, but I'm not holding out much hope."

"Will you take Jack?" Magic asked.

"Probably. Unless he doesn't want to go. He's getting kind of lazy in his old age."

"He seems pretty young to me," Magic said. "How old is he?"

"He just turned ten," Sara said. "A senior citizen in dog years."

"But he seems so lively and alert," Magic said. "How long do dogs live?"

"It depends on the dog and the breed," Luke explained. "Generally, the bigger the dog, the shorter their life expectancy. Labs normally live to twelve or thirteen. A few live longer."

"Oh, gosh, I didn't know that," Magic said, and then she started to tear up. The discussion of mortality must have made her think of her fiancé.

"It's the tough part of having a dog," Luke said. "They never live long enough."

"So, are you ready for some dessert?" Sara asked, changing the subject.

Magic didn't answer. But Luke did.

"You bet," he said.

"You don't even know what it is," Sara said.

"Doesn't matter to me," Luke said.

"It's week-old chocolate cake," Sara said. "I knocked the stale crust and green hairy stuff off it. You still want some?"

Magic listened and looked at Sara. Sara winked at her and said to Luke, "I can throw some licorice ice cream on it."

"Mmmmm, sounds delicious. How about you, Magic? You up for some?"

Magic started giggling. Then she started laughing. She had tears running down her cheeks, but she was laughing. It was good to hear her laugh. In a second, Luke and Sara were laughing too.

CHAPTER 13

Sara called Kristen Gray the next morning and told her what the medical examiner had said.

"So, Magic was right," Gray said. "I bet that other man, the one they called the Duckman, was murdered too."

"It seems like a possibility anyway," Sara said. "But with no body to autopsy, we will never know for sure on that one."

"And it sounds like some others in that same camp died in the past couple months," Gray said. "Did you ask Magic about them?"

"No, not yet," Sara said. "I think she's still in a bit of shock over losing her fiancé. I'll get a chance to talk to her later today or tomorrow."

"Does she know about the medical examiner's call?" Gray asked.

"No, not yet. I'll talk to her about that today. She was sleeping when I left for work."

"I bet she hasn't slept in a bed in, what, months or even years?" Gray said.

"She spent the night in the hospital, but nobody ever sleeps soundly in those places, what with all the nurses coming and going, and the machines hooked up to you."

"Is someone there making sure she doesn't just up and leave?"

"No, but I think she'll stay. She loves our dog, who is there. And I think she knows that being at our house is the safest, best place for her to be right now. My husband is going to check in on her every couple of hours."

"So, is there anything you can do to follow up on the death of Toby?"

"I'll call the Seattle police officer I talked with before," Sara said. "But from what you and Magic said, it seems like they may not be eager to push it too hard."

"I'm going to go back to the camp and talk to some of the other people there," Gray said. "Maybe I can learn something else."

"You need to be careful," Sara said.

"I've spent days and days in those camps," Gray said. "I'll be fine. If I find out anything that might help you or the Seattle police, I'll give you a call."

Sara told her to be careful one more time, and to stay in touch.

Gray said, "Talk to you soon" and ended the call.

As soon as Gray was off the line, Sara called Officer Donley with the Seattle Police Department.

"Agent McCain," Donley said without even a hello.

"Officer Donley, how are things in the Emerald City?"

"We're busier than a bunch of squirrels in a nut factory," Donley said. "For some reason, the criminals never take a day off."

"I know what you mean," Sara said. "Listen, I spoke to the King County medical examiner last night, and she said there's something fishy going on with the death of the young man in the homeless camp. He was injected in his neck, and there seems to be a strange foreign substance in his bloodstream along with large amounts of heroin and fentanyl."

"Any idea what the foreign substance is?" Donley asked.

"She didn't know yet, but she said as soon as she has the findings, she will be sending them to you. Or I assume it is you. She just said the Seattle Police Department."

Donley remained silent for a few seconds and then said, "Well, I guess that girl, Magic, was right. Someone did kill her boyfriend."

"It is starting to look like it," Sara said. "And her belief is he was killed because he saw someone kill the man who fed the ducks. Evidently, he died just a few days earlier."

"Yes, it was also ruled an overdose, but no autopsy was done," Donley said. "And I'm sure his body was cremated, so there is no way to know for sure."

"That's unfortunate," Sara said. "Magic said two other people died in that camp in the last few weeks. Any way to check to see if an autopsy was done on either of them? I think she said one was a woman."

"I can check, but if the person had no known relatives and we didn't believe the death was anything but an overdose, no autopsy would have been done."

"Would you mind checking anyway?" Sara asked. "I'd hate to think there is a serial killer out there killing homeless people."

Again, Donley said nothing for several seconds. "But why would anyone want to kill homeless people?" she finally asked. "That makes no sense at all."

"We live in a strange world, Officer Donley," Sara said. "And it is getting stranger all the time."

"Very true," Donley said. "If it is a serial killer, which I certainly hope it isn't, will the FBI get involved?"

"Not my call," Sara said. "But there's a high probability. We have all those brilliant minds back in D.C. who do nothing but profile serial killers. It could help."

"You don't sound very convinced," Donley said.

"I've been working several cases over here where Native American women have been murdered or gone missing. So far, the profilers haven't been much help."

"I've read some about that," Donley said. "Do you think it is a serial killer?"

"A couple of murders have been solved, and it has been acquaintances who have done the killing. But who knows on the others. If we can't find any bodies, there is virtually no evidence. It's very troubling and difficult."

"I'm guessing someone who is killing homeless people could be difficult to find too," Donley said.

"I agree," Sara said. "But let's see what the medical examiner says and go from there. If you get the report, would you mind forwarding a copy to me? I'll text you my email address."

"Can do," Donley said. "So, do you know where the girl is now? She might be in danger too."

"She is probably asleep on the couch at my house with a hundred-pound yellow Labrador retriever sleeping next to her."

Donley laughed. "That's good to hear," she said. "I'll let you know when I hear something."

"Thank you," Sara said. "I'll do the same."

After ending the call, Sara texted her email address to Donley and started thinking about the whole situation. It was hard to believe that anyone would be randomly killing homeless people for the thrill of the kill. The killings certainly didn't seem to have a sexual component. So why would someone want to kill residents of homeless encampments?

Her cell phone started buzzing, interrupting her train of thought. She looked at the screen on her phone. Luke was calling.

"Hey there," Sara said.

"Hey yourself," Luke said. "I just stopped to check on Magic. She seemed to be getting a little claustrophobic, so I invited her to ride along with me. She's getting ready to go now."

"Her clothes were in the dryer. Did she find them?"

"Yes. She told me to tell you thanks for washing them. Jack is going to join us. That seemed to perk her up, knowing he was coming along."

"If she feels like talking, try to learn more about her, and Toby, and the other people in the camp who died. But don't push it."

"Got it," Luke said. "I thought I would run out into the L.T. Murray and look around. She might like seeing that country."

"It'll be a big change from the camps in Seattle," Sara said. "Let me know how it goes."

"Will do," Luke said. "See you tonight."

* * *

They had been driving for about fifteen minutes before Magic said anything. Luke didn't want to push her, so he stayed quiet and just let her watch the scenery. They had driven along the Old Naches Highway, through apple and cherry orchards, and then up the Naches grade into the Wenas.

"When will those apples be ripe?" Magic finally asked, long after they'd passed the last orchard.

"They pick them in September and October," Luke said. "This area is famous for the apples that are grown here. They ship them all over the world."

Magic looked out at the farmhouses, many with horses and cattle in nearby pastures. After a while, she said, "Sara said that Jack saved your life. Is that true?"

"He did," Luke said. "A couple of times actually."

"What happened?" she asked.

"One time, we were tracking a bear that a poacher had wounded. It was holed up in some brambles, too thick to see into, but Jack smelled the bear just before it charged us."

"What did you do?" Magic asked, her eyes getting bigger as she looked at Luke.

"I shot it," Luke said. "Died at my feet. If Jack hadn't given me some warning, I'm sure the bear would have mauled me."

"Wow," Magic said. "Are there bears where we are going?"

"There might be an odd bear wandering through where we are heading, but I've never seen one out there."

Magic relaxed a little and then asked, "What was the other time?"

Luke told her about a guy that was living in a shack up in the Cascades who had killed a motorcycle rider and made it look like a cougar had done it.

"Jack helped track the man to his little cabin, and when we went in, the guy attacked me. Luckily, Jack was there and bit the man in the butt just as he was about to get the upper hand on me."

She snickered and then turned to Jack, who was sitting very regally, like a very important person in the back seat of Luke's truck. "Good boy, Jack!" she said.

Jack stuck his head between the front seats and licked Magic on the cheek.

After another couple minutes of silence, Magic asked, "So, just what is it you do?"

"I do a lot of things, but my main job is to protect the fish and wildlife in this area and make sure people are obeying the rules and regulations when they are out hunting and fishing."

Luke could see Magic thinking about that. Finally, she said, "So you just drive around looking for people who are breaking the law?"

"It's a little more detailed than that, but yes, I'm making sure people are obeying the laws."

"So, you are a cop?"

"My official job title is fish and wildlife enforcement officer. But I am technically a state police officer."

"I know several of the cops who came through our camp," Magic said. "They all seemed pretty nice. They wouldn't harass us or anything."

Luke didn't say anything.

"But they wouldn't believe me when I told them that Toby wasn't doing drugs anymore."

Magic pulled her legs up to her chest and wrapped her arms around them. Then she started rocking forward and back and started tearing up.

"When I met you at the river the other day, you said that you thought other people had been killed in your camp too," Luke said.

"What happened with them?"

She told Luke about the man who fed the ducks, how he never took drugs, and then died one night in the camp not long before her fiancé had died.

"Cops figured it was an overdose too," Magic said. "That's the easy explanation. If you live in a camp, and you die, you must have overdosed."

"But you don't think so?" Luke asked.

"No, I don't. I talked to the Duckman many times before he died. He was a really nice man. And he was always telling me about the evils of drugs and had really been encouraging when he found out that me and Toby were clean and were going to get married."

Another long pause followed. Luke could tell she was thinking back to her times talking to the man who fed the ducks.

"Never once did I see him shoot up," Magic finally continued. "And he never was high. I know what someone looks like when they are tripping, and he was never that way."

"And there were others who died recently in the camp?" Luke asked.

"Yeah, a couple of others. This one woman died only a few days before the Duckman. I don't know what her name was, but Toby and me, we called her "Dirty Donna" because she was always a mess. I mean, like messing herself and rolling around in the dirt."

Luke cringed at the thought.

"I know it's wrong, but I thought of it as a blessing when I heard she had died. She was in really bad shape."

"Another overdose?" Luke asked.

"I didn't hear for sure. But she was always high. She definitely could have OD'd."

"Anyone else?" Luke asked.

"Yeah, another man. But I didn't know who he was. I just heard about it."

"When was that?"

"Probably three months ago, or maybe not that long ago. I have trouble remembering when stuff happened. But I'll never forget about Toby and when he died. I hope the cops can figure out who killed him."

"And you think he might have been killed because he saw something he shouldn't have?"

Magic said nothing. Again, Luke could see her thinking.

Finally, she said, "I know he did. Toby told me all about how he saw a guy standing over the Duckman the night he died. And as soon as the man saw Toby watching through the tent window, he turned and ran."

"Toby thought the man killed the Duckman?" Luke asked.

"Yes, he did. And I bet he's the same man who killed Toby."

"Did Toby describe him to you?"

"Yeah, he said the guy was dressed like a homeless person but didn't act like one. Especially when he ran off."

"Did he see anything distinguishing, like hair color or eye color? Could he tell how tall he was?"

"No, he just said the guy stuck out. I mean, being around the people in the camps long enough, you get a feel for what's real and what's not."

"Can you think of any reason why anyone would want the Duckman dead?" Luke asked.

Magic thought about it for a minute and said, "Not one reason. He was the nicest man in the camp."

CHAPTER **14**

He had checked seven camps in the area over the past two days and had not seen the girl called Magic. He was working the overnight shift at the ER at Harborview, so he hadn't been able to check the camps at night. Sometimes the camp residents would get odd jobs for a few days. If the girl was working, she could be coming back to the camp at night.

It would be nice to know what she knew, if she knew anything at all. With each passing day, he was more convinced she knew nothing because if she had gone to the police, they would be patrolling the camps, and he hadn't seen any more cops than usual.

Doc had seen the young social services worker, or whatever she was, in another camp. She was carrying her clipboard and making notes as she talked to the different people sitting around the tents. He stayed out of her sight. He wondered if she might know where this Magic had gone.

That night he saw the young woman again. He was working his shift in the ER at Harborview, and she came in with a woman who was in obvious distress. The nurses rushed the sick woman into an examination room, took her vitals, attached an EKG to her chest, and put an IV with a saline drip into her arm.

Doc entered the room a few minutes later, and boom, there was the young woman he had seen at a camp earlier in the day, sitting in a chair next to the sick woman on the bed. He hesitated for a split second but realized she didn't recognize him.

"Good evening," Doc said as he looked at the chart showing the sick woman's vital signs. "What do we have here?"

"I came across this woman in one of the camps near the freeway," said Kristen Gray. "She was in obvious distress. I put her in my car and drove right over here."

"We'll check it out," he said with a reassuring smile as the woman looked at his face like she was trying to place where she may have seen it before.

As he worked through his examination of the woman, he asked Gray if she knew the sick woman's name. She did not. He asked other questions about her breathing when she found her, and if she was coherent and talking.

Gray said the woman's breathing was erratic, and she was not very coherent.

"But she could walk with you to the car?" the doctor asked.

"It took some coaxing, and she was pretty wobbly, but yes," Gray said, again studying the doctor's face.

"Have we met before?" Gray asked the doctor.

"Maybe," Doc said. "I see hundreds of people come through here each month. But I don't recognize you."

"Gosh," Gray said, shaking her head. "I swear we've met before."

"So, are you with DSHS?" Doc asked, changing the subject as he listened to the woman's heart with the stethoscope.

"No, I'm a grad student at U-Dub. I'm doing my dissertation

on the living conditions of the people who are residents of these camps. I just happened to be in this woman's camp."

"Well, it's a good thing you were," the doctor said. "My guess is she has suffered a mild myocardial infarction and needs to be checked out to see what may have caused it."

"She may be a drug user," Gray said. "That might be a factor in all of this."

"Yes, it might," Doc said. "We'll check it in the blood tests."

"I'm sorry I don't know her name or anything more about her," Gray said.

"That's okay," Doc said. "We get people from the camps in here frequently."

"Well, thank you for helping them. Many are in such bad shape. I'm surprised they aren't in here all the time."

"We help when we can," Doc said with another warm smile. "And thank you for what you are doing. This homeless situation is serious, and nobody seems to know what to do."

"There is no simple solution," Gray said. "I've learned that, for sure."

Doc paused for a few seconds and then said, "Would you be willing to meet me for coffee sometime? I'd be interested in hearing what you've learned and would really like to chat about this."

Gray looked at the doctor and didn't say anything. He saw the look of concern in her eyes.

"I'm not asking for a date. I'm happily married," Doc lied. "I just would like to learn more about your project and what you are seeing in the camps."

"I guess I could do that," Gray said after another minute of thought. "Maybe I could ask you some questions about the people you are seeing from the camps for my dissertation?"

"Sure," Doc said. "I'd be glad to help."

The doctor told her his name and phone number and said, "I'm working nights for the next three weeks, but we could meet most anytime during the day. Maybe here at the hospital cafeteria or at a Starbucks close to the university?"

Gray told him her name but did not give him her number. She wanted to think a bit more about it before totally agreeing to meet.

"I'll give you a call," Gray said. "What time would be best? You must sleep sometime."

"Call anytime," Doc said. "I grab a nap here and there when I can, but I always have my phone nearby."

Gray said she would call later in the week, thanked him again for looking after the woman, touched her arm, said, "Get to feeling better," and walked out of the exam room. The woman on the bed didn't respond.

Doc smiled. Kristen Gray bringing the sick woman to the hospital was most fortuitous.

* * *

The medical examiner's report arrived in Donley's email the morning after she had talked to the FBI agent in Yakima. She immediately forwarded it on to her and then took a few minutes to read it. The report showed that the young man named Toby, no last name, had enough heroin and methamphetamines in his blood system to kill a horse. The other substance detected in the blood was shown as a chemical compound.

Donley wrote $(CH_3CH_2{-}O{-}CH_2CH_3)$ on a notepad. Then she pulled up Google in a second window and entered the compound into the search bar. The compound was identified by the common name of ethyl ether. The description showed that it once was used as anesthesia but that over the years it had been replaced by safer anesthetics like nitrous oxide and halothane.

The medical examiner's report basically said that the young man had been knocked out by breathing the ether and then had been injected with the drugs that had caused his death.

She picked up the phone and dialed Agent McCain.

"Have you read the medical examiner's report?" Donley asked after Sara answered her phone.

"No, I haven't looked at my emails in the last hour. I just got out of a meeting."

"When you look at it, you'll see something very weird and very compelling that tells us Toby was murdered."

"I'm pulling it up now," Sara said. "So, what does it say?"

"He had small amounts of ether in his bloodstream," Donley said. "So, someone used an ether-soaked rag or something over his face to knock him out before he was shot full of heroin and meth."

"Ether?" Sara said. "They stopped using that in operating rooms as an anesthesia decades ago."

"That's what I just read," Donley said. "But that doesn't mean it isn't still around."

"No. But it is very strange that someone had it and was willing to use it."

"My thought is that Toby was a fit young man and whoever was planning on killing him decided he needed to do it without a big struggle. If he was going to kill him in the camp, he had to do it quickly and quietly."

"I can see that," Sara said. "Magic never mentioned hearing anything outside their tent."

"We definitely have a murder investigation on our hands," Donley said. "We'll start by interviewing everyone in the camp and go from there."

"Let me know if there is anything I can do to help," Sara said. "I'm hoping that Magic will stay with us for a while. If someone is killing witnesses to a murder, then she needs to stay away from there."

"I agree," Donley said. "We will need to interview her again, officially, as part of the investigation, but maybe we can do it via Zoom."

"If you need to talk to her in person, I'll be happy to escort her over there," Sara said.

"Sounds good. Thank you, Agent McCain. Talk to you soon."

After Donley hung up, Sara set her phone down and thought about everything. She reviewed the report again, and Donley was right. The medical examiner had basically said so the night before, but now there was no doubt. The ether in the young man's system proved he had been knocked out and then drugged to death. But why had he been killed? She would hopefully get a chance to talk to Magic about it soon.

Sara's phone started buzzing and chattering on her desk. Caller ID said the incoming call was from Kristen Gray.

"Hi, Kristen. I was just about to call you," Sara said after sliding the answer button on the screen.

"Did the autopsy results come in?" Gray asked.

"They did," Sara said. "Evidently, Magic's fiancé had ethyl ether in his system, along with fatal amounts of heroin and meth."

"Ethyl ether?" Gray asked.

"You're probably too young to remember that ether was once used as an anesthesia in the medical world."

"So, what does that mean?" Gray asked. Then she answered her own question. "You mean someone drugged him to put him out before shooting him up with drugs?"

"That seems like the likely scenario," Sara said. "Magic said Toby was in his twenties and fit. And she swears he wasn't using, so he would likely have been someone not easily subdued. A rag doused with ether held over his face would knock him out pretty quickly."

"Geez, who thinks of that stuff, and where would they get it?"

"Same place the killer got the other drugs that killed Toby," Sara said. "So the police have opened an official investigation and are going to be interviewing the camp residents and others who were there. You'll probably be getting a call from Officer Donley."

"Will they want to talk to Magic?" Gray asked.

"Yes, I'm sure they will," Sara said.

"How's she doing?" Gray asked.

"She's very sad, but she seems to be doing better," Sara said. "She's riding around with my husband now, so she's in good hands."

Gray wanted to ask "riding around to where," but she let it go.

"I'm glad she's there with you," Gray said. "Being over here in this camp would be the worst place for her."

"I agree," Sara said. "Stay in touch, and if I learn anything else, I'll let you know."

"Sounds good," Gray said.

"And please be careful," Sara said. "It's possible someone has killed at least two people in that camp, and we don't know why."

CHAPTER 15

"Look over there," Luke said, pointing through the windshield and to the left. "See that dark green bush? Look just to the right. See those two ears sticking up?"

Magic looked. Then she finally said, "Yes, what is it?"

"That's a mule deer doe," Luke said. "She's looking right at us."

"I don't see its face," Magic said. "Just the ears. How do you know it's a deer?"

"Mule deer have big ears, like a mule—that's how they got the name. And I know it's a doe, a female, because it doesn't have any antlers. If we watch for a minute, we might see that she has a fawn, or maybe even two."

"Really," Magic said. "That would be cool."

They watched the two ears above the sagebrush, and in a

minute the ears wiggled, and the doe stepped out from the brush. She took a couple of hesitating, cautious steps, like she wanted to start to bounce off, when two fawns stepped out behind her.

"Oh, how cute!" Magic said. "Why do the babies have white spots?"

"It makes them harder to see when they lay in the grass and brush. It's one of their defenses against predation. And they put off very little scent, so the cougars and coyotes and bears can't see or smell them."

"How old are they?"

"Probably three or four weeks old. They'll lose the spots in the next few months as they get bigger and shed their summer coat and grow their winter coat."

They sat and watched as the doe and her fawns walked off through the brush, up over a small hill and out of sight. Then they continued driving slowly up the rough dirt road.

"Do you really think you'll see where that guy is digging up mammoth bones?" Magic asked.

"I don't even know if that is what he's doing," Luke said. "But you never know until you check it out."

"And what if you don't find anything?"

"I will still try to talk to the gentleman who is supposed to be doing the digging. And I want to talk to the first guy, who started this whole game of whisper down the lane."

"Do lots of people turn people in for breaking the law?" Magic asked.

"More than you might think," Luke said. "There are only five of us enforcement officers working out of the office here, and we have thousands of square miles to cover. We can't be everywhere all the time, so it really helps when the people out in the woods and on the rivers are watchful. Most people, if they see someone breaking the law, will report it."

Magic sat quietly, contemplating things. After five minutes of silence, she asked, "How long have you been a police officer?"

"Twenty-three years," Luke answered.

"Have you ever shot anyone?"

Luke told her how he'd shot at the man who had shot him in the chest. Luckily, his Kevlar vest had protected him from serious injury. Another officer, a sheriff's deputy, had also shot at the suspect at the same time as Luke and had killed the suspect. Luke never knew if it was his or the deputy's bullet that had killed the shooter, and he didn't want to know.

Luke told about how he'd also shot the serial killer who had murdered several women and dumped their bodies in the Cascades. He and Jack had tracked the man for miles, and when the suspect started shooting at Luke, he shot the man in the leg with his rifle.

"And you were okay with that?" Magic asked.

"He was a serial killer, and he was shooting at me. I could have killed him, but I shot him in the leg to stop him," Luke explained. "And I would do it again in a minute if it was him or me, or I needed to protect someone else from being killed or injured."

"I don't think I could kill another person," Magic said quietly.

"Yes, you could," Luke said. "I don't know you well, but one thing I do know is you are tough. Look what you've been through. If someone was going to kill you, and you had the chance to kill them first, I know you could do it. You're a survivor. You would do it."

"I don't know," Magic said. "My mom killed the creep who was molesting me. And now she is in prison. I wouldn't want to go to prison for killing someone."

"You wouldn't go to prison if it was self-defense," Luke said.

The young woman went silent again, so Luke left her alone with her thoughts and kept driving, watching for anything that might tell him someone was out here digging up bones.

When they got up on one of the highest ridges and could see out into some sagebrush flats and down to the Yakima River, Luke stopped the truck.

"What?" Magic said. "Do you see something?"

"I see lots of things," Luke said. "I see the river and the sagebrush hills. I see wildflowers and trees. If I look closer, I'll probably see more deer, and birds—maybe even a bald eagle or a coyote."

"Really?" Magic said. "All that is out here?"

"Yes, you just have to look," Luke said as he pulled his twelve-by-fifty-powered binoculars out from behind his seat. "Let's get out and see what we can see. Jack needs to stretch his legs too."

Luke climbed out of the truck and opened the back door to let out the big yellow dog. Jack jumped out and immediately started sniffing the air. Magic climbed out of the truck and stood and then took a deep breath and stretched her arms and hands to the sky.

"It's beautiful up here," she said.

"Yes, it is," Luke said as he held the binoculars to his eyes.

"What's that smell?" she asked.

"That's the sagebrush," Luke said, inhaling the scent of the sage that encircled them.

"It's different. I've never smelled it before," Magic said. "I like it."

"I like it too," Luke said. "I never get tired of smelling it."

"You see anything yet?" Magic asked.

"I see four deer down at the river's edge and a bald eagle sitting on a tree branch not far from them."

"Shut up!" Magic said. "No, you don't."

Luke smiled. It was the first sign of the young woman's personality coming through.

"Yeah, I do. Come take a look," he said.

Magic ran around the back of the truck to where Luke was standing. He handed her the binoculars and slowly directed her to where she would see the deer and the eagle.

Finally, she said, "This is so cool. I can see now why you like your job. Getting to see this every day would be wonderful."

She kept looking through the binoculars and said, "Oh, I see some more deer! Another mama with two more fawns."

Luke smiled again. "Keep looking. You might see something else."

She ended up seeing some ducks on the river and some other

birds—magpies and crows mostly—but no more deer.

"I'd come up here every day if this was my job," Magic said as she looked around and inhaled some more of the sagebrush scent.

"I come up here every now and again," Luke said. "But I have so much area to patrol, it's hard to come here often."

"I bet you see lots of other cool things, don't you?" Magic said.

"I do, for sure," Luke said. "It's what I like about the job. And I meet some great people too. Like you."

Magic blushed a little and dropped her head so that she was looking at her old tennis shoes. "I'm not a great person," she said, kicking at a rock in the road.

"Yes, you are," Luke said. "You're young and courageous and you seem smart. It may not feel like it right now, but you have the whole world in front of you."

Magic thought about it for a minute and then said, "No one has ever said those things to me before."

"Well, they're all true. Sara and I were talking about it last night. She believes it too."

"She does?" Magic asked. "She seems so smart and beautiful. And she's an FBI agent."

"She's all those things," Luke said. "But she wasn't always an FBI agent. She went to school and became one. You could do it too. Or anything else you want to be."

"Could I get a job doing what you do?" she asked.

"I don't know why not," Luke said. "The Department of Fish and Wildlife is always looking for good candidates for a variety of jobs."

They chatted for a few more minutes, and Luke could tell that a seed had been planted. Something good could certainly grow from it. It would be up to Magic to make it happen, but with a little nurturing from people around her, there was no reason she couldn't do whatever she wanted.

"We better get down the hill," Luke said. "I have a couple other spots I want to check out."

He looked around, and Jack was nowhere to be found. Luke

whistled, and in a minute a small yellow dot appeared over the horizon about a quarter-mile away. Jack came loping back to the truck.

"Where you been, boy?" Luke asked, as if he expected the dog to answer him. "Come on, let's load up."

Luke opened the back door, and Jack jumped in. He was panting hard from the run back to the truck.

"Does he always come when you whistle for him?" Magic asked.

"Most of the time," Luke said.

"You have him well-trained," Magic said. "Did it take a long time?"

"No, not really," Luke said. "We kind of trained each other. He seems to know what I want him to do, and he lets me know when there is something up, like the wounded bear in the thicket."

Magic reached back and scratched Jack's ear and said, "Good boy, Jack."

Jack moved up between the seats, front feet on the center console, and gave Magic another lick on the cheek.

She giggled and told Jack to stop. But she didn't mean it.

CHAPTER 16

fter driving around the wildlife area for another two hours and seeing nothing that might indicate a dig, Luke turned the truck toward home.

"Sara wants us back by three," Luke said. "She wants to take you to town to pick up some things."

"I have some money," Magic said. "So I can pay for what I need."

"You can figure that out with Sara," Luke said.

He knew Sara wasn't going to let Magic pay for anything, but that would be between the two of them.

When they got to the house, Sara's car was already there.

"I'm just going to drop you off," Luke said. "I still have a couple things to do today. And can you take Jack in with you?"

Magic said, "Okay," climbed out of the truck, opened the rear truck door, and said, "C'mon, Jack."

"The door around the back of the house will be open," Luke said. "Just go on in."

Magic gave him a slight wave and turned for the backyard with Jack by her side. He watched the pair disappear around the corner. The young woman was a bit of an enigma. She did, in fact, seem very smart, but she was definitely naïve. Her world growing up had been anything but normal, and then her life in the homeless camps was most likely nomadic and barbaric.

Luke backed the truck out of the driveway and headed to the highway. He was going to see if he could find Quentin Nash at home.

* * *

As Luke drove up the gravel road to Nash's place, he wondered if he would be greeted by the old man again. He looked over at Sarah Stout's house as he drove by, and the woman was again tending to her roses. He honked the horn and waved, and she frantically waved at him with a "come here" motion.

Luke stopped the truck, backed it up, and pulled into Stout's driveway.

"Officer McCain," Stout said. "I was just going to call you."

"This is fortunate then," Luke said. "What's up?"

"Not that I was spying on Nash," Stout said. "But since our visit yesterday, I have been paying a little more attention to what is going on over there."

She hesitated, so Luke said, "And?"

"He came in last night, after dark, pulling a trailer with one of those little backhoe machines on it."

Luke looked over at Nash's house. He couldn't see behind the place, but he saw no trailer with a backhoe on it.

"I don't see it there now," Luke said.

"I heard him leave this morning before daylight. When it got light enough to see, I came out to water the flowers and looked over there. Nash's truck with the trailer and backhoe was gone."

"What does he do for work?" Luke asked.

"I'm not sure. But I've never seen a piece of equipment like that over there before. You asked if I ever saw any big bones over there, so it doesn't take Einstein to figure out he may be using the backhoe to dig up the bones."

"Well, that's one possibility," Luke said. "Or he could be digging a septic tank for a friend, or a line for some irrigation pipe, or a hundred other things."

Sara Stout looked at Luke with a sly grin and said, "But you don't really believe that, do you?"

"Let's just say I would like to find out for sure what he is doing with the backhoe," Luke said. "Have you seen him come back?"

"No, but I ran to town for a couple hours to meet a friend for lunch, so I wasn't here the whole time."

"Have you seen the skinny older man coming or going?"

"Haven't seen him at all."

"You didn't happen to see if the backhoe had any writing on it, like the name of a rental company or something?"

"It was dark, Officer McCain. I have good eyes, but I'm no owl."

Luke chuckled and then said, "Thank you, Ms. Stout. You don't need to spy on Nash, but I'd sure appreciate a call if you see anything else going on over there. You have my number."

"Yes, I do," she said with a smile. "This is kinda fun."

Luke climbed back into his truck, backed out of Stout's driveway, and headed to Nash's house. Like he did the day before, he drove up the driveway, but this time no one came out on the porch to yell at him, so he put the truck in park, kept the engine running, and jumped out of the truck.

He climbed the steps and found no doorbell next to the weathered front door, so he knocked. Luke took a step back and waited and listened. He heard no footsteps inside, so he moved to the door and knocked again, this time a bit harder. Again, he heard nothing from inside the weathered house. Either no one was home, or the old man was sound asleep.

"Or dead," Luke said to himself after remembering how sickly the skinny, gray-haired man had looked.

He took the opportunity to look around the place. From what he could see, nothing had changed. The wheelbarrow sat where it was before, the lawn mower was still in front of the garage door, and the gardening tools were still leaning against the dying apple tree. One thing was different, though. The old brown Chevy truck was no longer sitting next to the driveway.

Around the back, he found a galvanized hundred-gallon water trough that looked like it hadn't been used in years. And he noticed an old three-wheel Honda sitting against a rail fence, the grass and weeds growing up so they almost covered the big rubber tires. Luke couldn't remember the last time he saw one of those motorized tricycles. The things were dangerous to drive and had been outlawed years ago. Now everyone used motorized four-wheelers and side-by-sides.

A small wooden garden shed sat in the back corner of the yard. It, too, was weathered, with shingles missing from the roof. Luke wanted to take a look in the shed, but if he found something that might indicate Nash was excavating prehistoric animal remains, he couldn't use it for an arrest because he didn't have a search warrant.

Nothing Luke saw around the house would indicate that Nash was digging up bones or doing anything else illegal, so he headed back to the truck. He was just about to open the truck door when he heard a vehicle rattling up the gravel road. An older black Ford F-250 pickup was coming fast, a cloud of dust boiling up behind it.

Luke stood and watched as the truck slowed at the head of Nash's driveway, turned, drove past Luke's truck, and parked.

An overweight man with a black beard covering a round face climbed out of the truck and said, "What the hell do you want?"

"I think you know why I'm here," Luke said, hoping the man might just confess right there. "We need to talk about it."

The man said nothing.

"Are you Quentin Nash?" Luke asked.

"What if I am?" the man said.

"I just want to ask a couple questions."

"Unless you have a search warrant, I want you off my property," Nash said.

"I'll be glad to leave, Mr. Nash, but we've received some information that you may be digging up mammoth bones on state land, and I'm here to tell you that is illegal."

"I ain't digging up no bones," Nash said. "And whoever told you that is a liar."

"What are you using the backhoe for?" Luke asked.

Nash paused and thought about it. Too long of a hesitation, Luke thought. Thinking up a lie most likely. Or maybe he was wondering how Luke knew he had a backhoe here recently.

"I'm working for a friend, helping dig a sewer line."

"Can I get the friend's name?" Luke asked.

"No," Nash said. "It's none of your damn business. Now leave."

"I'll leave, Mr. Nash. But just know I'm going to keep an eye on you. Digging up anything on public land is illegal. Selling something you dug up on public land makes it worse. Such activities could earn you jail time and some hefty fines."

Nash turned and walked to the front steps and climbed them without saying a word. Luke got into his truck and watched as Nash walked in the house and closed the front door. A second later, the big man came out on the porch holding a double-barreled shotgun in two hands across his chest. He stood and stared at Luke as he backed his truck out of the driveway.

"You're up to something," Luke said to himself as he backed out. "And I'm going to find out just what it is."

* * *

Luke drove and thought about it. He was probably wasting too much time on all of this, but now he really wanted to know what Nash was up to, so he called Derek Day again.

"Yeah, hello?" Day said on the other end of the line after the phone had rung five times.

Luke pulled off the road so he could talk and take notes if needed.

"Mr. Day, Luke McCain calling."

"Oh, hey there, Officer McCain."

"Did you come up with a phone number for the guy you talked to about Quentin Nash?"

After a moment's hesitation, Day said, "Well, here's the deal. I talked to the guy who talked to the friend of Nash's, and neither of them want to talk to you. They're afraid of Nash and what he might do to them."

"I've just talked to Nash and asked about the bones," Luke said. "So he already knows that someone has said something about it. I just need to talk to one of them."

"Oh man," Day said in a worried voice. "I told Otis you'd still need to talk to him."

"Otis?" Luke asked. "Is that his first name or last?"

"I don't know. Everyone just calls him Otis."

"Alright," Luke said. "Give me his phone number and an address if you have one."

Day said he didn't have an address but gave Luke the phone number. Luke wrote it in his notebook, thanked him, and told him not to worry about Nash. If he did something, Luke said, the law would be behind him since he had already threatened the men.

"By then it might be too late," Day said. "The law ain't gunna do me a whole lotta good if I'm dead."

"He's not going to kill anyone over something like this," Luke said.

"Tell that to his wife," Day said and hung up.

Luke looked at his phone for a long ten seconds and wondered what that was all about. When he'd talked to Day earlier, the man said he didn't know anything about the disappearance of Nash's wife. Then he looked at his notepad and punched in the number for the man named Otis. As he waited for the phone to ring, Luke thought about what Otis's last name might be.

A second later, the ringing stopped, and a man's voice, deep and gravelly, said, "Hullo." The guy sounded drunk. Maybe, Luke thought, he was like the Otis on *The Andy Griffith Show*, the town drunk.

"Mr. Otis?" Luke asked.

"Yup, who's this?"

"I'm Officer Luke McCain with the Department of Fish and Wildlife," Luke said. "You have time for a couple of questions?"

"I don't fish or hunt, so I got nothing for you."

"Is Otis your first name or last?" Luke asked.

"Last," Otis said without offering a first name.

"You mind me asking what your first name is?"

"Nope," Otis said.

Luke quickly got the idea. The man with the last name of Otis was not going to be giving up much information.

"So, what is your first name?"

"Charlton," Otis said.

"Okay, Charlton," Luke said. He was about to say something else, but Otis interrupted.

"No one but my dear old mama, rest her soul, called me Charlton."

"So, what would you like me to call you?" Luke asked.

"Otis," the man said. "Everyone just calls me Otis."

"Okay, Otis," Luke said. "The reason for my call is I am following up on a tip I received about a man by the name of Quentin Nash digging up mammoth bones out in the L.T. Murray. You know anything about that?"

"I'm not ratting on anyone about anything, and if you see that Derek Day, tell him I may have a little something for him."

"So, there is something going on out in the L.T. Murray," Luke said. "Why else would the man say something about ratting on someone?"

"You can look all you want, but you ain't finding nothin' going on out there."

"How well do you know Mr. Nash?" Luke asked.

Dead silence.

"Can you think of someone else who might be digging up bones if it isn't Mr. Nash?" Luke asked.

"If there was someone else, I wouldn't be telling you about them neither."

"Okay, well, you've been a big help, Charlton," Luke said, using the man's first name just to annoy him. "Thanks for your time."

Then he hung up.

Luke replayed the conversation in his mind. Otis knew what was going on, and what he said, without actually saying it, was that Nash was digging up bones. He was going to do a little checking on one Charlton Otis.

CHAPTER 17

Kristen Gray had been busy visiting the different homeless camps around Puget Sound and writing notes for her dissertation. She thought about the doctor from the emergency room at Harborview and planned on calling him sometime, but she'd been too busy to do it right away. And there was something about the man that nagged at her. She swore she had met him before but couldn't place where or when it might have been.

She had just arrived at her studio apartment near the university after a long day visiting camps near Tacoma when her phone rang. She looked at the caller ID and saw it was the Seattle Police Department.

"Hi, this is Kristen," she said after sliding the answer button on her phone's screen.

"Hi, Kristen, this is Officer Donley with the Seattle PD. Do you have a few minutes to chat?"

"Sure," Gray said. "Let me take off my coat. I just got home."

She set down her keys and the phone on a small table next to the door, took off her coat, slipped out of her shoes, picked the phone up, and said, "Okay."

"So, as you know, we are now treating the death of the young man named Toby as a homicide. I know we've gone over some of this before, but I want to ask some more detailed questions about what else you might have seen that morning."

"Sure," Gray said again. "I'll help if I can."

Gray walked Donley through all the events of that morning, when, from the freeway, she saw some people at an encampment who were gathered around in circle. One of the women in the group, who she later learned was Magic, looked to be in hysterics, pulling at her hair and crying. When she arrived a few minutes later, she said, there were fewer people around, but there were still several standing in a circle and looking down. Magic had moved and was sitting on a nearby rock.

"I walked over to Magic, introduced myself, and asked her if she was alright," Gray said. "That's when she told me that it was her boyfriend, named Toby, who was dead."

"What did you do then?" Donley asked.

Gray explained that she'd then walked over to the group of four men and two women standing and looking at a young man, who, based on the ashen coloring in his face, was most assuredly dead. Still, she knelt and felt for a pulse but didn't find one. She described for Donley the people in the group the best she could and said she remembered asking if anyone had tried using Narcan on the young man, but everyone there said he'd been lying there most of the night. Everyone just thought he had passed out.

"That's when I dialed 911," Gray said.

"Anything else?" Donley asked.

"The woman in the purple coat and Seahawks stocking cap said that this was the fourth death in that camp in the last few weeks, and I remember thinking that seemed strange. She specifically mentioned a man they called the Duckman as being another resident of the camp who didn't do drugs either, but the police said he'd died of an overdose."

"We're checking into that," Donley said. "But with no body to examine, it makes it very tough to determine if his death was caused by someone, or if it was, in fact, an overdose, or possibly some kind of health issue like a heart attack."

"I hate the thought of someone killing homeless people for no reason," Gray said.

"Yeah, that's a tough one to figure out," Donley said. "Anything else you remember?"

Gray then remembered seeing the man watching her that morning.

"There was this man wearing an old Army coat with the hood up covering some kind of fur cap, standing, holding a bottle of booze, watching from a ways away," Gray said. "He sorta looked homeless, you know, by the way he dressed, but he didn't *look* like a homeless man."

"Anything distinguishing about him?" Donley asked. "Beard, mustache, color of hair, like that?"

"I don't remember any beard or mustache, and he was wearing that old hat covered by the hood. But I do remember his eyes. They seemed too clear, too alert, you know, not like someone who had just downed a bottle of cheap wine."

"Hmmm," Donley said.

"He saw me look at him, and a second later, he turned and walked away."

"Would you recognize him if you saw him again?" Donley asked.

"I doubt it," Gray said. "But I might recognize the eyes."

They talked for a few more minutes, about the investigation's next steps in broad terms, as well as Magic and Agent McCain.

"Are they coming here?" Gray asked.

"I'm going to try to get them to come to the station," Donley said. "Agent McCain said she would escort Magic here."

"Any chance I could be there too?" Gray asked.

Donley thought about it for a few seconds and then said, "Not for the interview, but I bet they'd be willing to meet you for coffee or lunch or something while they're here."

"When you talk to Agent McCain, could you ask her to call me?"

Donley said she would do that and then thanked Gray for her time and information.

"I hope it helps," Gray said. "It would be good to catch this guy."

* * *

Gray was eating a salad and reviewing her notes from the day Toby died. Suddenly, her phone rang again. She recognized the number.

"Hi, Agent McCain," Gray said.

"Please, call me Sara."

"Oh yeah, sorry," Gray said.

"So, you've talked to Officer Donley and gave her everything you remember about the morning Toby died?"

"Yes," Gray said.

"Is there anything else you remember since you talked with her?"

"No, and I've been thinking about it and looking at my notes from that day."

"You took notes?"

"Yes, it's part of what I do every day. I'm doing a study on the people who live in the camps around Puget Sound for my doctoral studies."

"Interesting," Sara said. "And nothing sparked anything else?"

"No, but when I was talking to the officer, I remembered seeing a man nearby watching everything from a distance. When I looked at him, he was staring at me. Kind of gave me the creeps."

"A homeless man?" Sara asked.

"That's just the thing," Gray said. "He was dressed like a homeless person—Army coat, weird fur hat, holding an empty booze bottle—but like I told the officer, he stuck out somehow. Something about his eyes. I've been to so many camps throughout my education, and he was the first person who ever made me feel unsafe with just a stare."

"Could he have been the killer?" Sara asked.

"I don't know, but the more I think about it, he might have been. He sure took off quickly when I looked at him and saw him staring at me."

"Killers will sometimes stick around and watch what happens," Sara said.

"What really worries me," Gray said, "is if he is the killer, he was looking at me long enough to know what I look like. Do you think I'm in danger?"

"I don't know," Sara said. "But you need to keep an eye out for the guy, and if you see him again, call Officer Donley."

"I will," Gray said. "So, how's Magic doing?"

"She's doing better," Sara said. "We did a little shopping today to get her some more clothes, and before then, she rode along with my husband, out in the country."

"What's your husband do?"

"He's a game warden."

"Like those people on that TV show *North Woods Law*?"

"Yes, something like that."

"I bet she liked that," Gray said. "I would, for sure."

"She still seems sad, which is understandable, but just being away from the camp seems to be helping."

"Are you going to send her back here?" Gray asked.

"She's free to go where she wants. We're talking about if she would like to go back to school or at least find a job and a place to live."

"And you're coming over here to meet with Officer Donley?"

"Yes, that's the reason for my call. She said you'd like to meet up while we're there."

"If you'd have the time," Gray said.

"Our SPD meeting is set for nine o'clock the day after tomorrow. We could meet you for lunch someplace."

"That'd be great. I'll find a place near the police station and will text you the address. We'll figure noon unless your interview goes longer than that."

"Perfect," Sara said. "See you then."

After ending the call with Sara, Gray went back to her notes to see if there was anything she might have missed that could help the investigation. She was looking forward to meeting with the FBI agent and Magic.

She was concerned about the young woman from the homeless camp who had lost her fiancé, but selfishly, she was even more excited to meet and talk to a real special agent with the FBI, even if the FBI agent was from Yakima. Gray would figure out a way to include the meeting and the discussion in her dissertation and believed it would add credence and authenticity to the paper. Which reminded Gray again about calling the emergency room doctor to set up a meeting with him.

After all these weeks and months spending time in the camps, it felt like things were finally coming together, and she'd have a dissertation that would warrant praise. Better yet, maybe her paper would get published and help cities around the country assist one of their most vulnerable populations.

Gray looked for the doctor's phone number, found it, pushed the numbers into her phone, and waited.

CHAPTER 18

All the way back to the office, Luke thought about his conversation with Charlton Otis. The guy knew something about what Nash was up to, that was for sure.

When he got to his desk, Luke ran Otis's name through the Washington State Patrol's database and found that the man had had two DUIs in the past six years and a couple of arrests when he was in his twenties and thirties—one for burglary and another for trying to sell stolen property.

The database showed a photo of Otis, who was completely bald, with a thick neck and a light brown Fu Manchu mustache. The information showed he was fifty-two years old, stood an even six feet tall, and weighed two hundred and fifty-five pounds. From the look of Otis's head and neck, Luke believed the man was more muscle than fat. Not a guy you would want to tangle with.

Then, because he had forgotten to do so earlier, Luke looked up the owner of the older Chevy pickup that had been in Nash's driveway the day before. Luke looked at his notebook and typed the license plate number into the system. It took a minute for the computer to spin up, and when it did, it showed that the legal owner of the 1977 Chevy Silverado was one Herman Nash, with an address in Goldendale, Washington.

Luke clicked on the driver's license for the senior Nash and found a photo of a younger version of the old man who had been yelling at him from the porch at Nash's house. The information on the license showed that Herman Nash was seventy-eight years old and weighed one hundred and ninety-three pounds.

The man Luke had seen on the porch looked to be ninety-three years old and weighed way less than a hundred and ninety pounds. Maybe his first impression of the man had been correct, and the elder Nash was fighting a terminal disease.

Just for the heck of it, Luke ran both Nashes through the Yakima County Sheriff's Spillman arrest record system and found out the apple didn't fall far from the tree. The records showed both men had been arrested for petty theft, bar fights, and driving while intoxicated. The senior Nash had been arrested twice for beating his wife. Luke wondered if it was Quentin's mother who his father had abused.

"Find any dinosaur bones?" Bob Davis asked from behind Luke.

"No, sir," Luke said as he turned in his chair to face Davis. "But I'm getting closer."

Luke went on to tell his captain about his discussions with Quentin Nash, Derek Day, and Charlton Otis, and about the neighbor, Sarah Stout, who had seen Nash pulling a trailer with a small backhoe on it.

"Sounds like something is going on," Davis said.

"I agree," Luke said. "Although I spent a few hours driving around out there on the L.T. Murry and didn't find anything that might point to mammoth digs."

"There's a lot of country out there," Davis said. "If he's behind a hump or over a ridge away from the road, you'd never see it."

"I got up as high as I could in a few places but didn't see a thing."

"Well, keep trying, I guess."

"If I get any more information, what would be the chances of getting a ride in a helicopter or one of the planes the biologists use on their big game surveys? We could cover a lot more ground."

"We could probably make that happen," Davis said. "But let's try to get more evidence that Nash is really out there digging."

"The other thing stuck in my craw is this whole issue of Nash's wife just disappearing into thin air."

"When did she go missing?" Davis asked.

"Twenty-three years ago," Luke said. "I know the sheriff's office did an investigation, but I'm getting a nagging feeling after listening to the neighbor and to Derek Day that there is more to the story."

"That's out of our jurisdiction," Davis said. "But if you find something, get it to YSO. I'm sure they'd be interested in re-opening the case file."

"I will," Luke said.

✳ ✳ ✳

Sara's car was in the driveway when he got home, but Luke's Toyota Tundra was not there. That meant Sara had taken it to go shopping with Magic. Sara preferred to use the truck when she was doing personal business, and although she could probably justify using her work-issued black sedan, she liked driving the Tundra.

When he entered the house through the back door, Luke found Jack waiting for him. The big yellow dog wagged his tail.

"Are you happy because I'm home or because you know I'm going to feed you?" Luke asked.

The dog didn't have to talk—Luke knew the answer.

"Go get your dish," Luke said and watched as Jack ran over to grab the plastic dog dish that sat next to the refrigerator.

Luke filled the dish with kibble, put a little warm water on it, and took it back over to the spot next to the fridge and set it down. Jack followed and sat. He looked at Luke and then at the bowl.

"Okay," Luke said, and Jack moved to the dish and started eating like he hadn't had anything to eat in days.

"Slow down," Luke said. "No one is going to take it from you."

Jack didn't slow down, and before Luke had time to walk into the bedroom to change his clothes, Jack was done with his dinner. Luke didn't know if eating that fast was good for the dog, but it had been that way since Jack was a puppy, and he'd been a very healthy dog over the years, so Luke let it go.

He had just changed and was going to take Jack down to the river for a walk when Sara and Magic pulled into the driveway.

"How'd the shopping go?" Luke asked as the women were getting out of the truck.

"I'd say it was a success," Sara said and nodded at Magic.

The young woman was wearing a whole different set of clothes than when Luke had dropped her off earlier. She was wearing a new pair of Wrangler jeans, along with a white tank top and some boots. The clothes were crisp and clean, and she looked great.

Luke looked at Sara, and she casually pointed at her own hair. Luke caught the cue and looked at Magic's hair. Even though her hair color was the same, the hair was slightly shorter, and it shone in the afternoon sun.

"Nicely done," Luke finally said. "I like the look, Magic, and your hair looks great."

Magic smiled and blushed a little but didn't say a thing.

"See?" Sara said to Magic. "I told you he'd like it."

Then she said to Luke, "Come help us bring these bags in" as she was opening the back door of the pickup.

Luke obliged. There weren't that many bags, but enough to know that Magic should have plenty of clean underwear, socks, and a couple changes of pants and shirts. There were probably some personal things in the bags too, he figured.

He hauled the packages back to the spare bedroom and put

them on the bed. Magic followed him in and thanked him.

"I'm pretty tired. Do you mind if I take a nap?" Magic asked.

"No, go right ahead," Luke said. "If you're hungry, we'll fix something to eat in a bit."

"That would be great," Magic said and laid on the bed next to the pile of shopping bags.

"Sara and I are going to take Jack for a quick walk," Luke said. "We'll be back in twenty minutes."

Magic, who already had her head on the pillow and her eyes closed, just nodded. Luke closed the door and went to the kitchen, where Sara was putting away a few groceries.

"Stopped at the grocery store on the way home," she said. "I'll get something started for dinner."

"She's going to take a nap. I told her we were going to take Jack for a short walk."

"Let's go," Sara said.

They went out the back door and hit the trail that headed down to the river. Jack, always the hunter, quartered back and forth ahead of them as they walked. The dog had made the same walk a thousand times, but he still searched for anything new that might have somehow arrived since his last walk. Occasionally, he'd flush quail or bounce a cottontail rabbit into the nearby trees.

"Did you get a chance to talk to her about what happened in Seattle?" Luke asked.

"Yes, but she's pretty reluctant to get into details. Talking about it makes her really sad."

Luke told Sara about his discussion with Magic earlier in the day.

"She's convinced that a man killed Toby because he witnessed another murder."

"Well, someone killed Toby," Sara said.

She told Luke about the call from the King County Medical Examiner's Office and her discussion with the Seattle Police officer investigating the death.

"They want to talk to Magic in Seattle, and I volunteered to take her over there on Wednesday."

"You think she can tell them anything else that might help?"

"You never know," Sara said. "Sometimes reliving it step-by-step might help shake a memory loose."

"Magic said that Toby's death was the fourth in their camp in four months," Luke said. "Toby's was a homicide, and it sounds like the Duckman was killed by someone. Any chance there is some nut over there killing homeless people?"

"I don't know," Sara said quietly as she thought about it. "I guess anything is possible. But I have trouble coming up with a motive."

"Toby was killed because he witnessed the Duckman being killed," Luke said. "What if the Duckman also witnessed a murder in the camp?"

"That's possible, but that would mean someone else was murdered there recently."

"According to Magic, there was a woman who died in the camp a few days before the Duckman died. I've been thinking about what she told me, and there might be a motive for her death."

"What's that?" Sara asked.

"She said the woman who died was in really bad shape. Defecating and urinating in her clothing, living in the mess, sleeping in the dirt."

Sara cringed, just as Luke had earlier in the day.

"What if someone is killing people who are in such bad shape that he, or she, feels like they are doing the person a favor? Kind of like an angel of death type of deal?"

Again, Sara thought about it as they walked.

Finally, Luke broke the silence and said, "Magic said another man died in the camp a few months earlier. That's just one camp. I realize the living conditions and the health issues these people face are not conducive to a long life," Luke said. "But four deaths in one camp in a few months seems excessive. I mean, how many people typically live in a camp? A dozen? Fifteen? A third or a quarter of the residents in one camp dying in that short period of time doesn't seem natural."

"I've chatted with a graduate student from the University of Washington who is doing her doctoral dissertation on the homeless camps," Sara said. "She was in the camp right after Toby died. I bet she'd have some data on that. We're supposed to have lunch with her after talking with the Seattle police on Wednesday."

"It's definitely worth thinking about," Sara said.

"Did you ask Magic about staying here for a while?" Luke asked.

"Yes, and she is agreeable, at least for the short-term. She said she doesn't want to put us out."

"If there is someone killing people in the camps over there, and he thinks she knows who it might be, then she could be in danger. I'd sure feel better if she'd stay with us until the police figure out what is going on."

"I agree," Sara said.

CHAPTER 19

The phone rang once, twice, three times, and then the doctor answered.

"Hello?"

"Hi, this is Kristen Gray. We talked the other day at the hospital emergency room."

"Ah, yes," Doc said. "The young lady doing the study on the homeless people."

"Yes," Gray said. "Would you have time for a cup of coffee sometime soon? I'm starting to write the first draft of my dissertation and thought I might ask you some questions about the people you have treated from homeless camps."

"I'd be happy to meet you sometime," Doc said. "I'm still on nights, so anytime in the afternoon would work for me."

Gray decided that since she was meeting the FBI agent and

Magic at noon on Wednesday, maybe she would try to meet the doctor after that.

"How about two-thirty on Wednesday at the Starbucks across the street from the hospital?"

"Let's see," Doc said, playing along. "I've lost track of the days. So, day after tomorrow?"

"Yes," Gray said. "But I could do it some other time."

"No, no," Doc said. "Wednesday at two-thirty works just fine. I'll see you at Starbucks."

After he hung up, he thought about the young woman. She had definitely seen him under the bridge at the camp after he had killed the young man, but she had not recognized him in the examination room at the hospital. Was it exposing too much to allow her to see him again? She had said she thought she knew him from someplace, but would she figure it out? He'd have to be careful. It was a risk, but one he'd have to take. She might be able to tell him what the girl named Magic knew about the murders and where she was located now.

Besides the two times he had gone back to the camp dressed differently to talk to the man and the woman, Doc had stayed away from all the camps in the area. He needed to get this last little problem solved so he could resume his work. There were people out there suffering needlessly. They needed to be in a better place. It was his calling.

"Don't worry," Doc whispered to himself. "Help will be coming soon."

* * *

After she hung up from her short chat with the doctor, Gray started thinking about the man who had helped the homeless woman in the emergency room. Somewhere in her subconscious she knew she had met the doctor before. But try as she might, she couldn't figure it out. Maybe when she saw him on Wednesday, under different circumstances, in different surroundings, it would come to her.

In the meantime, she wanted to have some questions prepared for the doctor that would give her some vital information for her dissertation. She was looking forward to Wednesday. Meeting with the FBI agent and Magic, and then the doctor—it was going to be a very good day.

* * *

The next morning, Sara called Officer Donley at the Seattle PD. She had been thinking about her discussion with Luke on their walk the previous evening. What if someone was killing people in the homeless camps to put them out of their misery?

Donley recognized the number on the readout on her phone and answered by saying, "Agent McCain, how may I help you?"

"I've been doing some thinking about the situation at the camp where Toby was killed. As you know, Magic said that three other people had died in that particular camp within a fairly short time. Would the SPD be notified every time a person dies in one of the camps around there?"

"Yes," Donley said. "Even if someone calls an ambulance, the ambulance operators are legally obligated to give us a call if the person is dead or dies."

"But there normally isn't an autopsy done if there is no suspicion of foul play?"

"That's correct. Unless a family requests it, and a high percentage of the time we have trouble just finding family members."

"I understand," Sara said. "Would you mind doing something for me? Can you give me the data on the number of people who have died in the camps over, say, the last five years?"

"I can pull together some approximate numbers," Donley said. "But camps are transient by nature, and often a homeless individual isn't named as such in a police report. I'll gather data from addresses and intersections where I know encampments have been located for longer periods. And the data will only be for King County. We wouldn't have numbers for Snohomish, Pierce, or the other counties in the area."

"That's fine," Sara said. "And if there has been an autopsy on any of these, could you include the findings in the report?"

"Will do," Donley said. "I'll have it for you when we meet tomorrow, if not before."

"Tomorrow would be perfect," Sara said.

After the call, Sara thought more about it. Then she picked up the phone and called the FBI office in Portland.

"Special Agent Sanchez," the man's voice said on the other end of the line.

"Hey, Sanchez, it's Sinclair."

Sara used her maiden name because she figured Sanchez, a man who she'd worked with for a year in the Portland office before moving to Yakima, would have forgotten her married name, if he ever knew it.

"Hey, Sinclair! How're things out there in no-man's land?"

"Couldn't be better," Sara said. "No traffic jams, no idiots trying to burn down the city. I'm loving it."

"Well, there is that," Sanchez said. "So, how can I help you today?"

She told him about what she was working on, unofficially, and asked if he could run down the same information regarding deaths in the homeless camps in Multnomah County.

"I guess the Portland PD would have some rough numbers," Sanchez said. "I hear about one every now and again on the news, but it doesn't seem to be an epidemic." He started to say, "And you know those people—"

Sara cut him off. "Yes, everyone realizes they are not living the healthiest lifestyle. But we know of two murders in a camp in Seattle, and it just got us thinking."

"Understood," Sanchez said. "I'll make the call now and get you what I find out."

"That'd be great," Sara said and thanked him for his help.

When she was off the phone, Sara started second-guessing everything. The two known homicides had to be an anomaly.

People died in the camps occasionally. There was no one out there who was killing people just to put them out of their misery. Right?

* * *

The drive from Yakima over Snoqualmie Pass was uneventful. They were stopped once for about fifteen minutes for road construction, but Sara had figured that into the drive time.

"I've only been over this pass about three times," Magic said. "Every time, they've been doing road construction."

"It's a continual thing," Sara said. "Some people will work their whole life on the freeway up here."

"Gee, really?" Magic asked.

"I don't know that for sure, but it seems possible. They never seem to be done with all the construction on this stretch of the freeway."

"What do you think the police will want to talk to me about?" Magic asked.

"They'll most likely ask the same questions they asked before," Sara said.

"They didn't ask me any questions before," Magic said.

"They didn't?"

"No, because when I left, they hadn't arrived yet. I figured the guy who killed Toby could be after me next, so I went to the bus station and bought a ticket over to Yakima."

"Why did you pick Yakima?"

"Toby and I used to talk about places we might go, and he had been to Yakima and liked it. He said it was sunny and warm when Seattle was cold and rainy. I figured it would be a good place to get away."

"Well, they'll probably ask you the same questions Luke and I have asked," Sara said. "Like how long you knew Toby, and what he might have told you about seeing the man you think killed the man who fed the ducks."

"Okay," Magic said. "I've seen different police officers come through camp from time to time, and they always seemed nice."

"I'm sure they're just interested in finding the man who did this to Toby," Sara said. "Anything you can think of that might help them in their investigation will be valuable."

"Okay," Magic said. "I'll keep thinking about it."

The young woman went quiet and after a few minutes, Sara looked over and saw that Magic was crying. She reached over and squeezed Magic's hand. She wanted to tell her something like "you'll get through this" but knew there were no words that would help. They drove in silence the rest of the way to Seattle.

* * *

The Seattle Police Department was a beehive of activity when they arrived. Police officers were coming and going. Other people were milling around in the lobby, some waiting for someone, others looking like they were totally lost.

Sara pulled out her FBI credential pack, which included her badge on a lanyard, and put it on. She and Magic walked up to the officer at the window in the lobby and asked to see Officer Donley.

The reception officer, an overweight man of about sixty, with a pudgy red face and a small ring of white hair just below a very shiny bald head, looked at Sara's FBI badge and then at her face and asked, "May I tell her who is here?" The man was in full uniform, and with the stiff collar and a tie tied tight up against his fat neck, it looked like his head might explode.

"Special Agent McCain," Sara said. "She is expecting us."

The officer picked up the handset of an old-style phone, pushed a few buttons, spoke quietly into the phone, set it back in the cradle, and said, "Officer Donley will be with you in just a minute. Let me get you some guest passes."

Two minutes later, an inner door opened, and a fit forty-something woman with caramel-colored skin and black hair cut short stepped through. She, too, was in full uniform.

"Special Agent McCain?" she said when she spotted Sara with Magic. "I'm Officer Donley."

Then she turned to Magic and said, "Hi, Magic. How are you doing?"

Magic just smiled but said nothing.

"Well, thanks for coming in today," Donley said, again to Magic. "This shouldn't take long. We just have a few questions."

"Can Sara be with me when you ask the questions?" Magic asked as Donley headed back to the door that led into the bowels of the building.

"Of course," Donley said with a reassuring smile.

They wandered through a maze of desks, most unoccupied, to a small room that could be called a conference room but might also double as an interrogation room. Sara spotted a small camera mounted up in one corner of the room. But there was no double-sided mirror in the wall.

"Please, have a seat," Donley said. "Would you like some water or coffee?"

Magic looked at Sara, and Sara said, "Water would be good."

"I'd like some too," Magic said.

Donley left and was back in twenty seconds with two bottles of water.

"So, Magic," Donley said as she was sitting in one of the two empty chairs at the table, "I'm so very sorry for your loss."

Magic gave the officer a sad smile and dropped her gaze to the bottle of water resting on the table.

"Can you tell me what happened that morning?"

Magic told the same story she had told to Luke and Sara about the morning Toby was discovered dead in the camp. She then went on to tell the officer about Toby seeing someone standing over the Duckman the day the man died in the camp.

"So, the man standing over the Duckman knew Toby had seen him?" Donley asked.

"Yes, because Toby said he yelled something at the guy as he was running off."

"Did he tell you what the man looked like?"

"He just said he looked like a homeless man, wearing a fur cap with the ear flaps down."

"Have you seen anyone like that in the camp before?" Donley asked.

"Only about a hundred times," Magic said. "But it was always different men—tall, short, Black, white, Hispanic. How could I know which man it might be?"

"Why did you leave before we got there the morning Toby died?"

"Because I was afraid. If someone killed Toby, and they knew we were together, they might want to kill me too."

They talked about how she got to Yakima and how she had met Luke and then Sara.

"We'd like to have her stay with us for a while," Sara said. "Until she is ready to get back on her feet."

"I think that's a fine idea," Donley said.

They chatted for a few more minutes, but with nothing more she needed to know, Donley thanked Sara and Magic for their time and said she would let Sara know if anything popped up in their investigation.

Before they left, Donley handed Sara a manila envelope.

"Here's the information you requested," Donley said. "You may find some of it interesting."

Sara thanked Donley and told her she would review the file when she got back to her office in Yakima.

As the two women were walking down the sidewalk back to Sara's car, Magic asked, "Do you think they will find the man who killed Toby?"

Sara knew it was a longshot at best but tried to be encouraging. "I hope so. I'm sure they will do their best."

CHAPTER 20

After Sara and Magic left for Seattle to make their nine o'clock appointment with the police officer there, Luke called Jack, and they loaded up in Luke's truck. He wanted to go back out to the L.T. Murray, but other things on his plate needed some attention first.

Captain Davis had called while Luke was eating breakfast and told Luke a call had come into the office from a woman who didn't give her name, claiming that a man from Yakima was killing hawks and eagles and selling the feathers to members of different Native American tribes around the Northwest.

The caller hadn't given the name of the man who was selling the bird feathers, possibly because she didn't know it, but did say that members of the Colville and the Muckleshoot tribes had purchased the feathers.

"Can you check into this?" Davis asked.

"Sure," Luke said. "I'll jump right on it."

How Luke was going to get the man's name, he didn't know, but killing hawks and eagles was a serious crime, and he needed to find out if it was true.

When he got to the office, Luke made a couple of calls. First, he called the WDFW Region 1 office in Spokane and talked to Mark Olson, an enforcement officer who patrolled the area around the Colville Reservation. Olson hadn't heard anything about the feather situation, but he said he would talk to one of the tribal police officers for the Colville tribe and see if he could find out anything.

Then Luke made a similar call to the Region 4 office in Mill Creek and asked Officer Sandy Harthorn if she could do some checking with the Muckleshoot police. She said she would and would call him back if she found anything.

Next, Luke took care of some emails and talked for a few minutes with one of the biologists in the office who had heard that Luke was looking for a possible dig site within the L.T. Murray Wildlife Area.

"You think the guy is actually digging out there somewhere?" Sheri Bronson asked.

Bronson was an attractive twenty-something woman, perfectly fit, with short, strawberry blonde hair. She had a sprinkling of freckles on her nose and cheeks that most women would have covered with makeup. Not Bronson—she was au naturel. If she had been living in the 1960s and was wearing a tie-dye T-shirt with a giant peace symbol or a happy face on it, she would have perfectly fit the description of a hippie. Or maybe a flower child.

Today, dressed in green slacks and a brown button-up collared shirt, the young lady was right at home with the many outdoor-loving Gen Zers who now made up much of the employee force in the Department of Fish and Wildlife's Region 3 office. Compared to Bronson and some of the others in the office, Luke sometimes felt old.

"I'm not sure," Luke said. "We received a tip about it, but I have looked around out there and haven't seen anything that might confirm it."

"I have a degree in paleontology," Bronson said. "I might be able to help a little."

"That would be great," Luke said.

He knew Bronson was one of the big game biologists in the office and wondered how a degree in paleontology would qualify her for studying black bears and mule deer.

Bronson saw the look in Luke's face and said, "I also have a degree in wildlife biology."

"So, an expert in prehistoric and current-day wildlife, eh? You were already way smarter than me with just the one degree," Luke said. "Now I really feel stupid."

Bronson laughed. "Don't give me that crap," she said. "You don't need a bunch of degrees on your wall to be good at your job, and from what I've seen and what others have told me, you are more than qualified."

"I knew my ears were burning for a reason, but don't believe everything you hear."

"Catching a serial killer and saving that FBI agent—that's pretty good stuff."

"Aw, it was mostly my dog doing the hard work on that one."

"So, you want some help or not?" Bronson asked.

"Yes, please," Luke said with his best charming smile.

Bronson started to tell Luke about alluvial plains and sedimentary rocks and the Missoula floods, and pretty soon his head was swimming.

Finally, when there was a break in the flow of information coming from paleontologist-slash-wildlife biologist Bronson, Luke said, "So, you are saying there might be mammoth bones someplace in that ocean of rock and sagebrush?"

Bronson gave Luke a look that said, "Haven't you been listening to me the last twelve minutes?" and then said simply, "Yes."

"Good," Luke said. "Any idea where I should concentrate my search?"

"Let's take a look," Bronson said and crooked her pointer finger at Luke.

He stood up and followed her to another big office with several cubicles in it. She got to her desk, sat in a rolling desk chair, and hit the mouse on her desktop computer. A split second later, she had pulled up Google Earth and narrowed in on their part of the world. It looked like a photo of the backside of the moon.

"This was taken after the last fire out there," Bronson said. "It looks pretty rough, but the fire might actually have made it easier to spot the bones."

Luke just nodded. He could see how that could happen.

"Little or no vegetation allows for the wind to erode some of the most open and vulnerable areas," Bronson explained.

"So, any spots in particular come to mind?"

Bronson moved the mouse, directing the cursor on the screen, which in turn moved the view of the photo.

"Here are a few spots to try," she said. "But as you will see, they are quite a distance from any of the major roads, so how likely is it that someone would just be wandering around out there and spot a femur bone or something?"

"Good question," Luke said. "The deer and elk were moved out of those areas by the fire, and from what I've seen, very few if any have moved back in. So the odds of a hunter just stumbling onto some newly uncovered bones are slim."

"That's what I was thinking," Bronson said. "And since it has been so dry, you probably would have seen tracks off the roads if there was a piece of equipment driving through the area. Not that a person couldn't walk anyplace with a pick and shovel and do some digging."

Luke thought about it for a minute and then said, "In a hundred and twenty thousand acres of the wildlife area, how would anyone know where to dig?"

"It would have to be a one in a million shot, or more," Bronson said. "So if there is someone doing this, they must have stumbled onto a bone somehow out there, or they were digging for another purpose and found a bone."

Luke looked at the map on the computer monitor again. He was very familiar with the wildlife area and recognized some of the spots that Bronson had pinned with a small red icon. Others he would have to go find.

"Can you print this out for me?" he asked.

"I could," Bronson said. "But why don't you just bring the photo up on your phone, and I'll share the pins with you?"

"Or we could do that," Luke said as he hit his forehead with the heel of his hand. He never would have come up with that idea, but he didn't want Bronson to know it.

Luke brought the map app up on his phone and located the L.T. Murray Wildlife Area. Bronson helped him transfer the pins. They had just finished, and Luke was looking at the map closely when his phone lit up with an incoming call. The ID said it was from the Region 1 office.

"Hey, Luke," Mark Olson said. "I talked with my guy on the Colville Reservation. He talked to a few of the tribal members, and they said they have bought some feathers recently. They use them on their traditional ceremonial clothing and headdresses. The seller said he had gotten the feathers from us, and we had gotten them from roadkills and other dead birds turned in by concerned citizens."

"Did they know if the guy they bought from lived in Yakima?"

"The Colville officer said the man didn't say where he was from, but the tribal members got the idea he lived in Washington. He told one of them that he lived about three hours from the Colville Reservation."

"That could be Yakima," Luke said. "Did they give a name or description of the fella?"

"No name, but he said they said he was a white guy, big, totally bald, and had a Fu Manchu mustache. They thought he might be a member of a motorcycle gang or something."

Luke immediately thought of the photo he had just seen of Charlton Otis. What were the odds? Slim, but not slim enough. There had to be three thousand white guys with bald heads and Fu Manchu mustaches running around the Northwest.

"This is a longshot, but I'm working on another investigation, and a guy that fits that very description popped up. I can send you a photo to send to the Colville officer. Maybe he can show it around to the people who purchased the feathers."

"Will do," Olson said. "If I hear anything, I'll let you know right away."

Luke thanked Olson, hung up, thanked Bronson for her assistance, and said he would be bugging her again soon. Then he went back to his computer to retrieve the driver's license photo of Otis so he could email it to the Spokane office.

Photo sent, Luke decided maybe it was time to meet Charlton Otis in person and get a read on the man. He looked up Otis's most current address and learned that he drove a black 2005 Hummer H2. He jotted down the license plate number and headed for the door.

The address listed for Otis was out in an area known as East Selah, close to the Yakima Training Center. When he found the place, Luke saw it was an old, white, two-story house that was in serious need of a new roof, a paint job, and about seven high school kids armed with lawn mowers, weed whackers, and maybe a chainsaw or two to tame the yard.

The driveway had been concrete back in the mid-1900s. Now it was dirt and gravel and chunks of rock and concrete ground into the dirt. Luke pulled into the driveway and saw the black Hummer sitting near the back of the house. A ramshackle shed, with the door open and light coming from within, sat just behind the house.

Luke stopped the truck, rolled down the window on the rear passenger door so Jack could leap out if Luke needed him, told the yellow dog to stay, and climbed out. He was standing next to his truck, assessing the situation when a big, bald man walked out of the shed.

The man spotted Luke, looked a bit surprised, turned around, quickly closed the door to the shed, and walked down the driveway.

"Can I help you, officer?" the man asked.

"Are you Charlton Otis?" Luke asked, but as the man got closer, he knew it was Otis based on the driver's license photo he had recently looked at.

Otis was a six-foot-tall man as his driver's license said, but now he looked like he weighed well over the two-hundred-and-fifty pounds listed on the license. He may have been a strong, fit man in his twenties and thirties, but now the fifty-two-year-old Otis carried most of his weight in a big beer belly and a wide rear end. He was dressed in black jeans and a leather vest that showed off multiple tattoos on his biceps and forearms. He was wearing heavy boots and had a dog chain attached to a belt loop that ran to his back pocket where Luke imagined his wallet was wedged. Like his license photo, Otis was still totally bald and sported a Fu Manchu mustache that framed thick lips.

"That's me. But like I told you on the phone, nobody but my dear sweet mama calls me Charlton."

Luke wanted to say, "I'm sure she'd be very proud of you" but instead asked, "How'd you know I was the one who called you?"

"Because I've seen your picture on the TV when you caught that truck driver up near the Canadian border who was killin' those women."

He just looked at Otis and then at the shed.

"So, why's you here?" Otis asked.

"I think you know why," Luke said.

"I told you on the phone, officer. I don't know nuthin' 'bout no bones being dug up."

"But you do know Quentin Nash?"

"Yeah, we worked together here and there over the years, and we played in a pool league at the tavern a while back."

Luke stepped closer to Otis and asked, "What you got going on in the shed?"

Otis gave a quick glance back over his shoulder and then said,

"Just sharpening my mower blade. The old lady says I need to mow the front yard."

Luke glanced at the tangle of eighteen-inch-high weeds, took a step toward the shed, and said, "Yeah, it's probably time. Hey, maybe you could show me how you sharpen a blade? I need to do the same thing at my place."

"I ain't got time right now," Otis said stepping in front of Luke and putting a hand on Luke's chest. "But come back with your mower, and I'll do it for you."

From Luke's truck, there came a low, steady growl.

"It's okay, Jack," Luke said but didn't take his eyes off the big bald man's face. He wanted to get a look in the shed, but he didn't want to push it, so he decided to switch gears. "You been up to the Colville Indian Reservation recently?" he asked as he took a step back.

Again, Luke caught a tiny look of surprise in Otis's eyes and then a quick glance to the left.

"I get up there once in a while," Otis said. "I got a couple of cousins who live up there."

"Are you Native American?" Luke asked.

"No, but my aunt married a member of the Colville tribe, so my cousins are members too."

"You know anything about someone selling eagle feathers up that way?"

Otis pursed his thick lips as if he was thinking about it and finally said, "No, sir. I don't."

Luke just stared at the man, and Otis stared right back.

Finally, Luke said, "Well, I won't keep you from your lawn any longer. Don't want your wife to be upset with me."

"She ain't my wife," Otis said sharply.

Luke handed Otis his card and said, "If you happen to hear of anyone digging up dinosaur bones or selling eagle feathers, you be sure to let me know."

"It ain't illegal for the Indians to own eagle feathers," Otis said.

"No, but it is illegal to sell the feathers. And if the person selling the feathers also killed the birds, well, they could end up in federal prison."

Otis said nothing else. He just stood and watched Luke get back into his truck and back out of the driveway. Then the big man turned and headed to the shed. Luke guessed the next time he came back, the lawn would be two feet tall.

CHAPTER 21

The three women planned to meet at Tat's Delicatessen not far from the police station in Seattle. When Sara and Magic entered the restaurant, Sara looked around and saw a young woman waving at them.

"Kristen?" Sara asked as they walked up to the table where Gray was sitting.

"Yes," Gray said and extended her hand. "Nice to meet you, Agent McCain. Hello, Magic."

"Hi," Magic said quietly.

"Nice to meet you too," Sara said. "Again, please call me Sara."

Sara and Magic sat, and after a waiter came over and took their drink orders, Gray said, "Thanks for agreeing to meet with me."

"You're welcome," Sara said. "I'm interested in your study and what you've learned after spending time in the camps."

Magic was looking around like she had just landed on Mars. Sara noticed it and asked, "Is everything okay?"

"I've been by this restaurant a thousand times," Magic said. "But I've never been in it before. Sometimes I would scrounge food from their dumpsters out back. I really don't feel like a belong in here."

"I understand," Sara said, although she really didn't. "But you deserve to be in here just as much as Kristen or I do." Sara handed her a menu and said, "Pick anything you want to eat for lunch."

Magic started looking at the menu, and so did Sara and Gray.

There was some small talk about the drive over the pass and the weather. Then Gray asked Sara about how she had become an FBI agent. Sara gave her the short version of her path from law school to becoming an agent, and when the waiter came back, the women all ordered. Magic decided on a Philly cheesesteak sandwich with fries and a Pepsi, Sara had a turkey sub, and Gray went for the eggplant parmesan.

"So," Sara said, "tell us about how your study is going on the camps around Puget Sound."

"It's going good," Gray said. "I've learned a great deal, and I've met some really nice people, like Magic here."

"And the ultimate goal of your work?" Sara asked.

"I'm writing my doctoral dissertation on my findings, and I hope that there will be some information that will help get people out of the camps and find them the help they need to improve their lives."

Sara was nodding her head when Magic said, "A lot of the people in the camps don't want to improve their lives. They are happy right where they are. If they can get the drugs they want, they're happy."

The other two women just looked at Magic and said nothing.

"But there are some who do want to better their lives," Magic said. "That is what Toby and I wanted. But we didn't know where to go or what to do, so we stayed where we knew people, where we felt safe, until we could make enough money to move on."

Again, Sara and Gray said nothing.

"But we weren't safe, were we?" Magic said as she started to tear up. "I don't think there is any way to make the camps safe."

"That is one of the things I wanted to discuss with you," Sara said to Gray. "Magic said that Toby and another man were most likely killed because they saw something, probably the murder of someone else in the camp. Have you seen anything like that in any of the other camps you've visited?"

"I've only seen a couple of deaths in the time I've been in the camps, and that includes Toby. I heard about the Duckman, and there was a death in a camp down near Tacoma, but it was an overdose. At least, that's what the police said."

Sara opened the file that Donley had given her and started looking at it. Gray and Magic picked at their food as Sara read.

"I need to spend some time with this, but from what I can see, there has been an uptick in deaths in the camps around Seattle over the past three years. In fact, overdose deaths seem to have doubled in that time."

"That seems extreme," Gray said. "But maybe the drugs coming into our region are stronger or laced with something that is more deadly?"

"Could be," Sara said and kept reading. A minute later, she said, "But in the three other autopsies done in that time, plus the one that was done on Toby, the cause of death shows an overdose of a mixture of drugs, including barbiturates and fentanyl. All of them are very similar. That doesn't seem right to me."

"Toby never used those drugs," Magic said.

"We know," Sara said. "He was drugged by someone else. Probably the same person who killed the Duckman."

"I told you about the morning I was in the camp when Toby died," Gray said. "I spotted a homeless guy standing under the bridge watching what was going on. He didn't act like any homeless guy I'd ever seen."

"That's what Toby said about the man who was standing over the Duckman the day he died," Magic said.

"And you've never seen him before or since in any of the camps?" Sara asked

"I don't think so. At least not since then. Maybe before, but how would I know?"

They talked a bit more about it, but Sara could see that it was very upsetting to Magic, so she told Gray that she wanted to study Donley's report some more, and if she had any other questions, she would give her a call.

"That's fine," Gray said. "And I have a few questions for you too, when you have the time, to help with my dissertation."

Sara put a credit card down on the table to pay for lunch, and as they waited for the waiter to come back and pick it up, she asked Gray, "So are you heading to one of the camps this afternoon?"

"No, I have an appointment to meet up with an emergency room doctor over by Harborview. He treated a woman from one of the camps I was visiting who was having some heart issues and asked if we could chat. I figured he could give me some information on how many of the people from the camps he sees that are coming in for medical issues not related to drugs or alcohol."

"That would be interesting," Sara said. "Hope it goes well."

The women said their thanks and goodbyes and headed in opposite directions on the sidewalk in front of the restaurant.

As they walked back to Sara's car, they passed a couple of men sleeping in the doorway of an empty building. Magic slowed, looked at them, and teared up again. Sara could only imagine what she might be thinking.

* * *

After lunch, Gray hit one of the nearby markets to pick up a few items and then headed to the Starbucks to meet the ER doctor. She was a little early, so she ordered a chai tea and found a place to sit at a table in the back. As she waited, she thought about the discussion she'd had with Sara McCain at lunch. The dramatic increase in homeless deaths Sara had mentioned was, frankly, disturbing. She wouldn't have learned anything about that if it hadn't been for the

FBI agent checking into it.

She was deep in thought when she heard a man's voice say, "Hello."

"Oh, sorry," Gray said. "I was thinking about something and didn't see you come in. Hello."

"I see you have a drink already," Doc said. "I'll go grab a coffee. I'm going to need the caffeine."

Gray watched the doctor walk to the counter and order. Then he turned and looked at her. Right then something clicked. It was the feeling that she had seen or met the man before.

The doctor waited at the counter for his coffee and then walked back to the table and sat down.

"So, Ms. Gray, what would you like to ask me?"

"First, please call me Kristen," Gray said and then she pulled out a notebook where she had written a number of questions.

"Gosh, Kristen," Doc said with a chuckle when he saw the long list of questions. "I'm not sure I have that many answers in my head."

"Don't worry," Gray said. "I won't take up too much of your time. I'm just mostly interested in how many indigent or homeless people you might see, say, in a normal week? And what are the typical or common reasons they are seeking help in the emergency room?"

Doc gave her his best estimate on how many patients they treated at the ER who looked like they were homeless, and he discussed several of the reasons why they came to the hospital.

"Usually, it's just for treatment of simple things like a cold or the flu," Doc said. "Sometimes they have an injury, like a laceration or a severe contusion that they would like looked at. Sometimes they have fallen and broken or sprained an ankle or wrist. It's your garden variety of typical emergency room injuries and illnesses. No different really than the rest of the population."

Gray was quickly jotting notes as the doctor spoke. She asked a few more questions from her notebook, and Doc answered each of them succinctly and professionally.

Finally, when it looked like she had no more questions, Doc said, "Now, can I ask you a couple questions about your study?"

"Sure," Gray said, pleased that a professional would be interested in what she was doing.

He asked her some general questions, such as what the average age of the homeless population was, and what portion were men versus women. Gray had those figures at her fingertips and told him.

"Those are just for the Puget Sound area," Gray said after giving the doctor the breakdown. "I've not surveyed any other areas, but my guess is it's similar in other cities."

"You brought that woman in the other night, which was admirable of you. Have you found any people who have died?"

"Yes, one, a while ago. A young man died in a camp over by the football stadium. Sad really." She decided not to tell him the police thought it was a homicide.

"Oh, yes," Doc said. "They brought his body into the morgue at the hospital. Sounds like someone killed the young man. What a tragedy."

Gray looked at the doctor, and he saw the wheels turning in her head.

"I have dinner sometimes with one of the medical examiners," Doc said. "She told me about the death of the young man."

"Yes, it's a sad deal, for sure. Scary to think someone can go into a camp and just kill someone by shooting them up."

"The medical examiner said he had a fiancé. I wonder how she's doing."

"She's hurting but doing better," Gray said.

"Oh, you know her?" Doc asked.

"Not really, but I happened to talk to her today."

"So, she's still around?" Doc asked. "I hope she's getting some help."

"She's actually over in Yakima," Gray said and, even though she didn't know why, she immediately regretted saying anything about Magic's location.

"Well, that's good," Doc said and changed the subject. He didn't want to push it too much.

He asked Gray when she was going to complete her dissertation and what she wanted to do upon graduation. They talked about all of that for another twenty minutes, and when the conversation wound down, he looked at his watch and said, "I need to get over to the hospital for a meeting. Congratulations on the work you're doing. I believe it's going to help many homeless people in the future."

Then he stood, shook Gray's hand, and turned for the door. As she watched him walk to the door, she was again overtaken by the feeling of meeting or seeing the man previously.

CHAPTER 22

Charlton Otis was up to no good. Luke knew that. Captain Davis said a woman had left the tip about the eagles and hawks being killed for the feathers. He wondered if it might have been Otis's girlfriend, or "old lady" as he had called her, who made the call. Plenty of tips that helped him catch poachers over the years had come from disgruntled girlfriends or wives. He would have to think about that.

"Let's run out to the wildlife area and see what we can see," Luke said to Jack as they drove west from Otis's place to get to the L.T. Murray.

When they hit the gravel road and the entrance to the wildlife area, Luke pulled off the road and opened the map app on his phone. He located the first pin from the map that Sheri Bronson had given him and started that way.

But before he got there, Luke took a turn off the road to visit the shooting range just east of the main road, not far from the entrance to the wildlife area. The state had spent several thousand dollars improving the area for the public to come sight in their rifles or shoot pistols and shotguns.

Concrete shooting tables had been constructed, and berms had been built to make the range safe and convenient. Most everyone who used the shooting range followed the rules, picked up after themselves, and were happy to have a place to shoot. Still, for whatever reason, there were a few who just had to shoot up the signs in the parking area, break glass bottles, tag the tables, and leave a mess of hulls, brass, and targets. Luke had never caught anyone doing these things, but he figured that one of these days, on one of his random checks, he would.

Today was the day.

He slowly moved down the road to the range area, and as he topped a small rise where he could see the tables, he stopped the truck and watched. A group of four young men, possibly high schoolers, were shooting AR-style rifles. Luke couldn't tell the caliber. They weren't shooting from the tables; they were standing in front of them while one kid was grabbing beer bottles out of a box and throwing them in the air.

As soon as the bottle went up, the three other kids would start blasting in a variety of directions depending where the bottle was thrown. If one of the shooters hit the bottle, it would break in the air, and they would do it again. If they didn't hit it, the bottle would almost always break when it hit the rocky ground. If the impact with the ground didn't break the bottle, then the kids would open up on the bottle sitting on the ground until it was broken.

Luke watched for a few minutes and then slowly rolled his truck down the hill into the parking lot. One of the kids noticed the truck and said something to his buddies. They all stopped shooting and headed to a newer Jeep parked nearby.

They were putting the rifles in the Jeep and starting to climb in when Luke pulled his truck behind the rig and got out.

"Hold it a minute, fellas," Luke said.

The four stopped and turned to Luke. One kid, a tall, gangly blond with a touch of acne on his chin still had a rifle in his hands.

"Please hand me your rifle," Luke said to the kid. "And the rest of you step away from the Jeep."

They all obliged. Luke took the rifle from the kid and checked the clip and the chamber. It was still loaded with a live round. Luke pulled the clip and ejected the round and set the rifle in the front passenger seat of his truck.

"Are you taking my rifle?" the kid asked.

"Not sure," Luke said. "Now stand over there with your friends."

Luke pulled each of the other rifles out of the Jeep. One after the other, he made sure they were unloaded before putting them in the front passenger seat of his truck as well.

"So, it looks like you boys were having some fun," Luke said.

All four boys just looked at their shoes.

"I need to see your driver's licenses and your Department of Fish and Wildlife parking permit."

The boys all reached for their wallets and started digging out their licenses.

One kid said, "We don't have a parking permit."

Luke pointed at the nearby sign that indicated a WDFW permit was required to use the shooting range. The new sign already had three bullet holes in it.

"It's the law," Luke said. "If you have a hunting license, you should have the parking permit."

"We aren't hunters," a short Hispanic kid said. "We just like to shoot."

According to their driver's licenses, the boys were all sixteen or seventeen years old and had Yakima addresses.

"Are you going to arrest us, mister?" a third young man asked. He was a chubby kid, average height with dark hair that was thick and curly on top and shorter on the sides. He was about to climb into the driver's seat of the Jeep when Luke had pulled up, so he assumed the Jeep was his.

"I'm not sure yet," Luke said. "You guys have broken several laws."

"Well, it won't do any good," the chubby kid said. "My old man is an attorney, so he'll get us off."

Luke chuckled. "Oh, is that how it works? You break a law, but because you are related to a lawyer, you get off scot-free. You better check with your father on that one."

"He's done it before," the kid said.

"Well, it isn't happening today, sorry," Luke said. "So here is what we are going to do . . ." He went on to explain that the boys were going to pick up every piece of broken glass in the range, along with all the brass and shotgun shell hulls in the area.

"We didn't shoot any shotgun shells," the Hispanic kid said. "And some of the spent brass was already here."

"How do I know that?" Luke said. "So, just to be sure, you're going to pick them all up."

"What if we refuse?" the chubby kid asked.

"Then I will arrest you, and we'll head to the jail," Luke said. "It's your choice."

"Arrest me," the kid said. "I don't care. My old man will get me off."

Without a word, Luke grabbed the kid, spun him around, and pushed him face-first into the side of his Jeep. He wanted to really push hard, but he restrained himself. He pulled his handcuffs off the back of his utility belt, pulled one of the kid's wrists around, and snapped the cuffs on it. Then he did the same with the other wrist.

"Hey, hey," the kid moaned.

"It's what you wanted," Luke said. "Now come with me."

He grabbed the kid by the elbow and marched him over to his truck, opened the back door, and moved the kid onto the back seat.

After he closed the door, Luke turned to the other three boys and asked, "Anyone else?"

All three boys were wide-eyed and shaking their heads, so Luke went to the utility box in the bed of his truck and pulled out three black garbage bags. He handed one each to the boys and said, "There you go. Get to work."

After a few minutes, the fourth boy, who hadn't said a thing, came over to Luke and said, "You're that game warden who found a tiger in the woods up by Cle Elum a few years ago, aren't you?"

"Guilty," Luke said.

"I saw it on the news and thought that would be such a cool job."

"It is a great job," Luke said. "Except when I have to deal with knuckleheads like you guys."

"I know," the kid said. "I told them we shouldn't do this."

"But you were right in there with them," Luke said.

"Well, sort of. I've been here the whole time, but I never fired a shot. The rifle I had wasn't loaded. It isn't even my rifle. All the rifles are Steven's, the kid you arrested."

Luke thought back to the rifle he took from the kid, and he was right—it hadn't been loaded.

"So, why didn't you stop them?"

"Peer pressure, I guess. Steven is pretty good at getting his way. I was just along for the ride. None of us guys have a car, and Steven's dad bought him this Jeep, so it's a way to get around."

Luke remembered the kid's name from his driver's license and asked, "Michael, is it?"

"Yeah," Michael said.

"Being along for the ride has gotten lots of people in big trouble," Luke said. "So, you might want to think about that before jumping in with Steven again."

"So, what's going to happen to us?"

"You have a phone?" Luke asked.

"Yeah," Michael said.

"Call one of your parents and have them come out here and get you. By the time they get here, you should have this area pretty well cleaned up. Tell the other two over there to do the same thing."

Michael went over and talked to the two who were picking up

broken glass. Each of them pulled phones out of their pockets and made a call.

"I wish you would have just arrested me," the Hispanic kid named Felipe said to Luke a couple minutes later. "My mom is going to kill me."

"Mine too," the lanky blond kid said.

"Good," Luke said. "Now, when you're done picking up the glass and empty rounds, go out and pick up all those shot-up targets."

He walked over to his pickup, and Steven started yelling at him from the back seat.

"Let me call my dad," he said. "I know my rights—I get to make a call."

"I haven't placed you under arrest yet," Luke said. "So, no, you don't get to make a call. But I'll be happy to make one for you."

He asked the kid which pocket his phone was in and was told the phone was in the Jeep, so Luke went to get it. Then he pulled his own phone out.

"What's your dad's phone number?" Luke asked.

"You're so smart—figure it out."

Luke thumbed the front of Steven's phone to start the unlocking process and stuck it in front of the kid's face before he knew what was happening. The facial recognition opened the phone. Luke opened the contacts list, scrolled down to the "Ds," found "Dad," tapped on the name, and then pushed call.

Three rings later, a man's voice answered, "Hi, Steven. What's going on?"

"This isn't Steven, Mr. Harrel. My name is Luke McCain. I'm an enforcement officer with the Department of Fish and Wildlife. Steven and his friends have been detained for several violations out here at the L.T. Murray gun range."

There was dead air on the end of the line.

"Mr. Harrel?" Luke asked

"What did they do, Officer McCain?"

Luke listed about seven violations, including endangering the public with a deadly weapon.

"There's no public out there, is there?" Harrel asked.

"There are private homes less than a half-mile away," Luke said. "I watched Steven shoot in that direction several times. Bullets from the caliber of guns the boys were shooting can travel for two thousand yards."

"So, what do you want me to do?" Harrel asked.

"Well, your son wants me to arrest him because he believes you can get him out of this trouble. I'll happily arrest him right now. Just the endangerment with a deadly weapon is cause enough for me to do so."

"What about the other boys?" Harrel asked.

"Their parents are coming to get them," Luke said. "I haven't decided if I am going to cite them or not. Right now, they are picking up all the broken glass from bottles they broke in their little shooting spree."

"Can't you let Steven do that?"

"I offered him the option. He chose to be arrested."

"Will you let me talk to him?"

"Sure," Luke said and opened the truck door. He held the phone up to the kid's ear.

Luke could only hear Steven's side of the conversation, but on this end, there was a lot of whining.

"But, Dad," Steven whined. Then he listened for another minute and said to Luke, "He wants to talk to you again."

Luke pulled his phone back and closed the truck door.

When all the talking was over, Steven's father had negotiated a deal with Luke. If he would take the handcuffs off, his son would immediately join his friends picking up the shell casings and glass. And for the next four Saturdays, the boy would be out there picking up trash. Luke could issue whatever tickets he saw fit, and Steven would be responsible for paying them.

Harrel asked Luke to confiscate the rifles and said, "Whatever you do with the ones you take from criminals, do the same with these. I just want them gone."

He also told Luke that his son would only be allowed to drive to and from school or to work, not if but when he found a job.

"He needs to earn the money to pay off the tickets," Harrel said.

"You have a deal, Mr. Harrel. Just so you know, I will be checking to make sure Steven is out here doing what you said he would do."

"I understand," Harrel said. "Now, if you will release Steven, I'll call him on his phone and I'll let him know the details of our arrangement."

After letting Steven out, removing the handcuffs and handing him a black garbage bag and his phone, the phone started chirping.

Luke smiled to himself. Hopefully these boys learned their lesson. He did give each of the boys a ticket for littering, and Steven received tickets for reckless use of a firearm and not having a parking pass for the area. All totaled, Steven's tickets added up to just over a thousand dollars. Luke hoped Mr. Harrel would stick to his word and make his son earn the money to pay the fines.

Over the next hour, he met three very unhappy parents, two mothers and one father, who each thanked Luke for making the boys clean up the area. Each young man shook Luke's hand before they left and thanked him for not arresting them.

When the three kids had left with their parents, Steven was still there picking up the smallest shards of glass.

"You better hit the road," Luke said. "I'll see you out here on Saturday."

Steven Harrel just walked over and put his black bag of trash in the back of Luke's truck, next to the three other bags the boys had placed there. Then he walked to his Jeep, climbed in, fired it up, and drove out of the parking lot without saying a word.

Luke watched as the Jeep climbed the little hill leading out of the area. As soon as it was out of sight, Luke heard the kid gun the Jeep's engine, kicking up a big cloud of dust, and listened as the rig roared down the bumpy dirt road.

Luke just shook his head. The kid was a slow learner.

CHAPTER 23

Doc had heard of Yakima, but he had never been there, so as soon as he arrived at the hospital he went directly to his office and looked it up on the computer. He found out that the city of Yakima was a hundred and forty miles from Seattle, on the east side of the Cascades.

He also learned Yakima's citywide population was about a hundred thousand, and nearly two hundred and sixty thousand people lived in the county. With that many people, he figured, there must be some homeless encampments. Especially with a river running right through the middle of the place. That was where the girl named Magic would most likely be found.

His schedule at the hospital would keep him from traveling anywhere for the next two days, but come Saturday, Doc planned on taking a little excursion to the other side of the mountains.

The young woman doing the study on the homeless was another potential problem. During their meeting, Doc had watched her closely to see if she recognized him, but he never saw any indication. For now, he wouldn't worry too much about the doctoral student. If she did recognize him, well, there were ways of making her go away too.

* * *

On the drive to her apartment, Gray thought about her meetings that day. She was glad to see Magic again, and happy that she was with the FBI agent. The poor girl seemed sad, but she also looked healthier than when Gray had talked to her in the camp the day Toby died. So that was good.

She was pleased that the police were not just giving the investigation lip service, and with Agent McCain involved, maybe the local cops would be motivated to keep digging.

Gray caught herself smiling.

Then she started thinking about the meeting with the doctor. He was certainly professional and seemed to be very caring. And the interest he'd shown about her study was genuine. Or it seemed that way to her. But there still was something about the man that nagged her. She thought about all the places she had been, and meetings she had attended, and could not for the life of her figure out where she had met him before.

The doctor said he didn't remember meeting her either, so maybe it was one of those subconscious deals where he looked like someone she had met at some point in her life. It would come to her, she thought. Or not.

* * *

Sara and Magic made it to the McCain house in Lower Naches just as Luke and Jack were climbing out of Luke's truck.

"How did it go?" Luke asked after the two women got out of Sara's car.

"Good, I think," Sara said.

"So, the police are seriously working the case?" Luke asked.

"Seems like it," Sara said and held up the file folder that Donley had given her. "The officer compiled some interesting information. I need to spend some time with it, but there might be something more to all of this."

"Well, you guys must have eaten lunch someplace, but Jack and I didn't, so we're starving. How about I change clothes, feed Jack, and we run to get something to eat?"

Sara looked at Magic. The young woman smiled and nodded.

"Sounds good," Sara said. "I want to change too."

Twenty minutes later, the three of them piled into Luke's Tundra and headed toward the highway.

"How about we run up to Whistlin' Jacks?" Luke asked.

"Oh, that would be great," Sara said. "I love the mountains this time of year."

"What's Whistlin' Jacks?" Magic asked.

"It's a restaurant near Chinook Pass," Sara said. "Sits right on the Naches River. It's a beautiful place to eat. Very peaceful and serene."

"We might see some deer, or elk, or even some bighorn sheep on the way up there," Luke said.

Magic's eyes lit up. "That would be cool," she said.

They talked on the drive up the mountain. Sara recapped the meeting with Officer Donley and their lunch with Kristen. Luke asked a few questions, and Sara answered them after waiting for Magic to do so. She knew the young woman was listening, but evidently, she wasn't in the mood to talk.

"Look, what's that?" Magic said, pointing to the open hillside just above a big turn in the river known as Horseshoe Bend.

Luke looked to his left and immediately spotted a small band of sheep. He pulled off the highway so they could take a better look.

"Bighorn sheep," Luke said. "Those are all ewes and lambs."

Just then, one of the lambs started chasing another one.

Magic giggled and said, "They're so cute." Then, after a

minute, she said, "It looks like the bigger ones have horns."

Luke explained that the females, called ewes, did have small horns and told her about the rams and how big their horns can grow.

"They butt heads during the mating season to win the right to breed," he explained.

"I remember seeing that on TV one time when I was young," Magic said. "Will we see any rams?"

"We might, but they probably won't be butting heads right now."

They didn't see any rams, but when they continued on, Sara spotted a doe and two fawns on the hillside not far from the restaurant. Again, Luke pulled over so they could watch the mule deer.

As they walked into the restaurant, Magic saw that there were tables out by the river. "Can we eat out there?" she asked.

"Sure," Sara said.

When the young hostess came into the lobby to seat them, Sara asked to be seated at an outside table, and they were escorted to the closest one to the river. After they ordered their food, Magic walked down by the river's edge. Sara followed.

"You're right," Magic said. "This is so peaceful. I love being outdoors."

"I do too," Sara said, taking in a big breath of fresh mountain air.

The two women stood in the early evening sun and watched the water flowing by.

Finally, Magic said, "I could listen to the river forever. That was the nice thing about the camp down by the river. You could hear it all the time." She was about to say something else, but a yell from Luke interrupted.

"Okay, ladies," Luke said from up the hill. "Our food has arrived."

"Coming," Sara said, and she and Magic worked their way up the riverbank to the table.

They enjoyed their meal. Luke had ordered a cheeseburger and fries, while the two women had fish and chips. Magic changed her order from a burger to the fish after she'd listened to Sara order.

"I've never had this kind of fish before," Magic said in between bites of the deep-fried cod. "Or at least not that I can remember. This is good."

When they were done with dinner, the waitress asked if they wanted dessert. Luke looked at Magic and saw that she didn't know what to say.

"Looks like they have pie and ice cream, and some kind of a brownie deal," Luke said.

Finally, Sara, who rarely had dessert, said, "I'm going to have a piece of huckleberry pie."

"Me too," Luke said. "Warmed with a big scoop of vanilla ice cream."

Sara and Luke looked at Magic.

Finally, she smiled and said, "Sounds good to me."

As the three of them ate their pie à la mode, they chatted about how good it was. Luke and Sara could see Magic savoring every bite.

When Magic finished, she laid her fork on her plate and said, "This was the best meal I have ever had."

The waitress brought the check and put it on the table between Luke and Magic. The young woman gave it a quick glance before Luke picked it up and handed it to the waitress with a credit card.

"I feel bad about you paying for everything," Magic said. "I appreciate it very much. Thank you."

"Happy to do it," Luke said and left it at that.

On the way back down the mountain, they looked for more animals in the dying daylight and spotted a group of five deer, a couple elk, and the same band of bighorn sheep on the hillside.

A few miles down the highway, Magic said, "I can't believe it has only been a week since Toby died. It seems like it was months ago."

Luke and Sara said nothing.

"I miss him so much," she said and started sobbing again.

When they were back in cell phone service, Sara's phone started dinging, indicating she had a voicemail waiting for her. She pulled the phone out of her pocket and checked the voicemail.

"Hey, Sinclair," a man's voice said on the recorded message. "This is Sanchez. I've got some interesting information for you on the deaths in the homeless camps down here. Give me a call."

After she clicked off the phone, Sara set it in her lap, looked out her side window, and said, "Huh."

"Good news or bad news?" Luke asked.

"I don't know," Sara said. And after another minute of thinking, she said it again slowly. "I don't know."

CHAPTER 24

After having to deal with the knucklehead kids at the shooting range the day before, Luke was determined to get out on the L.T. Murray Wildlife Area to check out some of the locations that Sheri Bronson had flagged for him.

He phoned his captain and told him his plan for the morning. Then he looked at Jack, who was basically sitting in Magic's lap on the floor of the living room, and decided the dog would much rather be getting loves from the young woman than riding around in the truck. Plus, he figured the big yellow dog would be good company for Magic versus her having to sit around the McCain house with nothing to do. Sara had dug out several books for Magic to read, but Luke wasn't sure she wanted to be reading.

"Can I walk Jack down to the river later?" Magic asked as Luke was headed for the door.

"Sure," Luke said. "It'll be good for him to get a little exercise."

He thought it would be good for her too. And he knew Jack would be protective of the young woman, not that there was much around there that could put her in danger.

"I'll be back around noon," Luke said. "Have a good walk."

The last thing he saw before he closed the door was Jack, prone on the carpet, head in Magic's lap, with the young woman massaging his head. Luke was positive he saw the dog smiling.

He had just turned onto the highway when his phone started ringing. He pushed the receive button on his steering wheel to answer the phone and said, "This is McCain."

"Officer McCain," a woman's voice said. "This is Sarah Stout, Quentin Nash's neighbor."

"Yes, Ms. Stout. How can I help you?"

"Well, I was just taking the garbage can down to the road and noticed that Nash has the digging machine at his house again."

Luke almost laughed and said something about Sarah Stout remembering to take the garbage out, but he refrained. She'd probably had a gullet full of those jokes.

"Is it still there?" Luke asked.

"Yes, it is. And there are three other trucks parked around his house. Trucks I don't think I've seen before."

"Okay, thank you," Luke said. "I was actually just headed out that way, so I'll take a look."

"Should I call you if he leaves?"

"No, that's okay. Like I said, I'm headed your way now."

Luke thanked Stout and ended the call.

It took seventeen minutes for Luke to get to Nash's house, and when he got there, sure enough, there were four trucks parked in the drive, including Nash's which was hitched to a car-hauler trailer with a Bobcat backhoe strapped down on it.

Luke recognized two of the other rigs in the driveway. One was a black 2005 Hummer H2, the truck owned by Charlton Otis. The other was the older brown Chevy pickup, owned by Nash's father, Herman.

Luke had a hunch about who the other truck belonged to, so Luke looked up the phone number for Derek Day and punched it into his phone.

"Hullo," Day said after the phone had rung four times.

"Mr. Day, this is Luke McCain calling."

"Um, yeah, what can I do for you?" Day asked nervously.

"What kind of a rig do you drive?"

"It's an older silver Ram. Why?"

Luke took a second quick look at the fourth truck sitting in Nash's driveway. The truck was silver but not a Ram. It was, in fact, a GMC 2500 Duramax Diesel. And unlike the other three trucks in the driveway, the GMC looked shiny new.

"Just wondering. Have you heard from Nash or Otis about what's going on with them?"

"I heard from Otis, thank you very much. He was madder than a bunch of hornets. Said he was going to chew a patch of hide off my ass the size of a doormat the next time he saw me."

"I didn't say a word to him about who I got his name from," Luke said. "He must have inferred it."

"I don't know what inferred means, but he figured out it was me. Now I gotta be watchin' over my shoulder all the time."

"Well, I'm sorry about that," Luke said. "But I need to get to the bottom of this dinosaur bone thing."

"I've been meaning to ask you something 'bout that," Day said. "Since I was the one that first called 'bout this, will I get some extra bonus points on my special hunt applications next year if you catch him?"

"I think that can be arranged," Luke said. "But I could pretty much guarantee it if you were to hear anything else about where Nash is digging or who he's selling the bones to."

"Ah, I don't know," Day said. "I'm already on Otis's shit list. If Nash found out I was snooping around, he might just kill me."

"Like he did his wife?" Luke asked

"Yeah," Day said and then hesitated. "I mean, I don't know nuthin' 'bout that."

Luke again thanked Day for his time, told him to call if he learned anything else, and said, "Have a good day."

"Yeah right," Day said. "Otis is madder than a wounded grizzly bear. How can I have a good day when I know he's out to get me?"

"Well," Luke said, "you can relax a bit because I'm looking at Mr. Otis right now, and unless you are at Nash's house, he's nowhere near you."

Luke pushed the end call button on the steering wheel without saying goodbye.

Four men had come out of Nash's house. Three of the men Luke recognized. Nash, Otis, and Nash's father were now standing in the driveway talking to a fourth man. Two of the men, Herman Nash and the unknown man, lit up cigarettes. Otis had a can of Budweiser in his hand.

It was nine-twenty in the morning, and Luke thought it was a little early for a beer, but that was just his opinion. He had parked his truck just out from Sarah Stout's driveway, and he was somewhat camouflaged by the brush along Nash's fence, so the men hadn't noticed him yet.

He grabbed his binoculars from under the passenger seat and took a closer look at the fourth man in the group. The man was shorter than the other three and had jet black hair that was slicked back. But that was all Luke could see because the unknown man was standing with his back to Luke's truck.

Then Luke looked at the silver GMC pickup. He wrote down the license plate number on his pad and fired up the laptop on his truck's center console. He brought up the state website for running license plates and tapped the keys to enter the GMC's tag number into the system. He pushed enter and waited.

A minute later, the information on the truck's owner popped up. It said the truck was owned by a man named Garo Cartosian. His address was in Kent, Washington.

Luke then looked up the driver's license for Cartosian, and a photo of a dark-haired man, with black eyes set over a wide nose on a pockmarked face, popped up on the screen. The license listed the man's height as five foot seven and his weight as two hundred and ten pounds. Cartosian was forty-nine years old.

He thought about just driving into the driveway and having another chat with Nash and Otis but thought better of it. He'd been told twice to leave the place, and from his first experience with the elder Nash, Luke felt the man was a loose cannon. He decided to just sit and watch for a bit to see what might happen. As he sat, Luke pulled up the computer again and did a search on Garo Cartosian.

A few seconds later, a newspaper story from the *Tacoma News Tribune* from back in 2001 popped up with the headline: "*Kent Man Wants to Buy Kennewick Man.*" The photo with the story showed a younger, thinner, black-haired Cartosian standing next to a bunch of bones in a box with the caption that read: *Garo Cartosian of Kent is an expert on prehistoric bones. The multi-millionaire has offered to buy some newly discovered prehistoric human remains for four million dollars.*

Luke scanned the story, but the cut line on the photo had capsulized it nicely. He remembered when the old human bones were discovered in the Columbia River near Kennewick and the battle that had ensued as the Yakama and other Native American tribes wanted control of the bones. He couldn't remember how long the court battle was, but Luke knew that ultimately the Native tribes had won, and they buried the Kennewick Man's remains in an unknown location near the Columbia River, which meant Cartosian wasn't able to purchase them.

"Interesting," Luke mumbled to himself after perusing the story and photo. Then he started thinking. Could Nash and his buddies have found the remains of another prehistoric man or woman? Maybe they just told those close to them they found mammoth bones when they actually had discovered ancient human remains. They might have read the story on Cartosian and figured he might be in the market for the bones and would be willing to pay millions of dollars for them.

Luke decided he needed to get a photo of the men, and Cartosian in particular. He put his truck in reverse and backed up until he hit Stout's driveway, and then backed up the driveway twenty yards or so. He pulled his Nikon digital camera out of the metal case in the back seat and put a long-range, one-fifty-to-six-hundred-millimeter lens on it. He sat in the truck and cradled the camera and lens on his arm on the edge of the window. Staying in the truck would give him a little cover and not make him so obvious, even if one of the men happened to look his way.

Luke took a few shots of the four men standing together and then zoomed in on Cartosian. The man was still not facing Luke, but now he could see a side view of the man. He took a few photos and waited. Finally, Cartosian turned, flicked his cigarette onto the gravel driveway, and stamped it out with his shoe. Luke pushed the shutter button as fast as he could and ended up getting eleven shots of the dark-haired man's face. The lens had brought Cartosian's face in close enough that Luke could clearly see the pockmarks he had seen on the driver's license photo.

He was still sitting and watching when there was a tap on the truck's passenger door window. Luke jumped at the noise, then turned and saw Sarah Stout standing there.

Luke lowered the window and said, "Get in."

Stout quickly opened the door and climbed into the passenger seat.

"Have you figured out what they are doing over there?" she asked as she looked at the camera sitting in Luke's arms.

"They're just talking," Luke said. "But I wanted to get a closer look at the short guy with the black hair, so I decided to use my camera lens."

Stout just nodded with approval.

"Do you think you could keep an eye on them, particularly Nash and his pickup with the backhoe, and watch to see which way he goes when he leaves?" Luke asked.

"Sure," Stout said. "This will be fun."

"Don't be obvious," Luke said. "Just kind of keep an eye out."

"My side kitchen window looks right over there," Stout said. "The weeds and brush along the fence make it harder to see, but I can see his truck in the driveway."

As he was talking to Stout, Luke watched as Cartosian walked over to his truck, climbed in, and turned around in Nash's driveway. Then he drove down the road Luke had just come in on. The other three men went back into Nash's house.

Luke thanked Stout again as she got out of his truck. He watched her walk back to her house in the rearview mirror and then he headed out to the wildlife area to see if he could find any clues to confirm Nash was digging out there.

CHAPTER 25

Sara called Sanchez on her way into the office the next morning.

"Hey, Sinclair," Sanchez said. "How are things over there in the desert?"

"Pretty nice," Sara said. She had seen the weather forecast for Portland and knew they were in for another day of rain in the Rose City. "Sunny and warm."

"Yeah, yeah," Sanchez said. "Listen, I found some interesting stuff on your question about the deaths in the homeless camps around here. I asked the Portland Police and Multnomah County Sheriff's Office folks to compile some numbers for the past decade."

"And?" Sara asked when Sanchez paused.

"I'll shoot you the reports, but it seems there was a spike in deaths during a three-year period about five years ago. It didn't seem to send up any red flags, but the numbers basically tripled during that period before regressing to the mean."

Sara thought about the numbers she'd read the night before in the file that Donley had given her. The numbers in King County had started to spike about the time they were dropping back down in Portland.

"It looks like something similar is happening now in the Seattle area," Sara said. "Email me your findings, and I'll keep looking into it."

She thanked Sanchez, razzed him by reminding him not to forget his umbrella, clicked off, and walked into her office.

The email from the Portland FBI office arrived a couple minutes later, and Sara opened it immediately. Sanchez hadn't exaggerated. The deaths in the homeless camps inside Portland, and in others outside the city limits, had started rising five years earlier and had dropped back down approximately three and a half years later.

"What would cause that?" Sara muttered to herself as she reviewed the numbers.

Sanchez had been off a little on his estimates. Sara did the math, and it was just over double the normal years leading up to the spike. Then she pulled up the information Donley had compiled. It seemed that right as the Portland spike was waning, the number of reported Seattle-area encampment deaths began to grow.

It had to be the type of drugs coming into the market, Sara thought, but was there any way of finding that out for sure?

Evidently, Donley could find only seven autopsies done in the past two years on people who'd died in the camps in King County. Those results showed that two people had died of natural causes, which might include heart attacks, liver failure, strokes, or complications due to pneumonia or other illnesses. The medical examiner had concluded that the other five had died of drug overdoses. Four had nothing but fentanyl in their system.

The other person, a white man, aged sixty-eight, had died from a strange concoction of drugs. Sara looked at the list of drugs in the man's system and then brought up the autopsy report on Toby. The drugs were identical.

Sara looked to see if the autopsy showed any needle marks in any unusual places, but there was nothing listed. She guessed the examiner had spotted the large quantity of drugs in the bloodstream and quickly concluded the man had died of an overdose. Which, of course, was true. But had the man given himself the deadly cocktail?

It could be a coincidence, but Sara wasn't buying that. She hadn't asked Sanchez if there were any autopsies done in the three years during the Portland spike in deaths, but there had to be some, so she called him to ask if he could run those down too.

"I'd be glad to," Sanchez said. "What are you looking for?"

"The evidence shows the young man who died in the Seattle camp a few days ago was murdered—killed by a mix of lethal drugs. I found another autopsy done on a man a year ago with the same drugs, in the same amounts, in his system. I'm wondering if any of the folks down your way had the same strange fatal brew in their systems."

"I'll see what I can find and will let you know," Sanchez said before hanging up.

Sara set her phone on her desk, sat back in her chair, and placed her hands together, pointer fingers at the tips of her pursed lips. Could there really be a serial killer out there preying on the homeless?

✳ ✳ ✳

Kristen Gray awoke with a strange feeling that she knew something today that she hadn't known yesterday. She rarely dreamed, and when she did, she almost never remembered the details in them. Some people could explain in great length the dreams they'd had the night before, all in amazing technicolor, but Gray wasn't one of those people. She was aware that something happened last night, either in a dream or in some unlocked memory in her subconscious, but she was struggling to remember what it might have been.

Sometimes when she did dream, and could remember bits and pieces of the dream, it was about something that happened in her childhood. Sometimes it was a happy occasion, like the time on Christmas morning when she walked into the living room, and there was the brand-new purple bike she desperately wanted sitting next to the Christmas tree. That dream came back to her now and again.

Unlike some of the dreams her friends shared with her, Gray never dreamed of running through a crowded mall dressed only in her bra and panties. Or, at least, not that she remembered. And Gray never had dreams that she was still an undergraduate, and it was almost the end of the semester, and she had missed all the English 101 classes and was panicking because she didn't know how she was going to pass the class. Her friends seemed to have those types of dreams often.

Gray occasionally dreamed of her favorite pet when she was a child, a black and white cat named Snoopy. She thought about that for a minute and realized, no, it had nothing to do with family pets. Whatever it was that was haunting her sleep last night, it wasn't coming back to her in her awakened consciousness.

Her plan for the day was to check in on a couple of homeless camps north of Seattle, up near Everett, and then she would head to the UW campus for a scheduled meeting with the professor who oversaw her doctorial project. But first, just like millions of other people around the world, she was going to stop at Starbucks.

When she arrived at the coffee shop just two blocks from her apartment, she saw the drive-thru line was wrapped around the building and almost out into the street. Since she was in no real hurry, she decided to go inside, get her drink, and spend a few minutes reviewing her notes to be ready for her meeting later in the day.

Gray ordered her tea, along with a scone, and went to an empty table in the back. Although this was a different Starbucks, the building and inside layout were almost identical to the one next to the hospital. And the table, she remembered, was in the same place where she had sat with the doctor the day before.

A few minutes later, her name was called by the barista, and when she looked up at the counter, everything snapped into focus. She immediately remembered what she was struggling to conjure in her mind. The doctor had been standing at the counter, waiting for his drink, and he had turned and looked at her. His eyes were the eyes of the homeless man standing under the bridge, staring at her when she was next to Toby's lifeless body.

Gray shook her head. That couldn't be right. It was just a dream. It wasn't reality, was it? But the more she thought about it, the more convinced she was that it had been the doctor near the homeless camp that morning.

What had he been doing there? Why hadn't he said something about it when she'd met with him the day before?

"Kristen," a man's voice said next to her.

Gray jumped and screamed.

"I'm sorry," the barista said. "I just wanted to bring you your tea and scone."

Gray looked around. People were looking at her, some laughing. She looked up at the young man with her tea and food. He was smiling.

"Oh, I'm so sorry," Gray said. "Thank you so much."

"Are you alright?" the barista asked. "You look like you've seen a ghost."

"I'm fine," Gray said and took the cup and scone from the man. "Thank you again."

She tried to take a sip of her tea, but her hands were shaking too much. What was she supposed to do now? Should she call the doctor and set up another meeting to ask him about why he had been there that morning and why he hadn't said something?

After thinking about that for a minute, she decided that was probably not a good idea. If he did have something to do with Toby's death, she too might be in danger.

The more she thought about the doctor being involved, the crazier it seemed. He, like all other doctors, was dedicated to healing the sick, not killing them. He had been so caring and nice when she had taken the woman with heart issues into the emergency room. Someone like that could never kill Toby, could they?

She had to be wrong. Gray decided to let it go and not say a thing. At least for now. She wanted to think about it some more. Most dreams aren't real, she knew, but the doctor standing at the counter yesterday wasn't a dream. And the homeless man with the wine bottle who had been staring at her in the camp hadn't been a dream either.

✳ ✳ ✳

Another email from the Portland FBI office landed in Sara's email that afternoon. She opened the email and saw that Sanchez evidently had some information on autopsies of overdose victims in Oregon.

The email read: *re: The autopsy information you requested. CALL ME. Sanchez.*

Sara picked up her phone and dialed the number for the Portland office. When the receptionist answered, Sara asked for Sanchez and was put on hold. The song "Hold On Loosely" by 38 Special came on as Sara waited. She wondered what music played when people were asked to hold when calling the Yakima office. Sara was actually enjoying the music when Sanchez cut in.

"Sanchez," he said.

"Hey, it's Sinclair. So what did you find out?"

"So, I'm still waiting to hear from the Portland PD, but the Multnomah Sheriff's Office got back to me quickly because they only had three autopsy reports for people who died in homeless camps during that three-year time period. Two seemed to be legit overdoses, with only fentanyl in their systems. But the third, a forty-two-year-old man, had several drugs in his system, and they were in amounts that could have killed a rhinoceros."

"Did they say why they did the autopsy?" Sara asked

"Yes. The man's sister wanted one done. She told the deputy at the scene that she believed her brother had finally hit rock bottom and was ready to stop using. She wondered if he'd died from some cause other than an OD."

"Do you have the sister's name and contact information?" Sara asked.

There was a pause, and she heard Sanchez tapping keys on a keyboard. Then he said, "Yep, got it right here. I'll email it to you."

"Thanks, Greg," Sara said, using Sanchez's first name. "I really appreciate it. Shoot me anything you get from Portland PD."

Sanchez said, "No problem, I'll talk to you soon" and was gone.

The email came a minute later, and Sara looked at the information Sanchez had attached. The dead man's sister was Marie Swanson, and she lived in Beaverton. If Swanson worked, chances were Sara might not get her at home, but she decided to try anyway.

She dialed the number and listened to the ring on the other end of the line. Three rings in, and a woman's voice said, "Hello?"

Sara identified herself and asked if Swanson might have a couple of minutes to discuss her brother's death.

"You mean someone is finally ready to listen to me?" Swanson asked.

"What do you mean?" Sara asked.

"I've been trying to get the police to actually investigate John's death. I was with him the night before he died. He had hit rock bottom and finally was ready to quit. For the first time in a long time, I believed him. I don't think he took all the drugs they said were in his system."

She went on to tell Sara a familiar tale of a man who had been gainfully employed and had a good life, but after a skiing accident, which caused him to have four surgeries on his right leg in a year's time, her brother got hooked on painkillers.

"When the doctor wouldn't prescribe more, he started buying opioids from drug dealers. It went downhill from there. My husband and I tried to help John, but all he wanted from us was money to buy more drugs. When we stopped giving him any, he came to the house and stole the jewelry my mom had given me before she died. He claimed it was as much his as mine."

"I'm sorry to hear that," Sara said.

"He lost his house, his girlfriend, all his friends really. I tried to keep in touch with him, but it was hard. Finally, the day before he died, he called me, crying, and said he was ready for help. I'd never heard that from him before, so I met with him at a camp down by the Willamette River."

"What kind of shape was he in when you found him in the camp?"

"Horrible," Swanson said. "He was nothing but skin and bones, and he was filthy, and I mean in the worst way. He didn't say so, but you could see and smell that he had messed his pants. He was crying and asking me to help."

"What did you do?" Sara asked.

"I tried to get him to come with me. I pleaded with him. But he wouldn't come. All he wanted me to do was bring him some clean clothes, and once he was in them, he said then he would come with me. So, I left him and told him I'd be back first thing in the morning with the clothes. But when I got there the next morning, the police were there. There was an ambulance. I knew they were there for him. I was too late. John was dead."

"I'm so very sorry," Sara said.

"So, do you think he was actually killed?" Swanson asked.

"We don't know," Sara said. "But we want to look into it more. When we find out anything, I promise I will give you a call."

After she ended the call with Swanson, Sara sat back and thought about it again. Something was going on, for sure.

CHAPTER 26

Luke had just driven through the entry gate into the L.T. Murray Wildlife Area when he looked ahead and saw an older Chevy pickup bouncing his way. He recognized the truck, and he recognized the truck's driver.

The driver pulled the pickup next to Luke, rolled down his window, and said, "Hey, Luke. Whatcha got going on out here?"

The man driving the old Chevy was Jim Kingsbury. Gray-haired and always tanned, the gentleman was a local character, mostly because he wore shirts with funny or thought-provoking sayings on them, and no one had ever seen him in the same shirt twice.

Sitting next to Kingsbury was his friend, the man with three first names, Frank Dugdale. Luke rarely saw one of the men without the other.

He wanted to get a look at Kingsbury's shirt, so Luke put his truck into park and jumped out. He walked over to the old Chevy and said, "I'm looking for a couple of hooligans who were reported to be up to no good out here. Have you seen them?"

Kingsbury was wearing a blood-red T-shirt with "NO INTELLIGENT LIFE HERE—BEAM ME UP!" printed in white letters across the chest.

"No, can't say that we have," Kingsbury said. "Frank and I were just out here sighting in our rifles."

"Someone came out to the shooting range and picked up all the glass and trash around the place," Dugdale said. "We were out here two weeks ago, and it was looking pretty shabby."

"Really?" Luke said. "Well, it's good to know there are some civic-minded people around."

He didn't mention anything about the kids picking up the glass a few days earlier.

"Probably some of those old farts," Kingsbury said. "Trying to get their community hours in so they can become master hunters."

"You mean older than you?" Luke asked with a grin.

"Hell yes, older than us," Kingsbury groaned. "How old do you think we are?"

Luke really didn't have any idea how old the men were. Both were active and in good shape. They could have been in their sixties or eighties. So, he didn't answer the question.

"You haven't seen anyone out this way dragging around a Bobcat on a trailer, have you?" Luke asked.

"Was one stolen?" Kingsbury asked.

"No, but we've had some reports of possible illegal digging out here recently," Luke said, leaving out the stuff about the dinosaur bones.

"You know, I do remember seeing someone pulling a trailer with a backhoe out of here when we were here shooting the other day," Dugdale said. "Didn't think anything about it at the time."

"What day was that?" Luke asked.

"Mmm, let's see," Dugdale said. "Two weeks ago yesterday."

"No, it wasn't," Kingsbury said. "Two weeks ago yesterday was a Wednesday, and I go to bingo on Wednesday, and I didn't go to bingo after we shot our rifles. We went to dinner over at the new steakhouse in Union Gap, remember?"

"You and that damn bingo," Dugdale said. "What a waste of time. You and about a hundred old ladies sitting and looking at bingo cards, dabbing them with those giant markers. I'd rather go to a wedding or take a beating."

"You're just jealous because all those women like to kibitz with me," Kingsbury said. "Besides, I won the blackout game that night and brought home two hundred and fifty bucks."

"And who bought dinner the next night?" Dugdale asked.

"I forget," Kingsbury said.

"Me. It was me," Dugdale said insistently.

"Okay, fellas," Luke said. "So, it wasn't Wednesday, but two weeks ago today?"

Both men in the Chevy sat and thought about it a minute.

"Yep, had to be that day," Dugdale finally said. "Damn bingo. I'd rather have a root canal than sit in the gymnasium with all them women. Half the time, you can't hear the number being called because of all the yakking going on."

"That's probably why you don't go," Kingsbury said. "This ain't Russia. You can go where you want, and so can I."

"Okay, fellas," Luke said again as he turned to get back into his pickup. "Holler if you happen to see another backhoe if you are out here again."

The men said "will do" in unison, gave a quick wave, and off they drove, out the gate and down the road. Luke could see one man talking and then the other in his rearview mirror.

Luke chuckled to himself. It was always something with those two. But it was good to know that someone, maybe Nash, had been out in the wildlife area with a backhoe. Maybe he could find tracks near the spots that had been marked on the map on his phone.

He drove to the first spot Sheri Bronson had pinned on his map. Luke drove slowly and looked for places where a tracked vehicle might have left the road and driven off into the sagebrush, but found none. So, he parked and hiked in the direction of the mark on the map. He guessed the spot was two hundred yards from the road.

When he arrived at the spot Bronson had picked on the satellite map, Luke spent extra time looking around. He started in small circles and made increasingly larger passes around and around.

Luke could see why the biologist had picked this area, as it looked like the wind and weather had scoured all the topsoil away over the years. Even the cheatgrass seemed to be having trouble growing there, and that stuff can grow on asphalt. He spotted some small white rocks in the barren earth as he made his circles but found nothing that might be any kind of bone, mammoth or otherwise.

Finally, after looking for almost a half hour, he headed back to the truck.

The next spot on the map was about three miles farther into the wildlife area. This time, the pin was placed three-quarters of a mile from the road. Again, as he got closer to the spot on the map, Luke slowed the truck to a walking speed and searched for any odd vehicle tracks heading off-road. Seeing none, he parked his truck, climbed out, and headed out through the wildlands, most of which was burnt and black from a fire there the previous summer.

As he walked, Luke saw signs that the burned area was starting to come back. He spotted a few plants emerging from the blackened landscape, including what he thought might be a Modoc hawksbeard with its dandelion-like yellow flower. It was nice to see some form of life appearing in a now-desolate landscape that used to be covered in grasses, native flowers, and sagebrush.

Other shoots of green were popping up here and there, and Luke saw several fresh deer tracks in the dry soil. The ungulates, especially the deer, knew that burned areas would at some point start producing tasty broadleaf plants and grasses that were good to eat.

Like he had done at the first spot, Luke spent time circling the area Bronson had picked, but again he found nothing that showed anyone had been digging there. He saw no bones of any kind popping out of the burnt and windblown ground.

When he got back to his truck, Luke looked at the time. He was a good hour from his house and he wanted to get back home around noon to check on Magic. He was confident she was doing fine, with Jack there to keep her company, but still, he had told her he would be home around noon, and he wanted to keep his word.

As he drove, he thought about everything he knew, and all the things he didn't, about the investigation. After seeing the man named Cartosian meeting with Nash and Otis, Luke believed there was something going on. But without any hard evidence that the men were digging on public land, there wasn't much he could do.

He decided he would give it the remainder of the day, and after that he'd have to move on and stop thinking about it. He would come back after lunch, check out the last two spots Bronson had highlighted and, if he found nothing, he'd be done with it.

* * *

Luke wasn't surprised to see Sara's car in the driveway when he got home. She was worried about Magic too, and so she obviously was home to check on her.

When he walked into the kitchen through the back door, the two women were sitting at the table eating soup.

Sara smiled at him and said, "Hi! Magic and I decided to fix some split pea soup. Would you like some?"

"Sounds good to me," Luke said. "Let me go wash up."

Jack came up to Luke and sniffed his pantlegs.

"Yeah, I went hunting without you, boy," Luke said. "Sorry."

"Did you go hunting?" Magic asked.

"Sort of," Luke said. "I went looking for more evidence that someone is digging illegally on the wildlife area. That's kind of like hunting."

"Find anything?" Sara asked as Luke was walking down the hall.

"Nope," Luke said from the bathroom.

He washed his hands and face and came back into the kitchen.

"What are you going to do?" Sara asked.

"I'm going to snoop around a little more this afternoon. Then I'm going to have to move on."

"Well, I'm planning on staying home this afternoon. So, you can take Jack along to keep you company."

Jack heard his name, and his tail started wagging.

"I might just do that. I have to hike into a couple other areas, and it will be good for him to get some exercise too."

As the three ate their lunch, Magic told of her morning spent walking Jack to the river and back, and Sara told them about her phone conversations with Sanchez and the Oregon woman who had lost her brother to a massive overdose several years ago.

"You mean like Toby?" Magic asked.

"Yes," Sara said. "Very similar. Except her brother hadn't gotten off drugs and was in very bad shape. He was super skinny and was living a horrible life, sitting in his own excrement."

Luke was about to take another bite of his split pea soup but decided he'd had enough.

"Sounds like the lady who died in our camp before the Duckman and Toby died," Magic said as she slurped another spoonful of the green soup. The discussion hadn't bothered her. "She was in horrible shape. It was almost a blessing that she died."

Sara looked at Luke, and he looked back, but neither said anything. They were both thinking about their earlier discussion on why someone might be killing homeless people.

"Well, I better get going," Luke said. "C'mon, Jack."

The yellow dog followed Luke out the door and jumped into the truck's back seat after Luke opened the door and said, "Load up."

On the way back to the L.T. Murray, Luke thought about the lunch discussion. If someone was, in fact, killing the most destitute and sickly people in the homeless camps just to put them out of their misery, who could it be?

He remembered Sara mentioning some college girl doing a study on the homeless. Could it be her? She certainly was in and around the camps, brushing shoulders with people living in those conditions. Maybe, he thought. But who would have access to the drugs, including the ether that was used to subdue Toby? Maybe a drug dealer? But why would they have ether? No one was buying that to get high. It could be someone in the healthcare industry. A doctor or a physician's assistant or a nurse? Even a janitor at a hospital might be able to get access to drugs like that. He would talk to Sara about that when he got home.

Luke arrived at the third spot on Bronson's list an hour later. The roads out in the L.T. Murray were rough dirt roads with rocks and ruts, so there was no way to drive faster than about ten miles an hour.

For the third time that day, he slowed to a crawl when he neared the spot on the map that Bronson had identified. Again, he saw no strange vehicle tracks, so he pulled the truck to the side of the road, stopped, and climbed out.

"Let's go, boy," Luke said after he let Jack out.

The yellow dog ran ahead and started quartering back and forth, just as he would when they hunted chukars in the sagebrush. But they weren't hunting partridge, so Luke paid little attention to Jack and looked at the map on his phone to make sure he was heading to the correct spot. He also watched the surrounding landscape for anything out of place.

When he reached the exact spot Bronson had marked, Luke again started an expanding circle as he searched for signs of freshly disturbed earth, or anything that looked like a bone.

During his search, he lost track of Jack, who had disappeared over the rise of a small hill a quarter-mile away. Luke had seen the dog headed that way and let him run. He knew all he had to do was whistle, and Jack would come running back.

After twenty minutes of walking circles, Luke concluded that he was going to find nothing of interest. He stopped, looked around for Jack, and didn't see him, so he whistled for him and started walking back to the truck.

Luke watched the small hill as he walked, but Jack didn't appear. So, he whistled again. A minute later, and he still didn't see Jack pop into view.

Sometimes Jack would get so involved with something he was doing, such as digging up a ground squirrel, he would go deaf to Luke's whistles.

"Dang it, Jack," Luke said to himself. "Come on!"

He whistled again and was just about to turn and walk to the hill to see what Jack was up to when over the hill he came. Luke watched as the dog got closer, and after a minute or two, he could see Jack was carrying something in his mouth.

Over the years, Jack had brought him live baby rabbits and injured birds, held so soft in his mouth they weren't harmed one bit, but as Luke looked closer, he could see it wasn't an animal or a bird in Jack's mouth. It was long and narrow and white, and it looked like a bone.

CHAPTER 27

Kristen Gray couldn't stop thinking about the doctor's resemblance to the suspicious man she'd seen after Toby's death. And the more she thought about it, the more convinced she became: it was him.

Still, she was having trouble figuring out why the doctor would be dressed as a homeless person. And why would he be hanging around in the camp? Certainly, he hadn't been responsible for Toby's death. That was inconceivable to her.

Gray almost called the doctor, not once but twice. If she could talk to him, he would assuredly tell her what he was doing there that morning. But each time she was about to push the send button on her phone after dialing his number, something in the back of her mind would scream "NO!"

She had spent the morning at camps around Everett and

Marysville and was heading back south on I-5 to Seattle for the afternoon meeting with her doctoral supervisor. The camp visits were good because they took her mind off the doctor, but now as she drove, the whole conundrum started grinding away at her again.

Finally, Gray decided she had to discuss this with someone. She thought about calling Officer Donley, the Seattle police officer, but decided she would try Sara McCain first. Gray had been impressed with the FBI officer at lunch and figured she wouldn't mind talking for a few more minutes to discuss the case.

After exiting the freeway and parking in an IHOP parking lot, where she could sit and talk without the distraction of the often-impossible Seattle traffic, Gray scrolled through her incoming phone calls, found the number for the FBI agent, and tapped on it to place a return call.

As she sat and listened to the phone ring, Gray wondered if the number was an office number or a cell number for the agent. A second later, she found out.

"Federal Bureau of Investigation. How may I help you?" a woman's voice said after picking up the call.

"Yes, Special Agent McCain?"

"No, this is her assistant. Special Agent McCain is currently out of the office. Can I help you?"

Gray thought about it for a few seconds.

"My name is Kristen Gray. I had lunch with Special Agent McCain and another young woman in Seattle yesterday. I really need to talk to her. Would you be able to give me her cell number?"

"I'm not allowed to do that, but if you give me your number, I can call her and give her a message. If she's available, I'm sure she will return your call."

Gray rattled off her number and told the assistant it wasn't life and death, but she did have some new information on the murder that took place the week before in the homeless camp in Seattle.

The assistant told Gray she would relay the message and phone number right away and thanked her for calling.

After she clicked off the call, Gray stayed in the IHOP parking lot. She wanted to wait and see if Agent McCain called. She looked at the clock and then out at the traffic flowing down I-5. It was the middle of the day, and still it was bumper-to-bumper for as far as she could see.

"Ugh!" Gray said and started her car. She was about to put the car in reverse when her phone rang.

She looked at the screen and didn't recognize the phone number. She figured it must be Agent McCain calling and tapped the green button to answer her phone.

"Hello?" Gray said.

"Hi," a man's voice said. "Is this Kristen?"

She gulped. Gray recognized the voice. It was the doctor from the emergency room.

"Yes, this is Kristen."

The doctor identified himself and said he had been thinking about their meeting and had some other thoughts on the subject of care for the homeless.

"Do you think we could meet again sometime soon?" the doctor asked. "I need to leave town tomorrow for some business on the east side of the state, but I'd sure like to chat with you again. Maybe this afternoon or this evening?"

The voice in the back of Gray's head was again screaming "NO!" Only this time it hurt her ears.

"Gosh, I'd love to," Gray said. "But I have meetings at the university the rest of the day. I'm just on my way there now."

"Oh, well, that's fine," the doctor said. "Maybe when I return, I could call to set something up?"

"That would be great," Gray said nervously. "Yes. Let's do it then."

The doctor thanked her and clicked off.

Gray was staring at the phone and shaking a little when the device started ringing in her hand. It startled her so bad she gave another little scream. Not as loud as the one at Starbucks, but a scream nonetheless.

She settled down, looked at the caller ID on the phone's screen, and saw it was a different number than the doctor's. Gray answered the phone with a tentative "hello."

"Hi, Kristen. This is Sara McCain. My assistant said you needed to talk with me."

"Oh, thank you so much for calling," Gray said, speaking quickly with the nervousness still in her voice.

"Are you okay?" Sara asked.

"Yes, I'm fine," Gray said after taking a big breath. "Do you have a few minutes to talk?"

Sara told the young woman she did.

"Remember I told you about the homeless guy I saw the day that Toby died, how he was staring at me from a distance and then took off when he saw that I had caught him looking at me?"

"Yes," Sara said. "You said he didn't walk like a homeless man."

"That's right. Well, you are going to think this is weird, but I think I know who he is."

Gray went on to tell Sara about taking the woman from one of the camps to the hospital, the run-in with the ER doctor, and their subsequent meeting at Starbucks to discuss holistic care for the homeless population. She explained how the doctor had turned and looked at her at Starbucks, and sometime during the night it had come to her—the doctor's eyes were the same eyes that had been staring at her the morning Toby was found dead.

"I've tried to tell myself a hundred times today that he isn't the guy, but I'm positive he is," Gray said.

"Well, then, you are probably right," Sara said.

"But that doesn't mean he had anything to do with Toby's death, does it?"

"I don't know," Sara said. "It seems a little strange that a medical doctor would dress up like a homeless person and lurk around the homeless camps."

"I know, right?" Gray said. "And the reason I was so jumpy when you called is he had just called me a moment before you did. He wants to meet me again."

"I'm not sure that is a good idea," Sara said.

"I told him I was busy," Gray said.

"Good," Sara said. "Now give me the doctor's name and approximate age, and I'll see if I can find out a little more about him."

"I didn't know what else to do," Gray said. "Thank you so much for talking to me."

"I don't want to scare you Kristen, but DO NOT meet with him again. And if you see him somewhere, avoid him. It's just a safety precaution."

"Okay. I will. I mean, I won't. I mean, you know what I mean."

"Yes, I do," Sara said. "Talk to you soon."

"Thank you again, so much," Gray said and ended the call.

✳ ✳ ✳

Doc thought the girl sounded awfully nervous on the phone. She hadn't seemed that way when he had spoken to her on the phone or in person the day before. He wondered if she had figured out how she knew him, or where she had seen him before.

He would have liked to meet with her again, just to see if she had heard anything more about the possible location of the young blonde woman who was living with the kid he'd killed. He was planning on going to Yakima tomorrow to see if he could find the girl. If she'd moved on to another city, it would be nice to know that too, so he didn't waste his time.

His original plan was to go over the mountains to try to find the girl on his day off, but he decided he should go sooner than that and had traded shifts with another one of the doctors. He had had to agree to take two shifts for the one he'd offloaded, but Doc was okay with that. He planned to work his original twelve-hour shift, and then, after heading home and grabbing a few hours' sleep, he would be on his way to Yakima. He had checked the weather for Central Washington, and it was supposed to be sunny and warm, into the lower eighties during the afternoon, so he altered his homeless clothing accordingly. When he'd worked the camps in

Los Angeles, he'd often worn light pants, sometimes even shorts, with dirty tank tops and big floppy hats.

The only problem with the warm weather get-up was it was harder to conceal a weapon. He'd have to find a shopping cart when he got there and carry some junk to cover his pistol.

Doc would figure it out. He always did.

* * *

After talking with Kristen Gray, Sara went to her laptop and searched the name Gray had given her. Then she called Sanchez one more time.

"This is becoming a habit," Sanchez said when he answered his phone.

"I know, sorry," Sara said. "We're possibly making a little headway on these murders in the homeless camp in Seattle. Would you be willing to check something else for me?"

"Good to hear about the headway," Sanchez said. "I still haven't heard from Portland PD on the autopsies by the way, but I know they're working on it. So, what else do you need?"

"Just on a hunch, can you check with the hospitals around Portland for the time period that the spike in the homeless deaths took place? I'm curious if a Doctor Brian Malloy worked for any of them. Probably as an emergency room doc. We think he is in his late forties."

"I can surely do that," Sanchez said. "You don't think this doctor is the murderer, do you?"

"I just want to see if he was around there during the spike in deaths," Sara said. "Like I said, it's just a hunch, nothing more."

"Will do," Sanchez said. "As soon as I hear on any of this stuff, I'll give you a call."

When she ended the call with Sanchez, Sara looked up the number for Donley at the Seattle PD. This was officially her case, and Sara needed to let her know what she was doing.

"Hello, Agent McCain," Donley said. "What did you think of the numbers we compiled on the deaths in the camps?"

"Interesting," Sara said. "And it got me thinking. So, I asked an agent down in Portland to see if he could get me the same report for Portland and Multnomah County for the last ten years, just for comparison."

"That's a great idea," Donley said. "Did you get the numbers?"

"I've gotten some, and interestingly enough, they had a spike in deaths there a little over five years ago. Then the numbers dropped about the time Seattle's started to grow."

There was a pause as Donley put two and two together.

"Well, that's not good," she said. "Is there any way to tell if the deaths in Portland were something abnormal?"

"I'm working on that now, looking for any autopsy reports from the three-year period that the deaths spiked there."

"Oh, man," Donley said. "One might come to the conclusion that there is a serial killer taking out homeless people. He started in Portland and moved up I-5 to Seattle."

"One might," Sara said. "We at least need to consider the possibilities."

Then she told Donley about the conversation she had just had with Kristen Gray.

"Jeez," Donley said. "I don't want to think about that."

"But we need to," Sara said. "I'm trying to run down background information on the doctor now and I'll let you know what I find."

"Let me know what else I can do to help," Donley said. "You think I should go talk to the doctor?"

"No, not right now. There is no reason to yet, and if he knows the police are sniffing around, he might just pack his bags and disappear."

"Okay," Donley said. "Thanks for keeping me in the loop."

Sara clicked off the call and started thinking about something Donley had said—*he started in Portland*. What if he didn't start in Portland, but had started somewhere else, like in Denver or San Francisco or any one of a hundred big cities?

She felt like she was on to something, but also like she might be getting ahead of herself. The only thing they knew for sure was Toby didn't overdose accidentally. He had been killed. Other than that, everything was speculation.

CHAPTER 28

"Come here, boy," Luke said as he kneeled to take the bone out of Jack's mouth. He had seen about a million dead animal bones over his career, and in an instant he knew Jack's bone hadn't come from a deer or an elk. He looked it over closely and would bet dollars to dog treats that the bone was a human leg bone. A tibia bone to be precise, the bigger of the two bones in a human's lower leg.

Jack was panting hard from the run, so Luke grabbed a bottle of water and gave the dog a good drink. Then he opened a second bottle and drank some water too. Luke knew he needed to call this in, but first he wanted to see where Jack had found the bone.

This time before heading out into the blackened wildland, Luke grabbed his pack. He had plastic bags, water, a headlamp, and other items that might come in handy, depending on what he found. Then he and Jack started marching to the rise in the hill where Jack had been just a few minutes before.

Luke didn't run to the hill, but he walked at a much faster speed than he normally would. When he reached the top of the rise, he was breathing heavily. Jack had run ahead of him, and before Luke was halfway to the hill, the yellow dog had gone over the top and disappeared.

When he crested the hill, Luke looked for Jack. The dog's yellow coat would stand out in the sea of black, but Luke still couldn't find him.

Finally, after searching left, then right, Luke saw a yellow tail sticking out of some rocks, the tip of the tail wagging ever so slightly. It was the same tail Luke would occasionally see when Jack went on point while hunting quail.

Luke hustled over to the pile of rocks and found Jack pretty much on point. The big dog was standing statue-still, peering down into a large depression in the soil that looked almost like a sinkhole. The hole was eight feet wide, ten feet long, and dropped at least six feet into the ground. Luke had seen pictures on TV of sinkholes sucking up cars and even houses in places like Florida and Texas, but he had never heard of one in Washington.

He walked up to take a closer look and saw more bones protruding from the dirt in the bottom of the hole, including the whiteish, round top of what could be nothing other than a human skull. Luke wanted to go down and dig it out, but this could be a crime scene, so he let his better judgement take over. Instead, he moved around the hole, looking for vehicle tracks and people tracks. There were no vehicle or tractor tracks, but on the other side he found boot prints. It hadn't rained in the region in weeks, so the prints could be a month or two old, or they could have been made in the past few days.

Luke bent and looked closer at the prints which barely made a depression in the black soil. The edges of the prints were not sharp. The wind had softened them some, telling Luke they were probably a week old.

Before Jack or anything else muddled the prints, Luke took his pack off, pulled his flashlight out, laid it down next to the print, and took a photo of it with his phone. That would give investigators an idea of the size of the boot if they somehow were destroyed.

He then took several photos of the sinkhole from all angles. Finally, he pulled a roll of pink flagging tape out of his pack and walked it around the perimeter of the hole, attaching it to the burned branches of sagebrush. It was a challenge because the branches tended to break when Luke touched them, but it was worth it so that the hole would be visible from the air, and from the ground, when the sheriff's investigators came to check it out.

Before he walked back to his truck, Luke took one more look at the bones. He was certainly no expert on aging such things, but if he had to guess, these bones were not eight thousand years old like the Kennewick Man's remains. These looked like they might be twenty or fifty or a hundred years old, but what did he know. He'd treat them as prehistoric until someone told him differently.

Luke had no cell service at the site, so when he and Jack got back to his truck, he radioed the dispatcher.

"Wildlife 148. Need assistance from YSO out here on the L.T. Murray Wildlife Area. I can't remember the code for potential prehistoric human remains found at a possible burial site."

There was some dead air, and then the dispatcher said, "10-4, Wildlife 148. Send your location please."

"Hold on," Luke said. He should have known they would need the GPS coordinates. Since he wasn't far from the pin Bronson had placed on his phone, he pulled it up and read off the longitude and latitude to the dispatcher.

"Those aren't exact, but whoever comes will see my truck, and I can dial them in from here. And you might want to send a paleontologist."

"Wildlife 148, repeat that."

"You might need to send a paleontologist, or maybe an archeologist. The bones are in a sinkhole, and who knows how old they are."

"10-4, Wildlife 148. I'll make the request."

A minute later, Luke heard a sheriff's deputy's voice on the radio telling dispatch he would respond. Luke recognized the voice as Bill Williams, a longtime Yakima County deputy who had periodically razzed Luke about his name being the same as the lead character on the old TV Western, *The Rifleman*.

"Hey, McCain. This is Williams," the deputy said. "Whatcha got going on?"

"Not sure," Luke said. "Definitely human remains. Basically, a busted-up skeleton. I wasn't kidding about sending someone who knows about this stuff."

"I'm sure dispatch is working on it. Where exactly are you?"

Luke told him to just follow the Durr Road about six miles out into the Wildlife Area, and he would spot Luke's truck.

"Roger," Williams said. "See you in a bit."

While Luke waited, he thought about the sinkhole and the bones. Had Quentin Nash found the hole and was trying to get Cartosian to test the bones for their age and validity? Maybe he'd taken a finger or toe bone from the hole and given it to the dark-haired man at the meeting the day before.

And what about the mammoth bones? Were there any? Could Nash have told a few of his cronies he'd discovered dinosaur bones when he had actually found human remains? He must have researched the Kennewick Man discovery and found out about Cartosian and decided to not tell anyone about the human bones, thinking he could make a big sale.

Of course, all of this was just conjecture on his part. Luke knew that. Still, it was a huge coincidence that these things were all happening within a very short period.

And finally, if it was Nash, how had he found the site? The man didn't strike Luke as a hunter, so what would he have been doing out here?

Thirty minutes later, Luke saw the dust plume of a vehicle coming up the road. He pulled his binoculars out from under the seat and took a look at the rig bouncing along. It was Williams in his Yakima County Sheriff's SUV.

It took Williams another five minutes to arrive, and after parking behind Luke's truck, the deputy climbed out of his rig. Williams was in his sixties, but, unlike a few of the other deputies on the force, he was still trim and fit, standing close to six feet tall and weighing a hundred and seventy-five pounds.

Back in the day, Luke knew that Williams had been a smoker, but he had given up the habit years ago. Still, put a cowboy hat on the man and a cigarette in his lips, and he would've been the ultimate Marlboro Man.

"Hey, Williams," Luke said. "I thought you retired."

Williams laughed and said, "No such luck. I'm having too much fun covering your tail."

The deputy had worked alongside Luke on several different cases over the years and was a good friend.

"So, what's this about prehistoric bones?" Williams asked.

Luke leaned against the side of his truck and told the deputy the whole story about the tip they'd received that Quentin Nash was digging up mammoth bones, and the neighbor seeing a backhoe on a trailer at Nash's house, and his chat with the big man Charlton Otis.

"I know those guys," Williams said after Luke had mentioned Nash and Otis. "We've had a couple of run-ins with both of them over the years. And twenty years ago or so, we investigated Nash after his wife went missing, but we never found anything that could tie him to her disappearance."

After a minute of thinking about it, Williams said, "Hey, you don't think those might be his wife's bones in that hole, do you?"

"It's crossed my mind," Luke said.

Then Luke told Williams about seeing Nash and Otis meeting with the dark-haired stranger named Garo Cartosian and how, after doing a search on the man, he'd found Cartosian had once been in the market to buy the Kennewick Man's remains.

"I thought you were supposed to be writing tickets to fishermen this time of year," Williams said kiddingly after hearing the whole story. "You're a little out of your lane, aren't you?"

"Hey, digging anything up on state lands is against the law, and who else is going to handle this stuff? Not the sheriff's department. You guys are busy helping old ladies get their cats out of trees."

Williams laughed. "Funny you should mention it. That is exactly what I was doing when your call came in," he said. "I had to leave some nice lady standing in her yard looking up into a maple tree at an orange cat named Garfield."

Luke began laughing along with him. "Did you tell her to call the fire department?" Luke asked.

"I did," Williams said. "Now, let's go check out those prehistoric bones."

Luke turned to head back to the sinkhole when he noticed another plume of dust coming from back down the road.

"Here comes another rig," Luke said. "Do you think the archeologist could be coming?"

"It would be a miracle if it was," Williams said. "Dispatch said they were having trouble figuring out who to call."

Wondering who it might be, Luke again grabbed his binoculars and took a look.

"Well, I'll be damned," Luke said, the binoculars still glued to his eyes. He was looking at a black Hummer H2, pulling a flatbed trailer with a Bobcat backhoe riding on it.

"What is it?" Williams asked.

"I believe it is Nash and Otis, in Otis's truck, pulling a backhoe this way."

CHAPTER 29

"What should we do?" Williams asked

"Let's just sit here for a minute and see what transpires," Luke said.

The two men watched as the black Hummer approached. When it was three-quarters of a mile away, it turned off the road and started cutting cross-country.

"Is there a road there?" Williams asked.

"I remember seeing a two-track, but it didn't look like it had been used in a while," Luke said.

They watched as the Hummer and trailer disappeared down into a swale and stayed out of sight. A big ball of black dust rose up behind the truck and told the men that the truck was still moving and that they were headed right to the other side of the hill where the sinkhole was located.

"They know about the hole," Luke said as he watched the dust ball move along. "They're headed right at it."

Again, Williams asked, "What do you want to do?"

"They obviously didn't see us sitting here," Luke said. "Let's work our way to the top of the hill and see what they're up to. If nothing else, I can cite them for driving off a green dot road."

"You have your armor on?" Williams asked, wanting to know if Luke had his Kevlar vest on.

"Always," Luke said. "You?"

"Yessir," Williams said as he walked to his SUV, opened the door, and pulled a pump shotgun from a rack in the rig.

Luke decided he would do the same thing. He was not the greatest marksman with the state-issued Glock pistol he carried in a holster on his belt, and he always felt better carrying the Remington 870 12-gauge pump gun he had in the locking mount in his truck.

"Let's go, Jack," Luke said. "But stay close."

The yellow dog knew what that meant, and he fell in right beside Luke as the two men started for the hill.

* * *

"It's just a little bit farther," Quentin Nash said to Otis as he bumped along the rough two-track. "Just around this hill."

"You really think there is more than one body in that hole?" Otis asked.

"I think so, but we'll know soon. And if the bones are as old as I think they are, we're going to be sitting pretty."

"What if the bones aren't that old?" Herman Nash asked from the back seat of the truck.

"Then we move on," Quentin said. "Maybe we can shoot us a few bald eagles like Otis. There seems to be money in that."

"Not like the million dollars that guy wants to pay us if the bones are as old as them other 'uns he tried to buy," Otis said. "Selling feathers to the Indians is chump change compared to selling old bones."

As they got closer to the hole, Otis noticed the pink flagging around it. "Did you mark the hole with some tape?" he asked.

Quentin looked and said, "What the hell?"

They pulled up near the sinkhole, and both Otis and Quentin climbed out.

"Somebody else has found it," Otis said, stating the obvious.

Quentin was looking around. Like around-around, for someone who could be watching them.

"We need to get the tractor off the trailer, dig this stuff up, and get the hell outta here before whoever put this flagging here comes back," Herman said.

Otis and Nash jumped to it, while the old man stayed in the back of the truck.

It took them five minutes to get the tie-downs off, put the ramps in place, fire up the Bobcat, and move it off the trailer. As Quentin drove the Bobcat, Otis pulled the pink tape away from the hole.

Nash was just backing the small tractor into place so he could work the backhoe down into the hole when he heard someone holler, "STOP!"

* * *

As they moved up the hill, Luke and Williams heard the truck stop and two doors slam. There was some talking they couldn't make out, then they heard the Bobcat's engine.

"Let's get to the top of the rise," Luke whispered. "Stay low."

Both men belly crawled the last few feet until they could see what was going on below them. Quentin Nash was driving the Bobcat, and Otis was removing the pink tape Luke had put up just an hour or so before. They watched Nash back the little tractor to the hole and start to drop the backhoe down into it.

"Let's go," Luke said and stood up. He shouted, "Stop!" and watched as both Nash and Otis turned to look at Williams and him coming down the hill. Both lawmen held their shotguns across their chests, ready to use them if necessary.

As soon as they saw Luke and Williams, both men started to

move. Nash dropped down behind the Bobcat, and Otis ran for his truck.

Williams shot his shotgun into the air and yelled, "FREEZE!"

The gunshot stopped Otis in his tracks, but Nash had disappeared. In the excitement, Luke had lost track of Jack, but a second later he saw the big yellow dog run behind the Bobcat and start growling and snarling.

The next thing he saw was Nash falling backwards into the sinkhole.

Williams held his shotgun on Otis and told him to lay face down in the dirt. The big man looked at the shotgun pointed right at his chest and slowly went to the ground.

Luke sprinted to the edge of the hole and found Nash trying to stand. The top of his scalp was bleeding profusely, and the blood was running down his face. Jack was still standing at the edge of the sinkhole, a low growl coming from his throat.

Luke was just starting to give Nash some instructions when a gun went off back where Williams was cuffing Otis. The shot was so loud, it made Luke jump.

He turned and saw Williams go down. He couldn't see the truck because of the Bobcat, so he couldn't figure out what had happened.

"Stay there," Luke hissed at Nash, and he went low around the Bobcat to see what was going on.

He peeked around the front end of the tractor and saw a double-barrel shotgun swinging his way from the back window of the Hummer. Luke ducked just before a load of shot peppered the Bobcat.

If whoever was in the back seat had fired one shot at Williams, and another at him, that meant at this moment he was reloading the shotgun. But if he had reloaded after shooting Williams, he still had one shot. Luke took a chance and jumped from the Bobcat. He fired once, twice, three times into the open window of the truck as he ran at it. He could see the buckshot hitting all around the window.

Luke sprinted to the open window, ready to fire another shot if necessary. He looked inside and found Herman Nash lying on his back on the back seat with blood coming out of a spot on his forehead. The man had his eyes closed and was moaning.

Luke grabbed the double-barrel shotgun out of the truck and threw it into the brush. He checked on Otis, who was still lying face down in the black dirt, handcuffs on his hands behind his back, then he jumped over to Williams, who was now sitting up.

"You hit?" Luke asked.

"Yeah, but I took most of it in the vest," Williams said. "I have a couple of spots on my leg and hip that are burning, but I'm okay. Where's Nash?"

"In the hole," Luke said and went to check on the man.

Nash was still just standing in the hole. He had both hands on top of his head, trying to stop the blood. Jack was sitting and watching.

"Come on outta there," Luke said and offered Nash a hand. Nash wiped his hand on his shirt, took Luke's hand, and was pulled up out of the hole.

"Did you kill my old man?" Nash asked.

"No, but he's hit. You both need some medical attention."

Luke placed handcuffs on Quentin Nash and went again to check on Herman Nash in the back seat of the Hummer. The old man was breathing, but he too was bleeding profusely from his head wound. Luke looked at his head more closely, and the wound seemed to be superficial. If the shot had gone through the man's skull and into his brain, he'd be much worse off, possibly dead.

While Luke was checking on Herman Nash, Williams had used his portable radio to call for an ambulance and more police assistance.

As they waited for help to arrive, Luke hiked back to his truck, grabbed his first aid kit, and packed it back to the Hummer. He got big bandages and put them on both Nash men, holding the pads in place with medical tape to abate the bleeding. When he was done, both men looked like something from an episode of *The Walking Dead*.

"You still think he buried his wife there?" Williams asked as Luke leaned against the Hummer and watched the men, who were now sitting next to each other. Williams had dropped his pants and was inspecting the wounds on his leg.

"Nope," Luke said. "I mean, why would he want to dig her up if he put her there?" Then he said, "Good thing the old man only had eight shot in that scattergun."

"Yeah," Williams said as he dabbed at the small holes. "And good thing he didn't miss to the left, or I might be singing in the boys choir."

Two more sheriff's deputies and an ambulance arrived within forty-five minutes. Williams and the two Nashes rode in the ambulance back to Yakima. One of the deputies took Otis to be booked at the county jail for having four dead bald eagles in the back of his Hummer.

"I told you," Luke said to Otis as they were loading him into the back seat of the deputy's rig after finding the eagles. "It's not going to go well for the person killing the birds and selling their feathers."

Otis just scowled at him. Then he said, "That damn Derek Day. I'm going to kill him."

The forensics people showed up a short time later, and Luke walked them to the sinkhole and told them what had taken place. When they had everything they needed from him, Luke whistled for Jack, and they headed to the truck.

* * *

Later that evening, as he explained all that had happened to Sara and Magic, they both looked at him with awe.

"Did you really think the old man hadn't reloaded his shotgun?" Sara asked.

"I thought it was a pretty good chance he hadn't," Luke said.

"Well, that was stupid," Sara said.

"I agree," Magic said and started laughing.

The young woman's laugh was contagious, and soon they were all laughing. Although every time Sara looked at Luke, he could see in her eyes that she was not happy with him.

"I'm going to go give Williams a call and see how he's doing. You ladies pick a place to go eat, and we'll go."

Changing the subject usually worked. Although this time, he figured they would be revisiting the situation again, in private.

CHAPTER 30

Doc had finished his twelve-hour overnight shift at the hospital at six o'clock, signed out, and stopped at his condo. He had gotten everything ready to go the afternoon before, and now all he needed was a few hours of sleep. He was one of those people who didn't need much sleep, but he did need some, especially if he was going to be driving two and a half hours to Yakima.

He hadn't set an alarm and was surprised when he saw he had only slept about three hours. He thought about rolling over and getting another hour but decided he should get going. Not that he was on any kind of schedule, but he wanted to find the girl.

Doc fought the midday Seattle traffic, wormed his way into the I-5 gridlock going south, and watched for the I-90 exit. Soon he was zooming past Issaquah, headed east toward Yakima.

He hadn't spent much time outside of the city since he had arrived two years before, and he was surprised by the beauty of the Cascade Mountains. Doc had done some reading about Yakima and was looking forward to seeing the area.

And he was looking forward to finding the young blonde woman named Magic. Learning what she knew, and who she had told, would determine Doc's actions if he found her.

* * *

Sanchez called Sara at a little past ten in the morning. "Hey," he said. "I've got some information on the doctor you asked me about."

"Okay," Sara said. "What'd you find out?"

"Well, you were right. I had to do some talking, but I found out that Dr. Brian Malloy worked as an emergency room doc at Providence St. Vincent Medical Center in Portland for three and a half years. The time he was there mirrored the increase in deaths in the homeless camps in Multnomah County almost to the month. It's eerie."

Sara thought about what her next step should be and said, "Okay, thanks Sanchez. If we figure out this guy is a serial killer, you'll get some credit when we catch him—if we catch him."

"Sounds like you're putting the cart in front of the horse just a little," Sanchez said. "This is just one small piece of evidence, and clearly it's circumstantial."

"I know," Sara said. "Did any information come in on the autopsies from Portland PD?"

"The lady at the medical examiner's office said there were seven done during that three-and-a-half-year timeframe. She's rounding them up and will send me the results on all seven as soon as she has them."

"Alright, that's great. Thanks, Sanchez. Let me know when you have them."

"Will do," he said and clicked off.

Sara thought about the conversation with Sanchez. He was

right. There was some evidence to suggest the doctor could be responsible for the increase in deaths within the homeless population around Portland and the Puget Sound, but who would really believe that? The biggest question was why the doctor, or anyone for that matter, would want to kill someone who was just struggling to live one day at a time.

Then she flashed back to the conversation she and Luke had had a few nights earlier. Maybe someone, possibly this doctor, was killing people to put them out of their misery. Magic had said the woman who died in her camp was in terrible shape, both physically and mentally.

It was the same story she'd heard from Marie Swanson in Portland. Her brother had reached a point where he was living in his own excrement. Could someone have seen him in this horrible state and decided to end his pain and suffering?

Marie Swanson's brother had died from a lethal cocktail of drugs. So had Toby. Sara didn't know if it was the same blend of drugs in identical quantities. But they did know that Toby was murdered. If it was the same amount and same kind of drugs that killed Swanson's brother, it wouldn't be too difficult to conclude that the same person killed both men.

It would be good to get the other autopsies. If there was one more person with the same amount of the same concoction of drugs in their systems, she would be convinced. Two of the same might be a coincidence. Three would mean there was a serial killer out there. At least in her mind.

* * *

As he dropped down the hill on I-82 out of the sagebrush, Doc could see a green valley filled with houses. The freeway took him along the Yakima River and through a gap in the hills that fed him into the city of Yakima.

The first thing he noticed were several homeless people wandering along the sidewalks and sitting against the fences. There were small groups of people here and there. He slowed and looked at the women. It would be fortuitous to spot the young blonde woman right away. But he wasn't that lucky.

He stopped at a gas station with a convenience store and went inside. He bought a bottle of water and chatted with the clerk at the counter.

"What's up with all the people along the street?" Doc asked.

"Most of them are from the mission," the kid at the cash register said. "They are housed and fed there, but they get booted out during the day. I think they encourage the people to go look for a job, but most just hang around until the next meal is served."

"Interesting," Doc said. "Over in Seattle, there are homeless camps all over the place—along the freeway, under overpasses."

"Oh, we got those too," the kid said. "Most of the camps are down by the river. Some are just back up the road a ways. You probably drove right by them before you came into town."

Doc paid for his water and asked the kid about the best place to stay the night.

"You might want to pass on the ones in this area," the kid said, nodding to an old Motel 6. "Go back out to the freeway and go around town. There's several closer to the downtown exit near the convention center."

He thanked the kid for the information, went to his car, looked to see if there was a Holiday Inn, found that there was, and pushed the button to put the address into his maps app to take him to the hotel. He would get a room and then go out and see if he could find some of the camps.

✳ ✳ ✳

Luke had been in the office all morning, filling out reports on the arrests in the wildlife area. And he'd had two meetings. One during lunch, and another right after. He knew Sara was at her office too, and even though he'd left Jack with Magic, he worried that she might be feeling a little cooped up and alone. So around two o'clock, he jumped into his truck and headed for home. If nothing else, he figured they could take Jack for a walk.

He wasn't surprised to see Sara's car in the driveway when he got home—she was probably thinking the same thing. He was surprised, however, to see Sara come out on the front porch and hustle to his truck.

"What's up?" Luke asked as he got out of the truck.

"Magic," Sara said. "She's gone."

"Is Jack with her?"

"No, Jack's in the house."

"Did she take all her stuff?"

"No, but her backpack is gone."

"She couldn't have gone far on foot," Luke said. "Maybe she just walked to the river?"

"Without Jack? I think she would have taken him if that was her plan. She could've hitchhiked someplace."

"I guess," Luke said. He could see Sara was worried, and so was he. "She's a grown woman and can go where she wants, but you would think she would have left a note or something."

"I didn't see one," Sara said. "If she left when we headed for work, she could be anyplace. Should we go look for her?"

"Let me grab Jack and go check some of the camps along the river. It's what she knows, so maybe she headed there."

"Okay," Sara said. "I'm going to drive around here and see if I see her."

Luke went in, rousted Jack out of his bed, and they loaded into Luke's truck. He drove down to the pathway access where they'd found Magic passed out next to the river.

Luke pulled into the parking lot, which was three-quarters full of vehicles. Plenty of walkers were using the pathway on the beautiful summer day. Luke parked the truck, climbed out, and let Jack out of the back seat. He knew where Moon normally hung out and decided he'd go see if the man with the crazy hair had seen Magic.

They went through two camps before they found Moon. It wasn't the camp Luke had seen him in before, so Moon had either moved or he was out visiting the neighbors.

"Hey, Luke," Moon said when he saw him coming down the trail. Then he said, "Hey, Jack!"

Jack ran over to Moon, who was dressed in a baggy pair of hiking shorts and some black Converse All Star tennis shoes with no laces. Moon gave the yellow dog a big hug. He wasn't wearing a shirt, and his hair looked even worse than it had before.

"Hey, Moon," Luke said. "How are you doing?"

"Aw, you know . . ." Moon said, then changed the subject. "Are you checking fishermen?"

"No. Actually, I'm looking for the young woman you spotted the other day who was having the health issues."

Moon put his hand up to the tangled mop of hair, dug a pointer finger into the mass, and scratched his head.

After a moment, he said, "Nope. Haven't seen her since she was carted off by the ambulance. Is she s'posed to be back down here?"

"No, but I'd like to talk to her again, so if you see her could you give me a call?" Luke asked. "You still have my phone number in your phone, right?"

"Yeah," Moon said and reached for the phone in his pocket. "I mean, I think I do."

Luke watched as the man opened the phone, tapped the screen a few times, and said, "Yep, here you are."

He thanked Moon and again mentioned that he was available anytime, for any reason, and told him to "call anytime."

"I will," Moon said. He gave a dismissive wave and wandered back over to the camp.

Luke and Jack headed downriver. He knew there were at least two more camps there and he wanted to check them out.

CHAPTER 31

Doc had spotted the Target when he pulled into the Holiday Inn parking lot and figured he could secure a shopping basket there. He got a room and took two bags in with him. The first bag contained his regular stuff, including a clean change of clothes and toiletries. The other duffel bag carried his homeless kit.

He changed into some well-worn ratty hiking shorts, an old Seattle Sonics T-shirt, and pulled gray sweatpants and a sweatshirt over the top. He put on running shoes and looked like your average person heading out for an afternoon jog. The only oddity was the backpack he carried. Not many joggers carried a backpack, but he figured if anyone did pay attention to him as he left the hotel, they might think he was dropping the pack off in his car before he went for his run.

In the pack were a pair of cheap hiking boots and a floppy hat in Desert Storm camo. After he grabbed the shopping cart, he would step out of the sweats, trade the running shoes for the boots, put on the hat, stash the running shoes and clothing in his pack, and assume the persona he had perfected over the years.

He also had the pistol and medical paraphernalia in his pack. The medical stuff included syringes and small vials of morphine, fentanyl, and ether.

The change from jogger to homeless person went without a hitch, done next to the Target in a location hidden from cars going by. He found a stray shopping cart, loaded his stuff into it, and headed for Yakima Avenue to cross over the interstate and on to the river.

It took Doc a half hour to push the cart close enough to the river. He stopped and got a lay of the land. There seemed to be a paved bike and walking path that ran right along the river, and he figured that was where he needed to be. He was just rounding a corner in the road when some kind of an ugly brown pickup truck came at him on the road. The truck slowed, and Doc saw the driver looking at him. There were antennas on the roof of the vehicle, and an insignia on the driver's door said the vehicle was a Department of Fish and Wildlife truck. He didn't look long at the driver, but what he saw was a big man wearing a tan shirt with a badge on his left chest. He wasn't positive, but he thought he saw a yellow dog looking out the back seat window.

Doc figured every state had game wardens, but he had never really seen one in person. He once watched a few minutes of a TV show that featured some game wardens working in Maine, or maybe it was Montana—he couldn't remember. He wondered what this game warden was doing. Since he was close to the river, Doc figured he must be looking for people who were fishing or hunting where they shouldn't be. At least, that is what the game wardens were doing on the TV show.

He pushed on, and after traveling along the pathway for

another ten minutes, he found his first camp. Doc left his cart on the path and moved through the brush to the tents and tarps.

✳ ✳ ✳

After checking all the camps and having no luck locating Magic, Luke and Jack walked back to the truck. When they were loaded, Luke called Sara.

"Any luck?" she asked.

"No, nothing," Luke said. "I talked to a few of the people in the camps, and none of them had seen her. So, I'm thinking she didn't come here."

"I didn't see her either," Sara said. "Do you think she might have hopped a bus back to Seattle or somewhere else?"

"She could have, I guess," Luke said. "I'm going to head home, and hopefully she'll show up."

Sara said she was going to call the bus pickup spot and see if they had seen Magic. "I'll see you in a few," she said.

Luke was just driving out of the park that connected with the pathway when he saw a man pushing a cart toward him on the shoulder of the road. The guy looked homeless, but he didn't look like Moon or the other people he had just been talking with. The man was wearing the right clothes, but he didn't look, what, dirty enough? Or weathered enough? It was something, but Luke couldn't put his finger on it.

The guy checked him out, but Luke never really saw the man's eyes, as he had a floppy hat pulled down over his face.

He looked at the homeless guy in his rearview mirror, but the man never turned around. He just kept pushing the cart toward the river.

✳ ✳ ✳

Forty minutes later, Luke and Sara were home, sitting at the kitchen table. Sara had called Greyhound, and they hadn't sold a ticket to anyone matching Magic's description. In fact, the only ticket they'd sold that morning was to an elderly man.

224

"What should we do?" Sara asked.

"Not much we can do," Luke said. "Hopefully, she comes back."

The words were barely out of his mouth when Luke's phone rang. He looked at the ID on the screen and didn't recognize the number. He answered it anyway.

"This is McCain," he said.

"Hey, Luke. This is Moon."

Luke was surprised to hear from the man. He put the phone on speaker so Sara could listen.

"Hey, Moon. What's up?"

"You told me you were looking for that blonde girl who had passed out by the river the other day?"

"Yes," Luke said. "Did you see her?"

"No," Moon said. "Wasn't her name Magic?"

"Yes," Luke said again.

"Well, I just talked to some guy who was asking about her," Moon said.

"You mean, someone other than me?" Luke asked. He thought Moon might be under the influence and could be confused.

"Yes, a guy who was kinda dressed like one of us, but . . ."

There was a long pause.

"But what, Moon?" Luke asked finally.

"But this guy wasn't one of us. Nobody has seen him before, and he looked too clean."

Luke thought of the man he had seen pushing the cart into the parking lot.

"What was he wearing?" Luke asked.

"Shorts, shirt, shoes," Moon said, then laughed. "I guess he'd get service at a restaurant. Oh, and he had on a big hat with a weird pattern on it."

"Like a Desert Storm camo pattern?"

"I don't know what that is, but it was kind of a camo pattern. The brim of the hat was down covering his face. But what I saw of his face was smooth and shaved. He weren't no homeless guy."

"Was he pushing a cart?" Luke asked.

"Not that I seen," Moon said. "But there's carts all around these camps, so who knows."

"What did the man say?"

"He just came into the camp and said that he was looking for a young blonde woman went by the name of Magic. I told him she had been here a few days ago, but then she had to go to the hospital."

"What happened then?"

"He asked if she had been injured, and I told him she had a heart attack."

"Did he ask which hospital she went to?"

"He did, but I told him I had no idea."

"What happened then?"

"Nothin'," Moon said. "He just turned around and walked back through the brush toward the trail."

Luke thanked Moon for calling and told him that if he saw the guy again, or the woman named Magic, to call him back straight away.

During the phone conversation, Sara started thinking about the call she had received from Kristen Gray. She had described the man she'd seen at the camp the day Toby died as someone who was dressed like a homeless person, but something had made him stick out to Kristen.

"That guy might be this doctor that Kristen Gray has identified as the man at the camp where Toby died."

Luke was skeptical. He couldn't wrap his head around the idea that a man who had taken an oath to save people could actually be killing them. Still, the man pushing the cart didn't look like the other homeless men he had seen.

"Let me run back over there and see if I can find him," Luke said.

"And I'm going to go to the hospital to see if he shows up there," Sara said.

Then she wrote a quick note to Magic on the chance she showed back up at the house. She asked Magic to please stay at the house, and that either Luke or Sara would be home soon.

* * *

Doc felt like he was getting close. The man with the wild hair had said he'd seen Magic in one of the camps, and now she might be in the hospital. He remembered from his internet research that Yakima only had one hospital in town. He needed to get back to the hotel where he had left his cell phone so he could call the hospital and see if Magic was still there. If she was, he would drive there for a visit.

He thought about all the possibilities as he hurried back to the hotel. He had put his pistol and medical kit back in the backpack, ditched the shopping cart, and now—with his sweatshirt and tennis shoes on—he jogged back across the freeway.

If she was there and knew who he was, it would be easy to slip some drugs into her intravenous line. He really hoped he didn't have to do that, but if he did, he was prepared.

When he got to his room, he quickly googled the name and number for the hospital, then used the landline phone to see if Magic was still admitted. The big problem was he didn't know her last name. Without that, they may not be able to tell him if she was there or not.

Doc placed the call and got the information desk. The woman there said they had no one with the first or last name of Magic admitted.

"Have you had someone there in the last five days with the first name of Magic?" he asked.

The woman did some clicking on the computer and said she could not find anyone with that name who had been admitted in the past month.

He thanked the woman and hung up.

* * *

Sara arrived at the hospital not five minutes after the doctor had called asking about Magic. She went through the main entrance and stopped at the information desk. She pulled out her FBI cred pack and showed it to the woman.

"Oh, my," the lady said. "Yes, how can I help you?"

"Have you had a man in here in the past hour looking for a woman named Magic?"

"No," the lady said, "but I just had a call from a man asking about any possible patients named Magic."

"Did he say who he was?" Sara asked.

The woman thought about it for a minute and then said, "No, he didn't. He just asked if we had a patient by the name of Magic. He said he didn't know her last name."

Sara thought about trying to get access to the hospital's phone provider to see if she could locate the call's origin, but chances were the man had used a cell phone, and she would need a judge's approval to get that. Plus, there had to be dozens of calls coming into the hospital every few minutes, and trying to determine which call had come from their suspect could be difficult.

She thanked the woman at the desk, and as she headed back to her car, she pulled out her phone and called Luke.

"Any luck?" Luke asked.

Sara told him about the phone call to the hospital.

"I wish we could find Magic and make sure she's okay," Luke said.

"At least we know this man hasn't found her yet," Sara said. "And I sure would like to find him to have a little chat. If he is this Dr. Malloy, I just have a gut feeling he's involved."

"I'm back at the park, so I'll have another look around," Luke said. "Someone should be at the house if Magic shows up there."

"I'm on my way there now," Sara said. "Let me know what's happening."

Luke said he would and clicked off. He was just about to reach for the door handle when there was a tap on his window. He jumped when he saw who it was.

CHAPTER 32

Moon wasn't a scary-looking guy when you saw him at a distance, but when the man was just inches away from your face, with his wild hair, scraggly face, and glaring eyes, he could frighten a blind man.

"Geez, Moon," Luke said after he rolled down his window. "You scared the crap outta me."

"Sorry," Moon said, breathing heavily like he'd just been running. "I was just about to call you again when I seen you driving up, so I ran over here."

After a long pause, Luke asked, "So, what were you going to call about?"

"I just seen that Magic girl, or at least I'm pretty sure it was her. She was dressed different than when she was having the heart attack down by the river, but I'm pretty sure it was her."

Luke jumped out of the truck, opened the back door so Jack could get out, and said, "So where did you see her? Can you take me there?"

"Sure," Moon said, still breathing heavily. "But I don't think I can do no more running right now."

"That's okay. Let's just walk," Luke said. "Lead the way."

Actually, Jack led the way, with the two men following.

"She was upriver at the big camp," Moon said, which meant nothing to Luke.

As it turned out, the big camp was only about three hundred yards up the pathway, and by the time Luke and Moon arrived, Jack was already there, sitting at Magic's feet. She was petting the big dog, then leaned down and gave him a big kiss on the top of the head.

"Dang," Moon said. "I wisht I was a yellow dog."

"Hi, Luke," Magic said. "I hope you're not here looking for me."

"Actually, I am," Luke said. "We think that guy who was seen at your camp in Seattle the morning Toby died is here looking for you."

Magic's face went from happy to concerned to sad in an instant.

"How would he know I was here?" she asked with tears in her eyes.

"I don't know, but he was here. And then when Moon told him you'd gone to the hospital when you passed out by the river the other day, he called there looking for you."

"Am I in danger, Luke?"

"Not if you stay with us. What are you doing down here anyway?"

"I came looking for Toby's knife. I had it in my pack, but it wasn't there when you brought it to me. It either fell out or someone took it. It was special to Toby. His grandfather gave it to him, and it's the only thing I have to remember him by."

"I think I know who might have it," Moon said, again scratching his tangle of hair. Luke wondered if he had lice or some other creatures living in the overgrown mane.

Moon said a guy named Arnie was bragging about a new knife he had and was showing it to folks.

"I think I saw him a while ago at the blue camp," Moon said.

"Do you want to take us, or can we find it on our own?" Luke asked.

"You can't miss it," Moon said, which told Luke he didn't want to go, maybe because he'd be accused of being a stool pigeon. "The whole place is made up of blue tents and blue tarps."

Luke, Magic, and Jack walked downriver until they saw some blue in the trees next to the river.

"This must be it," Luke said. "You want to stay on the path with Jack, or do you want to go down there?"

"I'm used to dealing with these people," Magic said. "In fact, let me do the talking."

Luke smiled and said, "We'll follow you."

When they got to the camp, there were three men and two women sitting in old beat-up metal chairs around a fire. It was eighty-four degrees, so the fire wasn't needed for heat. Luke thought maybe they were planning on using it to cook.

"I'm here to see Arnie," Magic said.

One of the women turned and looked at a man sitting next to her. Evidently, he was Arnie. Luke couldn't tell how old he was. He could have been twenty-five or forty-five. He was rail-thin, had thinning blond hair on top, with a long, thin, braided ponytail in the back. He had a scraggly beard, and like Moon, he was only wearing some hiking shorts.

Arnie looked at the woman next to him, then at Magic, then at Luke, and finally at Jack.

"Whatcha need?" Arnie asked.

"I'm here to thank you for finding my knife," Magic said. "It was my dead boyfriend's, and I appreciate you keeping it safe for me. In fact, I've got a little reward to give you for what you've done."

She didn't say one word about the possibility that the man had stolen it from her backpack.

Arnie fidgeted and again looked at Luke, specifically at the badge on his chest.

"Yeah, sure," Arnie said as he stood and reached into his back pocket. "Glad to help."

He handed the knife to Magic, and she leaned in and whispered something in his ear. Arnie listened while Magic kept whispering, got a funny look on his face, and turned back to sit on the stump next to the woman.

Magic said to Luke, "Let's go" and started back through the brush.

"Hey, what about the reward?" the woman yelled at Magic as they were walking away.

"He got it," Magic yelled back.

When they were well up the trail, headed back to the truck, Luke asked, "So, what did you say to Arnie?"

"I told him his reward was not having his testicles cut off and handed to him because that is what I might have done if you weren't there. I reminded him you don't steal people's stuff, or there are consequences."

"Hmmm," Luke hummed. He was impressed. He no longer thought of Magic as naïve. The girl was tough, for sure.

On the way back to Luke's house, Magic apologized for not leaving a note when she left.

"Honestly, I didn't even think about it until I was almost here," she said.

"How'd you get to the camp?" Luke asked.

"I walked some of the way, but I got a ride from a dude who dropped me off at the Walmart."

"Well, Sara will be glad to see you. She's worried about this guy and what he is doing here."

✳ ✳ ✳

Doc was at a loss. Yakima wasn't nearly as big as Seattle, but still it was big enough that he could search for days and never see the woman. He decided he would stay that night at the hotel, get up in the morning, get in the garb, and search the homeless camps one more time. If he didn't find her, he would head back to Seattle.

The more he thought about it, the more he felt that if the woman could identify him, the Seattle police would have been looking for him. He was confident that even if her boyfriend had told her about him after he'd spotted Doc killing the man who fed the ducks, she still couldn't ID him. The cops might know that the young man and maybe even the duck man were murdered, but they certainly couldn't identify him as the killer.

He would look for her in the morning. If he didn't see her, he would move on and stop worrying about it.

* * *

Luke was in the office earlier than usual the next morning and so was his captain.

"I heard you caught the guys digging up bones out on the L.T. Murray," Bob Davis said. "Good work."

"Thanks," Luke said. "And as a bonus, we caught a guy who has been killing eagles and selling their feathers to tribal members around the state."

"The sheriff called me a few minutes ago," Davis said. "He said Williams will be just fine, and the two Nash men will be okay. The younger one needed stitches in his head, and the other is still in the hospital, but he'll be okay."

"That's good, I guess," Luke said. "I wasn't shooting to hit the old boy, just to get him to stop shooting at Williams. He must have caught a ricochet."

"The sheriff also said that their forensics guy believes the bones they were digging weren't all that old. Maybe a hundred and fifty years or so. From a man, based on the pelvis bones. He doesn't know if they are Native American or maybe from an early white settler. Their DNA testing will figure it out."

"Looks like there were no mammoth bones after all," Luke said. "Just the human bones that Nash thought were old enough to sell."

"He'll be doing some time for that," Davis said. "And so will that Otis fella who was killing the eagles."

Luke was about to say something, but his phone started buzzing on his desk. There was no name on the caller ID, but he recognized the number from the day before. It was Moon calling.

Davis said, "Take it" and wandered away.

"What's up, Moon?" Luke asked.

"He's here," Moon said.

"Who's there?"

"The guy who's looking for that girl . . . Magic. You know, the guy in the big camo hat who is trying to look homeless but is not."

"Okay," Luke said. "I'm on my way. Do not follow him or even look at him."

"Okay," Moon said, but Luke wasn't convinced.

"I'm serious. Do *not* follow him. Where did you see him last?"

"He was at the big camp, asking about Magic again."

Luke thanked Moon, told him one more time not to follow the guy, and said he was on his way.

After quickly telling the captain what the call was about, Luke ran out, jumped in his truck, and headed to the river. On his way, he called Sara.

"The guy is back at the river, working through the camps and looking for Magic," Luke said after Sara answered.

"Okay," she said. "I'm at the house with Magic, but I'll head that way now."

* * *

It took some convincing to get Magic to stay at the house, but when Sara said Jack could stay with her, she relented.

"There is nothing you can do there," Sara said. "We're just going to check this guy out."

She wanted to say that Magic would just be in the way and one more person to worry about, but she didn't.

When Sara hit the highway, she flipped the switch to turn on the blue and red flashers in her grill and did eighty miles an hour to the off-ramp by the park.

Because she was closer and didn't have to drive through town, Sara arrived at the park three minutes ahead of Luke. She wanted to go looking for the man she believed to be Dr. Brian Malloy but waited for Luke.

Luke pulled in and parked next to her. As he was climbing out of his truck, he asked, "Do you have your vest on?"

"Yes," Sara said. She could tell by the bulkiness under Luke's shirt that he did too. "What do you think we should do?"

"Let's split up," Luke said. Because Moon had told him the fake homeless guy was last seen at the big camp, he decided he would go that way. "I'll go upriver, and you go down."

Sara said nothing, just looked Luke in the eye, nodded, and headed to the pathway.

Luke made it to the big camp in three minutes. When he walked into the camp, he saw a few people he recognized, but he didn't see Moon or the man he had seen the day before with the floppy Desert Storm hat.

He thought there might be one more camp farther upriver but decided to head back down to the blue camp.

* * *

Sara hadn't been on the pathway in a couple of years and wasn't familiar with where the camps were located. Some sat so far into the trees and brush that they were difficult to see. Still, she walked slowly down the path, eyes and ears open. Luke had reminded her that the man they were looking for was wearing a round floppy hat with a desert camo pattern.

Two joggers, a man and a woman, came up behind her and passed by, the man saying, "On your right" when they went by. Then an elderly man on an electric bike came at her on the path. He nodded and said, "Morning" as he went by.

She checked her pistol in its holster on her hip for the twentieth time and kept moving. She wasn't planning on having to use the gun, but she knew she needed to be ready. And if she did have to pull her pistol, she would need to be extra careful because there seemed to be plenty of innocent people using the pathway.

Sara kept one eye on the path, and another looking down toward the river in the brush. Ahead, she saw something blue off to the left down by the river and then saw someone coming out of the trees above the spot of blue. She watched carefully as the man emerged from the brush, and Sara saw the desert camo hat. She looked at the man's face, and it was the same face she'd been looking at in photos for the past two days.

"Dr. Malloy," Sara said, pulling her badge up to show him. "FBI. We'd like to talk to you for a minute."

CHAPTER 33

Doc had moved upriver looking for Magic in two camps and then had moved down. He asked several of the people if they knew Magic or had seen a young blonde woman recently. No one seemed willing to talk to him, so he moved downriver.

He went through the brush and into a camp made up of blue tents and blue tarps, where he asked again if anyone had seen the blonde woman.

"She was here yesterday," a woman said. Then she pointed a thumb at the man sitting next to her. "She hustled a knife from my old man."

Doc didn't quite know what that meant but asked, "Is she staying in one of the camps?"

"What's it to ya?" a half-naked man with wild hair asked.

Doc said nothing.

Then the woman said, "She was with a cop of some kind, and the cop had a yellow dog."

Doc thanked them and turned to go back through the brush to the path. He was surprised to hear the young woman was with the police.

He was thinking about that when he stepped out of the brush and onto the paved pathway. There was a tall, dark-haired woman standing ten feet away. She raised a badge and said, "Dr. Malloy. FBI. We'd like to talk to you for a minute."

In an instant, his head was spinning. How did the FBI know his name? And how had they found him here?

He smiled at the FBI agent as his brain ran through his options.

"You must be mistaken," Doc said calmly. His pistol was in his backpack, along with the drugs in his medical kit. The pistol would be impossible to reach in a hurry. "I'm just here looking for a friend."

"We know who you are looking for, Dr. Malloy," Sara said. "And we know why you are looking for her. In fact, we know quite a lot about you."

He had some options, but none of them were great. He could bull-rush the FBI agent. Maybe not the best option, as she looked fit and was probably trained to deal with someone coming at her. He could turn and run down the path away from her, but again, she probably would catch him in short order. Or he could dive back into the brush, down to the camp, and try to cross the river.

The best option, he thought, was to simply ask the FBI agent what she would like him to do and follow her directions. Running would be an admission of guilt. And he would like to know just what they knew. It couldn't be much. They couldn't know he had killed the kid or the man at the camp in Seattle. Could they?

* * *

Sara saw the man thinking about it. She had told him that they knew who he was and who he was looking for. He was running through his options, she thought. She was ready if he came at her or took off down the path. If he turned and ran back into the brush, that would be more difficult.

The doctor smiled at her again and acted like he was going to say something, but he noticed something behind her and turned quickly, crashing into the brush, running down the trail he had just come up on.

* * *

Luke was walking quickly down the path and came around the corner in time to see Sara standing there looking at the man in the desert camo hat. As soon as the man saw Luke coming, he turned and ran into the brush.

Sara was on the run the second the man bolted, and Luke sprinted to catch up with her. If the man was armed, it could be a very dangerous situation. He hoped she would proceed cautiously.

The man hadn't been in the brush five seconds, and Sara was barely off the pathway, when Luke heard a crash.

Luke moved quickly through the brush to where it opened onto the blue camp. He found Sara standing over the man who, just seconds before, had been wearing the floppy hat. Now hatless, the man lay motionless, face down in the dirt, blood coming from his head. Standing next to Sara was Moon. He had a big smile on his face. And a big, club-like piece of wood in his hand.

When she heard Luke come through the brush, Sara turned and said, "Found him."

"You told me not to follow him," Moon said. "But we heard the FBI lady here talkin' to him, and when he ran down this a way, I thought I might just slow him down for her."

"What did you do?" Luke asked, although he was sure he knew what had happened.

"I hit him in the forehead as he was runnin' by," Moon said with a smile. No shirt, wild hair, and goofy smile on his dirt-streaked face, the man looked like he should be in Borneo. "You didn't tell me not to hit him."

"Well, it did the job," Luke said, hoping that Moon hadn't killed the man.

Sara knelt next to the doctor and checked to see if he was, in fact, alive.

"He's breathing," Sara said. "But we better get an ambulance rolling."

While Luke called for the ambulance, Sara removed the small daypack from the doctor's back, moved his hands behind him, and put handcuffs on them. Then she rolled him on his side so that she could watch to make sure he was breathing without difficulty.

"Thank you, Moon," Luke said. Then he turned to Sara and said, "Sara, this is Moon." Then to Moon, "Moon, this is my wife, Sara."

"Your wife is an FBI cop?" Moon asked.

"Yes, she is," Luke said.

"Wow, and purty too," Moon said, looking at Sara. "How'd you get so lucky?"

"I ask myself that every day, Moon," Luke said. "I ask myself that every day."

* * *

By the time the ambulance arrived and the EMTs got down the trail to the blue camp, the doctor had regained consciousness. He didn't seem to know where he was, or why he was there. He kept trying to bring his arms from around his back but couldn't get them to work right.

Sara looked through the backpack and found the pistol and the small medical bag with syringes and vials of drugs. She pulled them out and showed them to Luke.

"One of the bottles is ethyl ether," Sara said. "The autopsy report said Toby had ether in his bloodstream."

Luke had no idea if the medical examiners could match certain vials of drugs with those in someone's blood, but if there was a way, he figured this guy's goose was cooked.

CHAPTER 34

Doc woke up the next morning in a hospital bed. His wrist was handcuffed to the bedframe. He had a humongous headache and had no idea how he had gotten there.

A nurse was standing next to one of the bedside machines, looking at the screen, watching the numbers change every ten seconds.

"Nurse, why am I in the hospital?" Doc asked.

"You received a pretty good blow to your head," the nurse said. "Your skull is not cracked, but you have a dandy concussion."

"Was I in a car wreck?" Doc asked.

"No, you were hit on the forehead with some kind of club."

Doc thought about that for a minute. He had no recollection of where he was when this had happened, or who had done it.

"I'd like to be released from the hospital," Doc said. "I'm going to be fine."

"I'm sure you are, but the doctor who is treating you wants to keep an eye on you for a little longer to make sure there are no lingering issues. As you know, this type of an injury can sometimes cause swelling and even bleeding on the brain."

"Why am I handcuffed to the bed?"

"You were escorted in here by an FBI agent who wants to talk to you before you are released."

"Did she say what she wants?"

"No, she did not," the nurse said.

* * *

An hour after Sara left the doctor in the hospital with strict instructions to keep Malloy locked to the bed, she received a call from Special Agent Sanchez in Portland. He told her that of the seven autopsies done on the people found dead in the camps in Multnomah County, three had an unusual mix of drugs in their system, in amounts that were excessive, almost identical to the deaths in King County. One man found in a camp near the Columbia River, who was described in the autopsy report as being very large, also had ethyl ether in his system.

"It looks like your guy was busy down here for a few years," Sanchez said. "Just on a hunch, I did some checking on several other cities along the West Coast, and both San Francisco and Los Angeles had noticeable spikes in deaths in the homeless camps. L.A. first and then San Francisco, just before the spikes here around Portland. I'm checking with all the hospitals in those areas to see if Dr. Malloy was employed there during those spikes, but it looks like the good doctor was working his way up the coast, killing people as he went."

* * *

As the evidence stacked up against Malloy, the FBI had enough to hold him, and they worked with Seattle Police to gather enough evidence so that the King County District Attorney could file charges for the murder of Toby Hausman.

A leak to *The Seattle Times* created a storm of interest, and when their reporters started doing their own investigating based on information they had received about the increase in deaths in the camps, the story exploded. There were hints in the leaked information that these increases were not confined to King County. Similar numbers could be found in Portland, San Francisco, and Los Angeles.

In a matter of two days, all the major newspapers and television news outlets in the country were reporting that a serial killer had been preying on the most vulnerable of the residents in the homeless camps in several West Coast cities and counties. Some were estimating that the newly dubbed "Homeless Killer" had taken as many as a hundred lives.

It didn't take long for them to figure out the man suspected of doing the killings was a medical doctor, which created even more speculation as to the motives for these murders in stories and op-eds. In one of the stories published by *The Seattle Times*, a young doctoral candidate from the University of Washington was interviewed.

According to the news story, Kristen Gray, a graduate student working on her dissertation about the homeless people in the region, said, "I hope this horrible situation brings more attention to the need for more help for the people who live in these conditions on a daily basis. I've met so many of these folks, and if we could get people on the ground, in these camps, so many of them could be helped into a better life."

The story told that Gray had been in a camp near Lumen Field when a young man, thought to be a victim of the Homeless Killer, was found. Gray believed she saw the killer a short time after the young man's body was discovered.

* * *

Eighteen months after Dr. Brian Malloy was captured in Yakima, he was tried and eventually convicted of killing Toby Hausman. The circumstantial evidence made for a strong but not ironclad case against the doctor. The jury was convinced, however, by an eyewitness description of the events that took place that night. The witness picked Malloy out of a lineup, and under sworn testimony during the trial, said that Malloy was the man she saw struggling with Toby. The witness had watched in horror as Malloy took Toby down with a cloth over his face and then plunged a needle into Toby's neck.

* * *

A day after the jury found Malloy guilty, Luke and Sara were watching the national evening news, and a story came on about the trial. The reporter said that Oregon and California were seeking extradition of the doctor so they could file murder charges of their own.

"Did you think Magic could do it?" Luke asked after the news story was over.

"Yes, I did," Sara said. "We talked a lot about it, and I was positive she could do it."

"Do you really believe Magic saw what happened?"

"It doesn't matter what I believe. All that matters is the jury was convinced, and a man that we are all positive murdered Toby, along with who knows how many other innocent people, will be in prison for the rest of his life."

Luke was about to say something else, but his phone started buzzing.

"This is McCain," Luke said.

"Yeah, Officer McCain, my name is Lars Atoli. I was an investigator for the Yakima Fire Department for several years. I'm sure we met somewhere along the line."

"Sure, yes, Lars. How can help you?"

"Well, I've found some bones out on the L.T. Murray Wildlife Area a while back, and I'm not sure who should know about it."

"Okay," Luke said. "What kind of bones are they?"

"I'm a bit of an amateur paleontologist, and I'd bet my next month's Social Security check that they are Columbian mammoth bones."

"The hell, you say," Luke said, pulling up the map he had on his phone. "So where did you find them?"

ACKNOWLEDGMENTS

Many thanks to amateur paleontologist Hans Solie for suggesting the idea of a mammoth dig on public lands. And for showing me where such treasures might be found.

Also, thanks to retired WDFW wildlife enforcement officer Gene Beireis for his ongoing assistance in making sure Luke is following proper procedures.

And to my brother Doug Phillips for helping me with the technical stuff, of which I have little knowledge, and almost no desire to learn. Thanks, bro.

Thanks to proofreader supreme Alta Conrad for her assistance in making sure my errors are caught and fixed. I appreciate it greatly.

Finally, to my sons, Kyle and Kevin. Thanks for being my steadfast supporters, sharing thoughts and ideas for book titles and storylines, while keeping me and my characters in the present, not in 1974.

ABOUT THE AUTHOR

Rob is an award-winning outdoor writer and author of the bestselling and critically acclaimed Luke McCain mystery series set in the wilderness of Eastern Washington and featuring a fish & wildlife officer and his yellow Lab, Jack.

Rob and his wife, Terri, live in Yakima, Washington with their very spoiled Labrador retriever.

www.ingramcontent.com/pod-product-compliance
Lightning Source LLC
LaVergne TN
LVHW091435230225
804353LV00001B/1